MISSING

**Suspense fiction
by
Alice Marks**

Missing

This is a fictional work. The names, characters, incidents, places, and locations are solely the concepts and products of the author's imagination or are used to create a fictitious story and should not be construed as real.

Missing:
ISBN-13: 978-1517684747
ISBN-10: 1517684749
Copyright © 2015 Alice Marks
Published by the author, 2015 with Golden Box Books
Editor: Pamalee Ford
Book cover art and book formatting: Erika M Szabo
www.authorerikamszabo.com

There is no South Corpus Christi Police Department, no Modell in Oklahoma and no Cielo Vista Clinic, Liberty Motel nor Vega Building in Corpus Christi. Actual place names are used fictitiously, and all characters and events are products of the author's imagination. My apologies to any physician or any law enforcement official who reads this book, doubts its credibility and finds resemblance. This is a fiction story.

All rights reserved. No part of this book may be used or reproduced in any manner whatsoever without written permission, except in the case of brief quotations, reviews, and articles.

DEDICATION

This book is dedicated to my husband, Sam, with special acknowledgement to the Port Aransas Pens Writers' Group, especially Devorah Fox for her inspiration, and to the members of the Duluth Ink Slingers Writers Group. I am indebted to two others who helped me immensely, Pam Ford, editor and Susan Marks-Kerst, Beta reader. Without the expertise and patience of my coach Erika M Szabo, you would not be reading this.

INTRODUCTION

I met this novel's main character for the first time in a run-down motel on the outskirts of Corpus Christi on an afternoon in September. She's 30ish, tall, slender, has long beautiful blonde hair. Her name, according to her passport, is Sandra Lewis. I checked later and she gave the desk clerk a different name. She's staying in room 204, the Liberty Hotel.

Two plastic Wal-Mart sacks and a navy blue gym bag have been deposited on the bed. One retail sack appears empty, evidenced by several new articles of clothing that decorate the faded floral bedspread. I glance at the register slip on the bedside table and discern that Sandra wears Faded Glory knee-length pants, listed on the sales slip, as well as one of three T-shirts. Pale yellow.

Sandra picks up something from the floor, an ivory silk long-sleeved blouse. She stuffs it one of the bags. I notice a reddish-brown stain on the front of the blouse.

The woman also throws something silver in the bag. With both Wal-Mart bags in her hands, Sandra retreats to the bathroom. I respect her privacy, do not follow but hear her voice. I don't know what she's saying, but it sounds as if she is talking to someone who isn't there with the name "Rhonda". From other sounds and the distinctive scent of hair dye I figure out she's changing the length and color of her coiffeur. She returns with a smart-looking short hairstyle, light brown.

The woman sits on the bed and removes a large manila envelope, and reads from the enclosed document.

"The Last Will and Testament of Rhonda L. Collins. Sandra D. Lewis, first cousin, only beneficiary...." Pawing through the gym bag she produces a passport. From the panic-stricken look on her face and her attempts to find something else, it is easy to tell it's not what she wants. She delves into the bag again and relief washes over her. Sandra has found another passport.

Having the advantage of being the invisible author, I move in closer and see the first passport bears the name of "Rhonda", the second "Sandra". The woman mutters something about a "bubble-headed Felicity" and states, "Precisely why I did what I had to do." She pulls out a driver's license with her name. It's not a Texas license. I stare into the blue bag and see a huge wad of money.

Befuddled, I wonder why this character has someone else's passport, why she has changed her appearance. What about that stain on the blouse? The will? Who's Felicity?

What did Sandra do?

Sandra orders a pizza. I'm left with a title for a book, MISSING.

CHAPTER ONE

Cut and color

Sandra Lewis gazed at her fragmented reflection in the cracked bathroom mirror. The woman yanked the brown scrunchie from her ponytail and freed voluminous blonde hair. An obscenity escaped her lips. Sandra recoiled. Rhonda never would have used such language. *Not Rhonda,* Sandra mused. *So refined with her season tickets to the symphony, her designer clothing and her preference for upscale restaurants.*

How Sandra had loved Rhonda and everything the successful family physician at Cielo Vista Clinic had accomplished and accumulated. She began to cry as she grieved the loss of that amazing woman with the townhouse and BMW. Though Sandra always would miss Rhonda, the doctor had needed to be eliminated. She admonished herself to stop blubbering. Time to get ready. "I'm Sandra Lewis, I'm strong. I don't waste time crying."

Some time ago the woman had decided if she found herself in trouble, she'd head for the border as fast as possible. Though uneasy about Mexico's widespread dangers, Sandra knew staying in South Texas would be far more hazardous. She refused to follow in her wretched father's footsteps, footsteps that led straight to prison.

Teary in spite of herself, Sandra wished she could have kept Rhonda's car. *I've got to get past this. I'm lucky I found another car so quickly. It's 3:00 now; I should be on my way in a couple hours. All this will be behind me soon.*

The run-away needed to make certain preparations. From a plastic Wal-Mart bag Sandra took newly purchased barber scissors and sheared off her long tresses. As she checked out the short, feathered look achieved in spite of the flawed mirror, Sandra applauded her previous experience as a hairdresser. Removing a box of hair color from the same Wal-Mart bag, Sandra Dee Lewis transformed herself from a natural blonde to a natural-looking burnished toffee brunette.

"Now I don't look a thing like Rhonda. When they go looking for her, it will be a woman with long, blonde hair. I won't be mistaken for her and I can escape with ease!"

A vacant depression in the wall and a severed cord indicated it once housed a hairdryer. Sandra, now transformed, found she didn't need it. "Rhonda," Sandra said, "I know the little patients love to feel your long pony tail. How they laugh when you flick it around and whinny. But, girlfriend, being able to towel dry this 'do' is quite liberating!" Realizing she had referred to Rhonda in the present, Sandra added, "Not that it matters to you now."

Unbidden tears streamed down the woman's face. "Oh, Rhonda, I'm so sorry." Sighing, Sandra summoned all her strength to do what had to be done next.

Sitting on the bed, she pawed through Rhonda's gym bag until she found a large envelope. She carefully read every word of the "Last Will and Testament of Rhonda L. Collins, M.D." Rhonda had consulted a lawyer about six moths ago during one of her spells of anxiety. She left everything to one described as her only relative, her sister, Sandra D. Lewis, with an address in Chicago, Illinois. No one in Texas but Rhonda had known about Sandra. None but Sandra knew the truth about Rhonda, the truth destined to ruin the doctor.

The Chicago address belonged to Brian Cavendish. Sandra had used it for years because she always kept in touch with her old friend and one-time lover, now a married man. By the time Rhonda's estate was settled, years from now, no one would suspect the heir who lived in Chicago had anything to do with Rhonda's sudden absence in Corpus Christi. Her mind raced. *Someone's bound to remember Rhonda flew back to Chicago a few times. If her friends here find out about the will and its beneficiary, they'll know about her sister.* She continued to reassure herself. *Nonsense, girl, you're safe because no one ever met you. After all I pulled one over on Brian, brilliant Brian, eight years ago. The man has never figured it out so why worry?*

How she wished none of this had become necessary. Eliminating Rhonda ranked as the hardest thing she'd ever done. Harder even than running away from home and never returning when she was fifteen.

"I blame that old bubble-headed Felicity," Sandra muttered, hands grasping her forehead with its throbbing pain.

Two separate voices in her mind bickered. *Someone in the office is bound to make the connection between that incident with Melanie's aunt and Rhonda's abrupt departure,* nags a quavering voice.

So what! Merely a case of mistaken identity, argues another surer voice.

The doubting frightened voice counters. *But, you know how persistent that old bat can be.*

"Precisely why I did what I had to do," Sandra speaks out loud.

After that internal debate, one of many to come, Sandra's thoughts returned to the will. *I won't be able to collect what's rightfully mine for a long time, but I'll be okay for now with the cash Rhonda got her hands on today. Good she tucked all that cash awards and more from paychecks in the safety deposit box these past few months. A fantastic idea, if I, who suggested it, do say so myself!*

Sandra dug in the gym bag again and pulled out the passport she needed for Mexico. Panic-struck when she saw the document belonged to Rhonda, she moaned, "I can't use this. They could have the border patrol looking for her. I know I put mine in Rhonda's gym bag with the rest of the stuff from her purse." Pulse elevated, the panicked woman began a frantic search on hands and knees over the disgusting sour-smelling carpet. With no trace she again rifled through the gym bag and sighed with relief when this produced the needed passport. Using the barber scissors, she reduced Rhonda's passport to confetti. *No longer needed.*

She flushed the evidence down the toilet with more success than she had earlier when she tried to dispose of Rhonda's cell-phone in the one in a restroom at a Stripes convenience store. She remembered the incessant ringing as water whirled around, the toilet refusing to swallow the phone.

At this same time Dr. Linda Hernandez, Rhonda's colleague and best friend, handed over a photo and a DNA laden hairbrush to the police department. Sandra, overcome with headache and exhaustion, pulled down the spread and stretched out on the sheet. *It's late afternoon, only 5:30. I think I'll stretch out for a quick nap before my trip. Maybe get rid of this headache. That is if I can ignore the wheezing and clanging of that AC unit.*

The bolder Sandra voice persisted, *No! Hit the road. Don't waste any more time.*

But she's so tired, pleaded the other voice.

Ignoring the first voice, Sandra stretched out on the bed and wondered how a bed could be lumpy soft and hard at the same time. Suddenly she remembered that sensation. The mattress on the trailer house floor, the bed she had shared with her two little sisters in a no-account town in Arkansas. Sandra tried never to think about that part of her life, but the memory of the bed somehow comforted her. In spite of her nefarious deed, she had no trouble falling asleep.

Hours later she awoke with a start. The bedside clock, if correct, said nearly 9:00. She switched on the television, listened to a teaser for the one station that had 9:00 PM news. A growling stomach reminded her how long it had been since she'd eaten. Noticing a card with the number for Domino's taped to the telephone, she ordered a small pepperoni and mushroom pizza, Rhonda's favorite. *You influenced me in so many ways, Dr. Rhonda.*

Sandra watched the news while waiting for delivery. The big news story concerned twin tropical storms in the Gulf headed towards Mexico. *Nothing on the news yet about a missing person.* The pizza arrived. Sandra opened the door only wide enough so it could be slipped in sidewise and handed out the money and tip the same way. The delivery guy thought little about it. *Another scaredy-cat woman traveling alone.*

During that transaction a news item on the television would have piqued Sandra's interest just as it interested the night clerk at the Liberty Motel. The ever-perky anchor reported, "A Corpus Christi couple told police this afternoon that they had returned home from a cruise and found their gray 2010 Ford Taurus missing from the garage. Before going to police, they had questioned their teen-age son, who has his own car and wasn't aware this parents' car was gone." A gray Ford Taurus, like the one Sandra had purchased this afternoon from some kid outside a Stripes store.

The desk clerk, Lupe, wasn't sure of the year, but remembered a late-model car fitting that description in the motel parking lot when he came on duty. He always checked out the cars. More than once the type of people who patronized this motel had been wanted by the police and traced through the car recorded when registered. Lupe had called in a few tips himself. His curiosity aroused, he thumbed through the current occupants to see who drove the gray Taurus though

conceded there probably were dozens just like it around Corpus. It wasn't likely this was the missing vehicle, but....
Ah, here it is. Marsha Watkins: Room 204. He couldn't make out the license number the owner had scrawled. Most customers had to dart out of the motel to find out what numbers and letters their licenses bore.

Soon the person borrowing the name Marsha peered around a corner of the lobby. It had worried the agitated woman that it might look suspicious if she didn't check out, but now she wished she'd just left. Her tension eased upon spotting a different clerk, not the one who had been there when she checked in, the cute plump girl with curly black hair who hadn't even asked for an I.D. or credit card when Sandra said she would be paying cash. She probably shouldn't have been concerned about someone so clueless remembering her at all. *No worries now! With a different clerk, my changed appearance won't cause comment, suspicion.*

"I paid, but I'm not staying the night."

Lupe smirked. He couldn't resist. "Didn't he show up?"

Showing the same indignation as Rhonda would have shown, Sandra glared at him but decided to play along. "You got that right, the jerk." She handed him the keys and left.

Lupe laughed and said under his breath, "No, Marsha What's-her-Name doesn't look like the criminal type. Just another poor senorita done wrong by her man. Nothing to report to the cops this time."

A few days later the "clueless" female clerk, Brenda Ellis, would prove she had a fine eye for details. After seeing the photo of Rhonda on television, she called the police department on Monday morning to insist the missing woman had checked into the Liberty Motel where she worked.

CHAPTER TWO

Physician Missing

This same Monday afternoon turmoil had erupted at the Cielo Vista family medical practice as restless children and irritated parents accumulated in the waiting room. One of the doctors hadn't returned from lunch. "I wanna see Docker Wonda now!" wailed one preschooler in her "outdoor voice" while her impatient mother didn't even attempt to shush her.

"It doesn't make sense," Amy, one of the nervous young receptionists, grumbled. "Dr. Rhonda's never late."

"I've called her cell and her home phone several times, but she's not picking up," replied the other receptionist, Carla. "How could she be late on a Monday when she knows we're always so busy?"

"What am I supposed to tell her 1:00 appointment and the others? It's almost 2:00," wailed Amy, tightly gripping the appointment book.

"Tell her Dr. Rhonda had an emergency and reschedule them for tomorrow."

Dr. Linda Hernandez stopped at the desk to drop off some insurance forms and questioned the backlog in the waiting room. Alarmed that her co-worker and best friend wasn't back from lunch, she offered to take any of her patients she could. As the afternoon wore on, the office workers spent all their time calling the popular doctor's patients to tell them that they would have to reschedule.

Concern for Rhonda replaced initial annoyance. Dr. Ronyl Brooks, head of the practice, took charge, "I'm calling the police."

"I'm sorry," the dispatcher at the South Corpus Christi PD began, "We can do nothing about a woman missing three hours, no matter how responsible she always is. Call back when it's been at least 24 hours."

Dr. Ron slammed down the receiver as his co-worker Dr. Linda entered the office. He told her the reaction generated by his call. Her face took on a stony look. "I have the key to her townhouse. I'm going there as soon as I can leave work."

When Linda reached Rhonda's home in Palmetto Estates, she pulled on a pair of latex-free gloves and over her shoes maneuvered booties she had secreted in her pockets before leaving the clinic. As she unlocked the door, she heard the frantic bark of Poppy, Rhonda's Chihuahua. Linda knew Rhonda always fed the dog as soon as she came home but first Linda called for her friend and looked in each room. No Rhonda. She fed the little brown and white pet. While he munched on his kibbles, she looked around more and found nothing to make her think Rhonda had been there since she left for work in the morning. Cereal bowl and coffee cup in the sink. The pecan-colored jacket that matched the pants she'd worn left on a chair by the door as if she decided at the last minute it was too warm to wear. She remembered well the classic ivory silk blouse her friend had worn today. She was with Rhonda when she purchased the blouse in San Antonio, on a recent girls' weekend.

<hr />

"That's beautiful, Rhonda. With your coloring and the ruffles at the neckline and sleeves you'll look like an angel in it."

"It's just plain too expensive."

"Oh, come on" Linda kidded, "You can afford it, especially after that 'Distinguished Doctor' award. Or, at least you could, if you didn't insist on spoiling my kids with gifts."

In the end Rhonda had splurged on the blouse, worn for the first time today.

Linda called the police from her cell-phone, "This is Dr. Linda Hernandez from Cielo Vista Clinic. I know you told our lead doctor it's too soon to do anything about our missing doctor, but you have to start looking now. She's my friend and I'm at her home. There's no sign of her being here since this morning."

The desk clerk couldn't ignore the hysteria in the caller's voice. "Could you bring us a photo?"

Linda grabbed a current one of both of them from an end table. Having watched too many detective shows, she went into the bathroom where she'd seen Rhonda's hairbrush. She took both to the South Corpus Christi Police Department.

"She'll turn up, they always do," an office pronounced with assurance.

But what if she doesn't? Linda's stomach knotted. She couldn't allow herself to think that something bad had happened to Rhonda. *But the police must start thinking that or they'll never look for her, and I'll never see her again.* It hit her. *Poppy shouldn't be alone. I didn't even let him outside. I don't like dogs, especially Poppy, but no matter what anyone will think, I'm not so cruel that I'd harm a dog or any other living thing.*

Rhonda's best friend returned to her townhouse with gloves and booties and packed up the dog, his food and bed. She'd called her family earlier to explain she would be late and would pick up supper. As she and the little dog waited in the Jack-in-the-Box drive-through, she called home to say, "I'll be there right away. I'm picking up food now."

"What-ya bringing?" Sam, her eight year old, the middle one, asked.

"Jack-in-the Box Burgers." Looking beside her at the tiny dog her sons adored, she added. "And a humongous surprise." She smiled at Poppy, who bared his sharp little teeth.

CHAPTER THREE

A run for the border

Sandra saw lightning to the southwest as she headed out of the motel parking lot, but it shouldn't slow her down. In no time she'd be in Mexico, where she planned to dump the car and find a coach to Mazatlan. Rhonda and Linda had loved it when they vacationed there last March during the week when the clinic closed because of traffic congestion in Corpus brought on by hordes of Spring Breakers.

The nagging voice had made her feel guilty about poor little Poppy. She **had** to stop at Rhonda's townhouse to check on him.

That voice had turned hopeful. *Would it be possible to sneak in there, grab him, and smuggle him into Mexico?*

The controlling voice wasted no time in screaming, *Absolutely not! You don't need that complication.*

Sandra agreed. "I love that dog, but I have to stick to the plan and get to Mexico as soon as possible. I'm so far behind schedule but it's probably better I waited until it was dark." About then her car hit one of Corpus Christi's famed potholes, and she was sure she'd damaged the muffler. It didn't seem louder, and through the rear-view mirror she couldn't see any car parts scattered behind her. She continued to Palmetto Estates, where Rhonda lived. Total darkness had descended.

She started to turn right to Rhonda's street but spotted a squad car parked in front of Rhonda's townhouse. Backing up the gray Taurus, Sandra continued straight until she could circle around and, from the opposite direction, enter the alley behind the townhouses in the row where Rhonda had lived. She turned off the air conditioning; opening the window, she strained to listen. Could she hear Poppy's piercing bark? Nothing. A ray of hope! Perhaps a neighbor had reported incessant barking to the caretaker, and he or she had rescued the little pet as before when work had made Rhonda late.

Leaving the complex by a back exit, Sandra still avoided driving near the squad car. The soon-to-retire officer, Hank Barton, assigned to keep an eye on the townhouse in case the missing doc returned, had seen a driver start to turn down Spoonbill, where he was parked. The driver backed up and went straight on Reef. Didn't seem suspicious to him. *It's easy to get lost here with all the rows looking alike. I had a helluva time finding this address.* In the dark he hadn't noticed a car resembling a stolen Taurus. He looked for a missing blonde woman, not a missing gray vehicle.

Sandra hated more delays but needed gas. *Sure easier to use a credit card,* she thought as she filled the tank. *I'm probably calling more attention to myself paying with cash but I'll only have to do it once.* The attendant, engrossed in reading a tabloid, barely looked at her customer as she handled the transaction. She didn't hold the twenties up to the light or pen them, and she sure didn't ask for an I.D. Incompetent workers, Sandra's pet peeve, now worked to her advantage.

In the unlikely case someone followed her, the woman on the run headed northwest towards San Antonio before doubling back and turning south towards Mexico. Ignoring a "Don't Mess with Texas" sign and not noticing a sign that "Hope Comm. Church has responsibility for cleaning this mile of highway", she tossed out the bag containing the hair and stained blouse, both belonging to Rhonda. She'd been careful to avoid getting her handprints on any items. She felt certain that no one saw her. No one followed her.

As soon as she could, Sandra doubled back to Corpus Christi and headed towards the border, south through the desert area where throughout the years bodies or bones of many missing persons had turned up. She wondered how long until the police searched for Rhonda here. *I just can't think about it.*

Little traffic on the road south to Brownsville. Some truck traffic in the northbound lane. No check station to stop her going south. The events of the day played through her mind. *Could I have done anything else? No. Do I regret it? With every fiber of my body.* Brian had warned her eight years ago that what she wanted to do could land her in prison for a long time. She'd ignored him, saying he wasn't the only one in that line of business that could help her. "I took my chances, and I'm not giving up now," she stated out loud with mustered confidence.

She decided to turn on the car radio. Nothing like music to drown out her troubled thoughts. Furious, she discovered someone, probably the kid who sold her the car, had removed the sound system. *Creep!* Troubling thought occurred. *Did the kid sell me a stolen car?* She reassured herself: *I doubt it. He looked awfully clean-cut. I didn't ask any questions and neither did he. Obviously, he needed cash, maybe for college tuition. Oh, geesh, now you're sounding like Rhonda. Probably a druggie who got more money from selling the sound system and car separately, which means this car could be stolen.* Sandra had hit the nail on the head as would be revealed in days to come. Already law enforcement agencies throughout the state had received an alert about the car she drove.

As light rain turned heavy, fear about the deteriorating weather eclipsed her worries over the car. *This is getting really bad. I didn't think a tropical was going to hit for days. I should have gone to the west and down to the border. No, it's always been the plan to get out of the country as fast as possible.* Increasing discomfort accentuated by the rain made her wish she had gone to the restroom when she stopped for gas.

Heavy walls of rain gushed down. Visibility dropped to zero. Sandra pulled off to the side of the road. She'd planned to stop anyway and accomplish what needed to be done as quickly as possible, and this place was as good as any.

Having completed what needed to be done, Sandra now shivered in her soaked clothing. She listened to the machine gun-like sound of the rain pelting the car roof and found herself transported back in time to another rainy night in a trailer house in Arkansas. Over the years she had tried to bury all the memories of her Arkansas beginnings, but that old bumpy motel bed had triggered thoughts of those miserable early years and that fateful night when her dad stomped out of the trailer after beating her mother. Driving drunk, with a suspended license, Daddy was in the wrong lane and had a head-on collision that killed a couple and their child.

She remembered snuggling with her younger sisters in the back bedroom as rain pounded on the metal roof. She made up a game to distract the little girls from their parents' current drunken battle in the living room. Sandra quickly banished the scene from her mind and gave it free rein to go over what had happened to make this midnight escape necessary.

It concerned Sandra how Rhonda must have looked to others when about noon, she, obviously distressed, left the clinic in a rush. She'd panicked because of a chance encounter with a visitor to the clinic from Oklahoma, Felicity Ritter, known to many as "Fe". She had insisted the two of them had a history together. Rhonda seemed to lead such a lovely, serene life. Only Sandra knew how she worried that something like this might happen. Sandra knew exactly what Rhonda was thinking when she took off. How could she run out on her responsibilities, abandon her poor patients, her colleagues, everyone who depended on her? What would become of her dog? How could she leave Linda, who'd been more like a sister than her biological sisters? Or, him? Though she had tried often enough. Basically, how could she give up the wonderful life she had made for herself, the life she loved? Sandra knew that Rhonda would depend on her to make the right decision.

Sandra continued to piece together the order of events. Rhonda's purse that she'd left in the BMW outside the credit union would reveal she'd visited another financial institution after leaving the clinic. C*areless! I should have taken that receipt.* After Rhonda left the credit union, she took a deliberate detour into the public restroom in the hallway outside the credit union. At that point Sandra understood the woman she knew so well hovered near the brink of aborting the escape. She'd champion the right thing to do was return to the office. Confess. Take the consequences. Such a good person but they were in this together. Sandra, ruthless Sandra, had to take charge.

A short time later Sandra Lewis wearing the outfit Dr. Rhonda Collins had put on that morning left the restroom and exited the building into the parking ramp. Looking around, Sandra found herself alone on the ramp but had to work fast before someone observed her. Luck was on her side because a man, who had a 12:30 assignation with Rhonda, had spotted her BMW. He had waited for their meeting but unable to wait any longer, this man who knew Rhonda intimately, just missed Sandra when he entered the building to look for Rhonda. If Sandra had seen the man, she would have been disgusted. Though having many flaws, something she would never do was commit adultery with a married man. She wondered what people would think if they knew Rhonda slept with none other than Dr. Linda Hernandez' husband.

She unlocked the BMW on the passenger's side and laid Rhonda's purse on the seat. From it she extracted the large amounts of cash, documents and cell-phone. Earlier when she had grabbed the purse in the restroom, she had taken out what else she needed, being as careful as possible not to leave finger prints on anything else.

Reaching over the seat to grab Rhonda's gym bag, Sandra stuffed into it the cash and papers as well as Rhonda's gold hoop earrings, a watch and a scalpel the doctor had had kept for protection. From the bag Sandra took the doctor's cross-trainers, which she exchanged for the pumps. She also grabbed a black hoodie from the backseat and put that on, covering most of her hair. She put the pumps next to the purse, deliberately leaving Rhonda's wallet with ID, credit cards and cash in the purse. She locked the car.

Checking to see if there was anyone near and seeing no one, she returned to the restroom. Not a soul saw her return to the car, open and close the trunk with a look of great distaste on her face. *That's the smell Rhonda was talking about. She planned to have the car detailed. Said she was afraid to open the truck because of the odor and laughed that someone had planted a body there. Little did she know...*

Sandra remembered the dark glasses in the purse and retrieved those. She again locked the door and tossed Rhonda's key ring with the car and garage remotes under the car. *Neither of us will need these.*

Rhonda had prepared to take flight by withdrawing cash. Now Sandra was the one needing to flee in case someone mistook her for Rhonda with her clothes and long blonde hair. Rattled as she felt, Sandra had to stay calm and think. Finding enough coins in the pocket of the hoodie, she extracted The Corpus Christi Caller Times from a news box. She perused used car ads. Finding one that caught her eye, she called the number listed.

A kid saying he was eighteen, who sounded about ten, agreed he'd meet her within the hour at a nearby Stripes Convenience Store. Sandra had milled around the crowded shop where many people bought quick lunches. The burritos smelled especially tantalizing so she bought two and nibbled on them waiting by the door but keeping one eye on the line at the restroom.

A tough-looking kid, all tattoos and body piercings, entered the store and looked around. Sandra approached him, but he wasn't selling a car. Twice more she stopped teen boys and hoped no one noticed this behavior. Another, much better groomed than the other three, came in and looked around. Sandra asked him the same question. He motioned her to step outside and showed her a gray sedan, a late model. "I forgot to tell you. I need cash," he mumbled.

"Sure, how about $700? It's all I have," Sandra lied. He didn't argue about the ridiculously low amount, took it and completed the transaction by handing her the keys.

Sandra returned to the Stripes store to see the long line at the restroom had diminished to one. She took her turn so she could fling Rhonda's cell phone down the toilet. It had rung constantly since 1:00 with calls from the clinic and rang still as it swirled around in the water. She wasn't about to reach into a foul toilet to retrieve it and figured the water would ruin it anyway. It would erase her call to the kid about the car and another call Rhonda had made. She decided what to do next, buy a few necessities at a Wal-Mart not in the area.

After making it through the usual Wal-Mart crowds, she'd located a motel where no one would look for Rhonda. Now she sat worried to death by the side of the road. She talked to herself, just to hear a voice. "Hope I didn't waste too much time at that miserable motel. I had to get out of those clothes and color my hair. The police will be looking for a missing woman with long blonde hair. If I'm stopped for anything, I don't want to be mistaken for her. They could search the car, find the gym bag. I'm still worried about this car. What if it's hot? I need to ditch it as soon as soon as possible."

"Should-haves" filled her mind as she contemplated any other mistakes made so far. *Should have thrown the cell down a sewer. Should have asked the seller if he stole the car – no, I know that kid would have lied. Should have left the motel as soon as I finished coloring my hair. Should I have used a different color? Definitely wasted too much time.* In present time as Sandra became increasing uncomfortable, she lamented not relieving herself when she'd stopped. The runaway sure didn't want to go out in the rain again.

I've tried not to leave a trail but what if I screwed up along the way? For sure, I should have left sooner and beat this storm.

It's not too late to turn back, whined the voice she'd named Rhonda. The other, more like her voice, disagreed. *You have to keep going.*

Even though the rain still could be termed torrential and lightning jagged the sky, Sandra decided she needed to be on her way to the border. "Maybe it's letting up," she kidded herself. Turning on the ignition and starting to pull over, Sandra saw the red and blue flashing lights of a patrol car, coming up beside her.

"OH, NO!!"

Sandra's heart started beating so hard she thought it would burst through her chest. Her mind raced, too. *Somehow they've traced the car and think they've found the missing doctor because someone thinks they recognized Rhonda buying it. Or worse, somehow through her lawyer they know about the will and they've made the connection between Rhonda and me. Either way, I'm...*

A trooper tapped on the window. Sandra unrolled it, tears welling in her eyes as she pictured being taken away in cuffs.

"Are you okay, Miss?"

Her mind continued its race. *I don't look a thing like her now and I'll just tell the truth about the car. I bought this one from a kid at Stripes to drive to Mexico to see -- to see my sick aunt.*

"Miss? I asked if you're okay."

"Yes," Sandra stammered as convenient tears dripped down her cheeks, "It's just this awful storm…"

"That's why I've stopped you. This is from that first tropical storm but now they think the second will come in as Hurricane Leo. Evacuation may become necessary but for now we're closing all traffic south. If you follow me, I'll show you a crossover where you can head back north. It's for your own good."

Sandra couldn't believe her good fortune. She wasn't being arrested. Another chance. She grabbed it. Thanking the officer profusely, she followed his directions and drove north to Corpus and then towards San Antonio.

I'm going to find another motel, somewhere inland, and come back as soon as the weather clears. I'll find a nice motel. I deserve it.

Sandra Lewis passed several motels that don't meet her specifications as she traveled northwest. Hours later she wound up in San Antonio and spotted a motel near the airport that looks very nice. Not wanting to be associated with the car, she parked it a few blocks away from the motel in an office building lot and walked to the motel. Walking alone is something she never would have considered if she'd had an inkling of the crime rate in that area.

A thug followed her. Sandra heard footsteps behind her. Not daring to look back, she turned a corner. The footsteps continued behind her. She heard labored breathing and imagined a man's hot breath on her neck. Her heart pounded as Sandra regretted throw throwing away the scalpel that

Rhonda always carried. The doctor had maintained it was small and light to carry and could do real damage if you knew what to do with it.

The person continued to tail her as she came closer to the motel and fear had mounted until Sandra could barely breathe or walk. If she screamed, would anyone hear? Should she try to run? She used to be a fast runner and, at least, she wasn't wearing heels. Her heart now beat so hard she expected it to blast out through her yellow t-shirt.

The thug, who'd made a study of female clothing, came close enough to see cheap clothes and a gym bag instead of a coach purse and decided the woman wasn't worth robbing. He'd give her a break and look for more promising prey. He turned around and walked back into the darkness. Again luck was with Sandra as she heard the retreating footsteps.

At the motel she signed in with another false name. The night clerk asked if she had a credit card and I.D.

She answered, "Never use credit cards. Scared silly about identity theft, I'm paying cash."

"I still need an I.D. and I need your car license number."

"I came in a taxi from the airport," Sandra lied.

"Fine, then just your I.D."

Sandra made a big show of looking in the gym bag she carried. "I know it's in here some place." She sighed as she began a frantic search and didn't have to pretend panic as she threw herself on the mercy of the desk clerk. "I'm afraid I lost it, maybe the last time I showed it to security in the airport. What will I do? What WILL I DO?" she screamed.

The motherly clerk took pity on her. "Please, calm down. Just write down your name and address, and if you find your I.D., bring it down to me."

"Oh, thank you, thank you." Sandra couldn't have been more sincere. She wrote down the fake name she'd given and added Brian's address.

She took the keycard and found the elevator that would take her to a room and a few hours sleep before dawn.

CHAPTER FOUR

Hand-wringing

Too overwrought to eat or sleep, Linda finally fell into her bed the same time Sandra did at the San Antonio motel, about 3:00 Tuesday morning. Rain pounded the roof. The scent of their fast-food supper still lingered in the house as the evening replayed itself before her.

She had tried but couldn't eat her hamburger, which she'd passed over to her husband, Dave. He'd shown concern for Rhonda, who after all was his friend, too, but it seemed his friend's disappearance hadn't affected his appetite.

In private before supper his wife had explained to Dave about Rhonda's failure to return from lunch break and her fear that she had been taken away against her will. He thought Linda was over-reacting, but he knew how much her friendship with Rhonda meant to her and wasn't about to say that.

Linda had told her three sons that she had volunteered them to take good care of Poppy while their favorite auntie was on a trip. She disliked being untruthful but would spare them what had really happened for now. Monday evening, listening to their laughs and Poppy's excited yipping, she repeatedly dialed Rhonda's land phone. Voicemail soon filled up with her calls and, no doubt, those of others with the same message of caring and a request to be called back. *If the police check the phones, they will know how concerned everyone is, especially me.* She tried the cell phone, which she'd begun calling from the clinic as soon as Rhonda hadn't returned. Until about 1:30 that afternoon it rang and rang. Later it appeared not to be working, which could mean anything from a battery not recharged to something much worse. *No, I don't want to think about that.*

She looked for Dave, who was in their room reading a handgun magazine with the television blaring in an attempt to mask the noise of the kids and the visiting dog's infernal yap. Irritated that he could be so complacent with their friend missing, Linda shouted over the television, "I'm going to post Rhonda's photo and what happened on Facebook."

Anything but complacent, Dave had worries of his own about Rhonda. Neither of them wanted to hurt Linda, and last night Rhonda had decided to break it off once and for all. He had tried to talk her out of it, but Rhonda threatened to tell Linda if he wouldn't end the affair. He did what he had to do, regardless of how it turned out, and in case someone had spotted him at the Vega Building, he didn't want anything on Facebook that might implicate him. "Not yet, Linda. Have respect for Rhonda's privacy. There's probably a perfectly reasonable explanation for this." Then with a look towards the living room he added, "Have you tried calling her? Probably she's home, worried silly about that miserable little beast."

Linda glared at him and in a shaky voice answered, "I've called her every few minutes since I've been home. I don't think either you or the police department are taking this seriously enough."

The contrite husband beckoned to his wife. "Come here, Babe. I'm sorry. I understand you're worried." He held his wife, and dried the tears she'd been holding back all day. "You know I love Rhonda, too."

Linda couldn't help thinking. *At times I think he seems to love her a little too much.* She chided herself for being so petty at a time like this.

After they put the kids to bed and coaxed Poppy into his bed in the living room, Dave, apologized to his wife about the timing of a business trip the next day, singing, "I picked the wrong time to leave you, Lucille." That brought a small smile, but then a frown. "But you just got home from one last night."

"I know, Hon, I don't like it any better than you do, but it's my job," he commented while thinking with regret, *And I won't be stopping at Rhonda's on my way home this time or ever again.*

He went back to the master bedroom to pack a bag. He wished Rhonda's disappearance act were some kind of attention getting scheme his ex-lover was pulling, but he knew otherwise. It was over. Really over.

In the living room the little dog whined pitifully. Linda remembered Rhonda always covered him up at night because Chihuahuas she had said, even in South Texas, chill easily. She found an old sweater and wrapped him in it. He fell asleep.

She turned on her laptop, and didn't post on Facebook. Instead she left messages on the website links for "News Tips" of the three local television stations and the local paper. Linda described Rhonda and the clothes she wore and an expressed fear for Rhonda's well being. Later Dr. Brooks would call the same tip-lines. He couldn't remember what Rhonda wore but described her BMW in detail

In the homes of every Cielo Vista staff member that Monday in September, all speculated about what had happened to the doctor they liked so much. At the Brooks' home Dr. Ron asked Melanie, his wife, "Did you see Rhonda when you brought your aunt to visit the clinic?"

"I most certainly did. She seemed in a really big hurry. I thought at first she had an errand to run or was meeting someone for lunch during her break but I don't think that was it because she seemed a little agitated." Melanie paused, wondering if what she was about to say could have any significance. "Ron, something else happened. When Aunt Fe saw Rhonda, Auntie insisted she knew Rhonda but called her a different name. I can't remember what is was and I should because she kept saying it. I believe the last name was a man's name with an 's' at the end, maybe Adams – no, that wasn't it. Andrews? Roberts?"

Ron spoke more harshly than he intended, "Please get on with the story. We could spend all night sitting here playing Rumpelstiltskin."

"Okay, okay. Auntie insisted that Dr. Rhonda used to be her hairdresser. I assured her that Dr. Rhonda might resemble her hairdresser but she's been here for years. Then she said that her hairdresser left years ago and, of course, commented that she didn't like the new hairdresser because her perms are frizzy. I told her that she might be a little confused and could be thinking about when she lived in Modell not in Tulsa. At any rate, she seemed to forget all about it when I said we needed to grab you for lunch before I took her to the airport."

Ron, mulling over all of this, commented, "If it were anyone but your nutty aunt, I'd say there's a possibility that Rhonda worked her way through med school as a hairdresser, but she went some place out east, not Oklahoma. But how did Rhonda react?"

"She looked confused, smiled and left while Aunt Fe railed about her rudeness because Rhonda hadn't even acknowledged her."

Ron puzzled out loud, "Could something have happened with one of her patients to upset her? Tomorrow I'll take a look at her Monday schedule. Maybe someone who had an appointment with her realized something not quite right. Now

I plan to relax and enjoy an evening without having to listen to your aunt and her constant chit-chat."

That same evening neither of the young receptionists, Carla and Amy, had any compunction about posting on their Facebook pages. Amy told in detail how she was at the reception desk and saw the doctor leave for lunch and didn't return on time, then, at all. It wasn't like her -- no way and she feared that she had been abducted. Carla posted a very similar message except with her own colorful theory that a sick, rich old man knew that Rhonda recently had been named Distinguished Young Doctor and had her kidnapped to be his private physician, just like the rich and famous. This and any kidnapping theory would be proved wrong, but throughout the night, as Sandra drove to San Antonio and settled at the motel, that news spread.

By the end of the week the disappearance would become the lead on all stations and on the front page of the paper. On Monday's late newscast only one television station had a brief mention that Linda waited to hear. A Breaking News reporter, young and eager, stood outside in the rain and darkness by the sign for the Cielo Vista Clinic. With little to report, he pointed to the signboard and stated, "Ten hours earlier a doctor left this clinic for lunch and never returned. One of her frantic co-workers described her as slender, about 5-8, in her late thirties, wearing a silk ivory-colored blouse with ruffles, pecan colored pants and matching shoes and purse. She was last seen driving her black BMW from this clinic parking lot." He added, "We contacted the police at South Corpus Christi PD, near the clinic." With narrowed eyes and in an exasperated tone, he uttered, "They refused to comment." Then smiling, "If you have seen someone fitting this description, tell it to our tip-line. Back to you in the studio." The anchors shook their heads and pursed their lips in empathy and turned to the well-known meteorologist, who began, "I hope she didn't drive south of here because they're experiencing very heavy rains on the

Brownsville Road, due to those twin tropical storms in the Gulf, responsible for the deluge now. It's likely the second storm will turn into Hurricane Leo, but we should be okay since its path -- look right here -- will take it into Mexico."

Knowing she couldn't sleep, Linda didn't turn off the television after the news. Instead Rhonda's best friend, Linda, listened to rain and watched mindless late night fare until after 3:00 AM.

CHAPTER FIVE

Bring on the PD

Hurricane Leo ranked as the main topic of conversation Tuesday morning in Corpus Christi. Hurricanes, someone was bound to point out, 'always hooked', which meant it could wind up in Texas, maybe even in Corpus. At Cielo Vista, everyone agonized out loud about Rhonda and the weather.

The phone rang incessantly at the recently established South Corpus Christi Police Department, SCCPD, located south of the main thoroughfare, South Padre Island Drive, known as "S-P-I-D" and "Spid". Irate citizens wanted to know what the police were doing about the "abducted" doctor.

"We don't need this kind of pressure from the public," stormed the hotheaded, often unconventional, Chief Hernando Ortiz. Reeking of cigar smoke, the rotund chief with a rogue black mustache began morning roll call with his tirade. "She's an adult, not a toddler, and it hasn't been a damned twenty-four hours. I thought we were doing more than enough sending Hank out last night to do surveillance at the doctor's Corpus residence."

The Police Department desk clerk chimed in, "Not only that but I agreed to have one of the doctors bring in a picture yesterday." She extracted the photo from a file cabinet behind her. "Here it is."

"I saw a better one on Facebook," offered young, pretty dark-eyed Maria Gonzales, a uniform who had spent a year as a street cop. She recently had transferred from the downtown station in hopes of becoming a detective here.

Chief Ortiz fumed, "Facebook? I thought everyone saw it on the news. Who knows how many more calls we'll get from Facebook crazies."

"Here's a note from last night," a clerk volunteered. She read the scrawled message: "A reporter from one of the TV stations called and we said 'no comment'."

"Somebody did something right," Ortiz snarled.

Already accustomed to Ortiz' explosive reactions, Marie offered, "I saw a photo on one of the 10:00 news shows last night and also this morning. It was the Facebook photo. From what I've learned this doctor's really a big deal. She won the Distinguished Young Doctor award a while back. I think that's a national..."

The Chief cut her off with a look, "Since you've taken so much interest in the woman, I'm sending you to the clinic to find out everything you can from their staff."

Even with her MA in Criminal Justice from the University of Texas, Maria wasn't quite prepared for this. "But I've never..." stammered Maria.

Ortiz spoke calmly. "Don't worry. It's just to placate everyone. We know an adult who disappears usually does it on purpose, and there's been no ransom request yet, which makes it more likely she's run off."

Officer Gonzales registered her disbelief and inadequacy. "You -- you -- want me to do this on my own?"

Ortiz swore in English and then Spanish for emphasis, "Yes, I just *promoted* you to a plain-clothes detective because of your fancy education and obvious preoccupation with this so-called case."

"Oh." Maria couldn't believe it. *This is what I wanted, but...* She blurted out, "But isn't it customary to send out two detectives?"

Out of patience, the gruff Chief employed more blue and *azul* words. "For a real case, yes, but what the h-e-double toothpicks, Belkin go with her. Might as well waste the taxpayers' money on two cops chasing their tails." This wasn't standard procedure but it wasn't the first time Ortiz deviated.

"Sure," agreed Sgt. Stan Belkin, who wasn't opposed to spending time with the cute-looking newbie. " But I need to know, did Hank's watch amount to anything?"

"*Nada* -- no lights, nobody came. At 11:00 they needed him for a robbery at a liquor store on Saratoga. That's what we're supposed to do," he added sarcastically, "fight crime, not look for some gal who probably had an argument with her boyfriend and wants him to suffer worrying about her. Then looking directly at the newly appointed detective, he added, "I don't care if she's a Big Deal doctor who won some fancy prize."

On the drive to the clinic, Sergeant Belkin lectured his new partner. "People watch two damned much television. Because someone is missing a couple minutes, they assume they've been abducted or worse. Just like Chief said, adults take off usually because of a complicated personal relationship or cash flow problems." Warming to his topic, he went on," A few take on new identities, go to foreign countries; no one finds them. Most return when they've had time to realize what they've done isn't working." He paused and added, "Then there's some that run after committing a crime, and because of massive attention, law enforcement locates them. Nine times out of ten that happens on television or movies!" Belkin laughed at his witticism and smacked the steering wheel for emphasis.

Gonzales silently seethed at the patronizing speech, especially since she knew with her MA she had considerably more education that Belkin. Sounding as defensive as she felt, the brand-spanking-new detective commented, "I understand that's why we aren't eager to get involved right away, but somehow this seems different."

Belkin raised his eyebrows, "Bullsh! This is a waste of time, but here we are, Cielo Vista Family Clinic."

As Sandra still slept in San Antonio, the veteran detective Sergeant Belkin interviewed each staff member in private without giving Gonzales much of a chance to ask anything. She hadn't had time to change out of the uniform she would no longer wear as an undercover so appeared as the low-ranking uniform that had gone to work that morning. Belkin wore a well-cut suit over his skinny frame. With his height, chiseled features and graying hair, he looked so much more imposing.

The clinic included five doctors, including the head one, the missing doctor, two other female doctors and another male, all young. The staff also included two receptionists, six nursing assistants and two RNs, plus a host of technicians. Only three of the technicians had been at the clinic Monday, and none were present after 10:00 AM. They would know nothing about the missing doctor leaving about noon.

Speeding through the interviews, Belkin acted bored with the answers to questions he'd asked about the doctor's character and whether she had any known enemies or problems. Gonzales' expressive eyes shone with compassion as she recorded what each had to say in a small red polka dot spiral notebook, which she preferred to the black issue one she'd been given. All stated pretty much the same thing: the missing woman was the definition of virtue, a competent, award-winning doctor, not a person who would run away from responsibilities. No known enemies, personal problems not apparent. Each person interviewed worried that something bad had happened to her.

The receptionists were last, and to hurry things along, Belkin interviewed them together. Dr. Ron, clinic owner and head physician, being the only one available, had to take over their jobs. After a few minutes of listening to a roomful of yowling kids and cutting off patients who called for appointments because he couldn't figure out the phones, he considered raising Amy and Carla's salaries or hiring more office help.

During the interview, Carla restated the theory that she'd put on Facebook about the rich old man having the doctor kidnapped. With tears in her eyes, Amy insisted, "Dr. Rhonda would be here now if she could. I just know -- I mean, I feel -- someone kidnapped her." Then offering another theory she and Amy had discussed earlier in the morning, "Or she fell and hit her head and is wandering around Corpus with amnesia."

Belkin bit his tongue. He wanted to tell those two twits that amnesia happened only on soap operas and the same for most adult kidnappings. Gonzales continued to look troubled and intrigued with their theories. Belkin dismissed the two young women and told his subordinate. "I want to talk more to that female doctor who says she knew the missing woman best. I have more questions for her."

They cooled their heels, appropriately in the waiting room, for twenty minutes until Dr. Linda had a few minutes between patients. Belkin then asked her to tell anything else she knew about Dr. Rhonda.

Dr. Linda spoke as if quoting something rehearsed, having found the right words when sleep evaded her Monday night. Certain she's be interviewed, Linda wanted the police department to know Rhonda definitely should not be considered "just another missing person".

"I've known Rhonda for the eight years she's lived in Corpus and practiced here. She is a model doctor, easy to work with, and the patients love her. We go to the same church, and we've become quite close." Linda Hernandez described all the holidays Rhoda had spent with the Hernandez family and how much the three children loved their generous adopted aunt.

Belkin, tapping on a table with impatience, interrupted the monologue to ask, "Do you know anything about her life before coming to Corpus?"

"No. She said she had no family and never mentioned her life prior to coming here." Linda avoided saying she often had pondered that previous life which Rhonda wouldn't discuss. *No, I won't say that. It might look like as if Rhonda was hiding something.* Instead she said, "Several times she flew from here to Chicago to spend weekends with a friend."

Gonzales thought of something to ask, "Male or female?"

"I assumed female, but …"

"Could've been a boyfriend?" Belkin asked.

"I doubt it. Rhonda never dated." Belkin thought twice before commenting on why a woman as good-looking as everyone described the missing doctor, wouldn't date. That gave Gonzales a chance to express her own idea, "Could it be she didn't date because her boyfriend was in Chicago?"

"I'm **sure** she would have told me," was Linda's emphatic answer. "We shared the details of our lives with each other all the time," she said while thinking *I certainly shared so much with Rhonda, but Rhonda shared little with me.*

Belkin took over, "Did she ever give you the number where she stayed in Chicago?"

"No." That wasn't completely true. Rhonda had given her the number once in case of emergency after she bought Poppy, but told Linda not to share that information. The best friend didn't intend to say anything unless it became necessary. Breaking a confidence didn't serve any purpose right now, besides not sure she could find the number.

"Okay, that's a life detail the doctor kept to herself." Sarcasm matched the Chief's in Belkin's voice.

Linda frowned as the detective continued, "Let's get back to her departure yesterday, what she was wearing, if she seemed upset when she left, anything at all."

Linda described the doctor's shade of tan pants as pecan with matching shoes and purse as well as the ivory silk blouse with ruffled collar and cuffs Rhonda had worn to work Monday, the same description given the media. She also described the BMW but didn't know the license number.

"Easy enough to look up," Belkin responded as Gonzales asked, "Was the doctor wearing jewelry?"

"She usually didn't wear much to the clinic, just a watch and earrings. Monday she wore largish gold hoops and a delicate yellow gold watch, warm colors to go . . ."

Belkin cut her off. "Did she seem strange -- like upset -- the last time you saw her? And when was that?"

"I saw Rhonda leaving an exam room about noon. She seemed in a big hurry, maybe had an errand to run during lunch break. Rhonda does that sometimes."

"Did anyone else see her leave?" Belkin prodded.

"Probably the head nurse, Sheila, when picking up her purse from the nurses' station, and probably the receptionists. I just want you to understand Rhonda would never leave her patients or her friends willingly. She just wouldn't."

The officers nodded and asked to talk again to the nurse and receptionists.

Both receptionists admitted they'd been busy on the phones and hadn't seen the doctor leave in spite of what both had implied on Facebook.

Something of more interest came from Sheila, the head nurse who turned out to be quite a chatterbox.

"I saw her about noon when she picked up her purse. We keep all our purses in the nurses' station, which no one is supposed to know." Then she laughed. "But I guess it's okay to tell y' all."

Belkin rolled his eyes. "Anything else?"

"Well, I just had been talking to two women and I know they were still in the hall. She would have passed them if she went out the front door, and I assume she used that door since the waiting room was empty; it's closer to where we park, and…"

Belkin interrupted, "And who were the two people you were talking to?"

"One was Dr. Ron's wife, Melanie, and the other was her aunt, an elderly woman from Oklahoma, Tulsa, I think. Melanie was taking her aunt on a tour of the clinic. Anyway, I know Rhonda passed them after I returned to the station, because I heard the aunt -- she has a really loud voice, like someone hard-of-hearing. Anyway she must have thought Dr. Rhonda was someone else. She kept calling her "Sandra something", and Miss Melanie told her she was mistaken."

Belkin's eyes lit up. "Back up. How did the doctor react to being called by someone else's name?"

"I couldn't see her and I didn't hear her say anything."

The officers thanked Nurse Sheila and requested that the receptionists tell the staff they would call or come back if they had more questions. After the officers had left, Dr. Ron, unimpressed, muttered something about hiring a private investigator.

The rain that had let up by morning, started again as the officers drove from the clinic. As they climbed into the patrol car, Belkin spoke with satisfaction. "There, now that should make them happy. We're done."

"Done?" Gonzales asked in disbelief. "Shouldn't we interview the doctor's wife and the aunt and take a look at the missing woman's residence?"

Belkin gave her a look. "Bullsh. I didn't hear a thing in there that makes me think anyone has committed a crime. We wasted an entire morning. Unless positive proof, like her body shows up, we're through with this."

Gonzales started to protest, "But somehow I feel . . ." Belkin cut her off with an uncalled-for remark. "Don't give me any of that female intuition crap."

The new detective's dark eyes flashed anger, but she looked straight ahead and said nothing. Most of the men she knew were Hispanic, the majority race in Corpus Christi. Belkin wasn't Hispanic but he sure had the same macho-man chauvinistic trait of Hispanic men, even her sweet boyfriend. After a time she looked over at Belkin.

"What you thinking, Gonzales?"

She fudged, "All of her co-workers believe something terrible happened. That should count for something."

"Didn't you learn in cop school, excuse me at You-Tee," (and he gave her the Hook'um Horns University of Texas hand sign) "that the persons closest to a supposed victim are the least reliable? Too close to be objective, Gonzales. I still contend the doctor had reason to disappear that none of her co-workers, including her best friend, know about. As far as that goes, I'm not sure her self-appointed best friend is being completely honest."

"Why would you say that?'

"Just a gut reaction?"

"Oh, is that anything like female intuition?" Gonzales asked in her sweetest possible voice.

Belkin didn't answer, but this conversation began the uneasy relationship between the seasoned Sergeant, long-time police academy alum, and the inexperienced college-educated detective.

Gonzales thought for a while before she asked, "Shouldn't we consider the person the doctor visited in Chicago? Maybe he or she holds something against Dr. Rhonda."

"That's a long shot without a phone number, address or gender."

"But if we got a warrant and search her townhouse, we might find her address book or something." Maria's voice trailed off.

Missing

"Gonzales, I repeat. We need concrete proof something has happened to her before we proceed. Let's grab lunch and check back in."

"Sure," Maria agreed but her mind was on something besides lunch and she hardly tasted her Whataburger and Diet Dr. Pepper. *I know Belkin thinks I'm worthless. Okay, so I panicked when the Chief asked me to take the case and he appointed this hotshot to baby-sit me. It's true I haven't done or said anything this morning to impress Belkin, but what if I show everyone that a brand-new FEMALE detective can be the one to crack this case wide open?*

CHAPTER SIX

Two people, two motels, two plans

In spite of her exhaustion, Sandra's mind gave her no rest at the motel in San Antonio. The Sandra voice whined, *"When will the weather clear so I can go to Mexico?"* The voice she'd named "Rhonda" nagged, *"What about Poppy? He needs to eat and go outside. And Linda? She must be worried sick about her best friend."*

"What if my car is being towed right now?" asked the Sandra voice, the voice that yesterday had seemed calmer and more confident.

Finally about 7:00 AM Tuesday, blissfully unaware an investigation into Rhonda's disappearance soon would begin at the clinic, Sandra fell into a deep sleep.

Ignoring the "Do Not Disturb" sign on the door, the housekeeper had rapped on Sandra's door several times after the 11:00 checkout time. No response. Galina needed to prepare the room for the next guest because it looked like a hurricane could be headed towards the Texas coast. The many evacuating coastal residents, the "Coasties", would need every available room in San Antonio. Assuming the person staying for only one night had left, she tried to use her master keycard. No, the chain was in place. She pounded hard and still heard nothing, no voice, no shower, no hairdryer. Once her friend Juanita had found a dead man in one of the rooms, and the thought of finding someone like that scared the liver out of her. The desk clerk didn't like being bothered with "nuisance calls" from housekeepers, but in desperation Galena called.

The desk clerk rang Sandra's room. The phone's harsh sound usually awakened sleepers immediately, but it rang several times until someone answered.

"Ma'am, are you all right?"

When the phone finally awakened Sandra, she'd looked at it and answered in a muggy voice, "I'm all right but I must have overslept."

The voice on the phone nagged, "It's past check-out time. Could you hurry?"

While talking, Sandra had switched on the Weather Channel and saw the hurricane the state trooper had predicted now headed towards Texas. An evacuation had been called, which meant highways would turn into one-way escape routes. Sandra started to panic, but counted to ten like a wise woman had once taught her.

"Are you still there?"

"Yes, but would it be all right if I stay for another night? With the weather and all?"

"Certainly, I'll put another night on your credit card. Wait, your record says you paid with cash. Just give me your card number. I'll book it again for you."

"That's not necessary. I'll bring the cash down right away." Sandra hung up.

Dressing, she contemplated this new complication. *I could leave now and drive to El Paso and then cross to Mexico, but as long as I committed to pay big bucks for another night, I better hang out here and figure out a better plan. I make too many mistakes when I rush and don't think things through.*

After she paid for the room, Sandra left to find a restaurant she remembered seeing last night. *Right before that jerk started following me and scared me silly.* She found it.

Breakfast served all day. She tucked into a huge meal of scrambled eggs, sausage, hashed browns and pancakes. It seems days since she had eaten, days since she had been on the run, days since Monday when her life turned upside-down. It was only Tuesday.

Returning to her room, Sandra sat cross-legged on the bed and thought over her options. After sleep and food she felt more clear-headed and wondered about the car. She got up and walked to the window. Due to another stroke of good luck, Sandra realized she could see the parking lot where she'd left the gray car. The car remained in the same place, though now surrounded by vehicles of all kinds. She paced a bit and sat down again. Rhonda-inspired doubts plagued Sandra, who still worried about Rhonda's dog. *I know. I'll call Linda this evening. I owe that much to her since Rhonda cared so much about her. I don't know exactly what I'll tell her…*

Sandra began practicing, using a low throaty voice, "Dr. Hernandez, I'm calling for Rhonda. She wanted me to tell you that she's okay and someday she'll explain everything to you. For now she wants you to keep it a secret that I called you."

Of course, Linda would plead for more information but she'd interrupt, "I don't have much time but I have one more request. Could you check on Poppy?" Then she'd hang up.

Sandra looked at the clock radio on the bedside table. Linda wouldn't be home for a few hours. Sandra couldn't risk calling her at work. Maybe she'd wait until after supper at the same restaurant. Then Sandra went over everything done to cover any tracks.

Ditching the car while I'm at the motel was brilliant just in case the kid sold me a hot car. I've paid cash for everything and I didn't use either Sandra or Rhonda when I registered at motels. I took care of the hair so don't look like either of us. I made sure anyone who saw me enter her car would think it was Rhonda because I had on her clothes. Of course, my driver's license and passport have my name if I get stopped for anything; I just couldn't show it to that desk clerk when I'd given her a different name. I should have gotten new forms of I.D. -- I've had experience with that -- but it's not like I had time to change my identity. For better or worse, I am Sandra D. Lewis.

Her mind took a detour back to the day in a little Oklahoma Panhandle town where she first had used that name. She had introduced herself as Sandra Dee Lewis to spunky Lurene, the woman who became more of a mother to her than her own mother ever had been. Unlike her mom with her addiction to sweet ice tea laced with vodka to solve all life's problems, Lurene taught her to control anxiety and anger by counting to ten.

Not quite twenty years ago, a gangly injured teen limped into Smokey's, the bar and grill Lurene owned, currently empty of customers. When the owner asked her name, Ronnie Lee Jackson began to sob. In time the girl gave Lurene the name she gave herself when she ran away from home, Sandra Dee after her favorite star from movies and Lewis for "Sherri Lewis" in the in the reruns of the old kiddies' TV show with Lamb Chop that her little sisters loved.

Lurene guessed it wasn't the kid's real name but she accepted it. "A new name for a new beginning. Sounds okay by me." She said that after the young girl had confided everything about a truck driver with bad intentions and a little about why she'd run away from home. Before the girl spilled everything, Lurene had wrapped her sprained ankle and treated all her scrapes and bruises. The big-hearted woman cooked her a burger that the kid wolfed down as if she hadn't eaten in days. As business started to pick up with her regular bar customers, Lurene sent the girl to a back room to rest on a cot.

Sandra smiled as she remembered how Lurene loved to tell this story. "Now I had lots of experience with strays, dogs and cats, that is, but I never had a stray kid before! Let me tell you, the same saying holds true: 'Feed a stray once, and it's yours!' That's why Sandra Dee lives with me now."

Sandra reminisced more about all Lurene had done for her. Besides giving her a place to live and feeding her, the big-hearted woman, who loved Sandra like the child she and her late husband had wanted, always had time to listen to her. Once when she was feeling homesick, she told her about her two little *cousins*, "Rainey" and "Midge".

"Rainey? I bet that was short for Lorraine," Lurene offered.

"You're right!" responded Sandra Dee, who thought this woman was the smartest person in the world.

"Now let's see. 'Midge'--I had a friend in high school named Marjorie that we called 'Midge. Is that why you call your cousin that name?"

"No, that's her name. She was so tiny when she was born that my mom -- I mean her mom, my aunt – said she was no bigger than the midge that's a tiny bug."

Sandra could tell her anything. Her first memory of her dad was of him carrying her on his shoulders to each bar in town, grabbing a quick beer and then on to the next to "show off his cute little daughter". She loved her dad so much then. With unexpected tears she told how her mother kept her away from the trial that convicted her dad. She never saw him again, and really didn't care because he'd beaten her mother countless times. Then her mother abandoned her. She cried again as she talked about the foster home with her tormenters. Lurene listened and held her when she cried.

Besides comforting her, Lurene helped Sandra grow up. Lurene found her charge's first job, a poultry house where Sandra Dee candled eggs. Even now, Sandra gagged thinking of the putrid raw smell of chicken blood and wet feathers that permeated the whole place. It took years before she could eat eggs and still avoided all manner of fowl. She remembered with pride how being able to contribute towards room and board made her feel better about herself.

Later Lurene taught her to drive and took her to the next town to get her license. Then she loaned her an old red Chevy pick-up so she could deliver newspapers on a rural route, which paid better than her egg job. In time her new friend let her work at her business, first cleaning, later cooking. During slack times the mother-substitute helped her study for her G.E.D. Sandra never would forget what Lurene did when she passed all the tests in the top percentile. She put a closed sign on the bar/grill one afternoon but invited all the patrons to come to a graduation party that included a bakery cake with "Way to Go, Sandra!" in red icing plus Hawaiian Punch, decorations, and presents. All afternoon the happy woman beamed with pride at her stray's accomplishment.

Though Lurene never wanted Sandra to work at the bar, she turned her acquired daughter into a first-rate bartender when the girl came of age. She agreed to this only because she had started feeling unwell. The day Lurene learned she had terminal cancer, Sandra took over running the business.

How I'd love to see Lurene again! Knowing this was beyond possible, she still fantasized about driving up to Oklahoma to see her one more time before she left the country. Just to have Lurene assure her she still loved her in spite of what she had done in Corpus.

Her two biggest fears arrived to end her magical thinking. *What if old Felicity took her story to the police, and they listened to her and somehow connected me to Rhonda's disappearance? Or, what if the car is hot and the police throughout the state are looking for it or what if they're looking because someone at the first motel gave the police the license number?* In either scenario she'd imagined, the law could be right behind her. She needed to leave the country as soon as possible. *I shouldn't have overslept. I shouldn't have slept at all, just kept driving to another border town last night.*

Too late for that. Sandra considered whether she should wait out the storm or leave for El Paso. Without making a decision she decided to take advantage of the motel's claim of free WiFi and computer and went downstairs to see if she'd find anything about the doctor's disappearance via the Internet. Accessing the Tuesday Corpus Christi newspaper, she found nothing about the doctor but with drumming heart, Sandra read a blurb about a Corpus couple coming home from a cruise and finding their gray Ford Taurus missing from the. Garage. The license number matched the Taurus she'd bought. A sixteen-year old son, with a car of his own, told his parents he didn't even know their car was missing.

That lying possum! Now I have to get rid of the car. Of course, if I'm stopped, I could honestly protest that I just bought the car and haven't had time to get the title changed. But I have absolutely no proof and I'd have to show my driver's license, and if my name has been linked to Rhonda, then ... I lucked out not having to show a license last night, but that won't happen again. Or what if I could be arrested for scamming the kid out of the car by paying a token price?

Before leaving the computer, Sandra checked out one of the Corpus television stations. She saw the same story about the gray Taurus. Under "Breaking News" she gazed at a photo of Rhonda, the professional one she'd had taken when young Dr. Collins received the award. A brief item stated that Corpus Christi physician, Rhonda Collins, had been missing since noon the previous day and that her co-workers suspected foul play. A police investigation had been launched. More info promised at 5:00 PM.

Sandra took several deep breaths and shut down the computer. *I need to leave the country before the police connect the dots between the car and me and between Rhonda and me. But now I'm afraid to drive that car even a short distance.*

Missing

Retiring to her room, Sandra switched on a movie, "Terms of Endearment", to occupy herself until she could access the 5:00 PM update on Rhonda. Another woman sat before the computer when she went back downstairs, and it didn't look as if the computer would be free any time soon. Sandra went back to the familiar restaurant for a hot roast beef sandwich with mashed potatoes and gravy. She heard considerable talk about Leo and the influx of Coasties. Returning to the motel, she found the same woman hogging the computer.

Back in her room, she called Linda's home. One of the boys answered. In the background Sandra heard Poppy's familiar yapping. *Bless Linda! She rescued Poppy. What a dear friend!*

As she hung up the phone without saying anything, Sandra prayed a silent prayer of gratitude that Poppy was okay. *I've never prayed before in my life. Rhonda, you and your church going sure did something to me.*

Finally Sandra had her chance at the computer. The update had little more information than the noon report except they had sensationalized the mystery of the disappearance even more and reinforced the foul play theory. At 10:00 there would be an important update. Sandra didn't have a chance to use the computer then because she was too busy making phone calls from her room. She'd hit on a new escape plan, one that didn't include that stupid car lacking a sound system.

In another motel in Phoenix, Dave Hernandez's thoughts centered on his relationship with Rhonda and his anxiety, even now that she was gone, that their affair could be exposed.

He had met Rhonda at a picnic for the staff of the Cielo Vista Clinic, where his wife was employed as a family physician. Rhonda had just started working there. At the park she had a flat on her ancient red pick-up, which he fixed for her. Soon after he'd talked her into buying a car more fitting her position though she seemed so reluctant to part with the old beater.

That was what, seven, eight years ago? They had been attracted to each other and began having an affair at her townhouse. As much as he craved the beautiful, sensual Rhonda, he coveted her calm, serene home so unlike his with one noisy son arriving right after another. Then Rhonda and his wife became very close, making an awkward situation even more so. He loved his wife and didn't want to hurt her and told himself that Rhonda was only a dalliance, the first and only one he'd ever had. However, as he fell more in love with the other woman, he knew he was in trouble. He could never divorce his wife, and before she found out about him and her best friend, he had to end the affair. Rhonda was quick to agree as she didn't want to cause pain for the woman who had become like a sister.

However, in spite of the best of intentions, Dave kept finding himself in Rhonda's bed. The only thing that ever marred their time together was the yappy little dog she bought a few years ago. In spite of that, he really thought that loving two women would work indefinitely for him. On Sunday night Rhonda was the one wanting to end things. He did everything to talk her out of it, but she said she cared more for her relationship with Linda than a tawdry one with him. That stung. He persisted in arguing that they needed each other.

She overplayed when she threatened to tell Linda. He couldn't let that happen and the next day texted to ask Rhonda to meet during her lunch break. He wanted to be the one, not the woman, to end everything.

CHAPTER SEVEN

Clues/News

After returning to SCCPD from the Tuesday morning interviews, Belkin went his way and Gonzales, thrilled to be away from him, went hers. First she accessed Vehicle Registration and found Rhonda's car license number. She wrote it down in her polka dot notebook and listed all she had gleaned from the interviews: colleagues suspect foul play, missing doctor had no known enemies, very popular with all, recently won a national physician's award, often ran errands during her lunch break, seemed in a hurry when she left the clinic in her car around noon Monday, a visitor had called the doctor by a different name.

Numerous callers from the Coastal Bend who thought they had seen the missing doctor inundated the Police department tip-line. Though all her colleagues said she wasted her time, Detective Gonzales listened to each and every one of the taped calls.

The Community Credit Union employee, who had accompanied the physician to her safety deposit box, recognized her on television. She wasn't one of the callers because she wouldn't violate any customer's privacy rights. Later a police order would compromise such rights.

Different callers to the police tip-line reported to have seen the doctor at one of the many Wal-Marts that proliferated in the Coastal Bend, this one in Kingsville. Others saw her at a restaurant in Port Aransas, a yogurt shop on Padre Island, a coffee shop in Corpus. Another saw her walking a huge black dog, maybe Newfoundland, on Ocean Drive. Still another swore on his mother's Bible that he saw her in a boat in the bay with two dark-skinned men. One who identified herself as a Cielo Vista patient felt sure she had seen her shopping at the new Corpus Christi Sam's Club on Spid.

Maria examined every recorded call and didn't need her hotshot partner to recognize that all of these sightings occurred before the time Rhonda allegedly left the clinic. Several callers claimed they had seen her on Monday morning or even on Sunday. She discerned one male voice had called three times. He reported having seen the doctor three different times in three different places, all about 11:00 AM Monday. *Crackpot.*

Another call came in. A male voice stated, "I'm sure I saw the missing doctor at a Stripes Store around 1:00, 1:15 Monday afternoon. My name is Dan and you can reach me at . . ." Quickly Maria broke in, identified who she was and asked if the caller could describe the woman.

"She was wearing light brown pants and a shiny white blouse. She also was wearing a black hooded sweatshirt, only not zipped up. What made me look at her twice was the hood part looked really big, like she had a whole lot of hair tucked under it, and blonde hair stuck out the front."

As soon as the caller stopped for a breath, Maria asked if he would meet her at the same Stripes to answer more of her questions. In spite of the pouring rain, he agreed.

Maria concluded, *a nice guy, not a crackpot.*

As they stood at the end of the an aisle, Maria first wanted to know if the caller could tell her the color of the woman's shoes, purse, but he couldn't. She went over everything he had told her on the phone, and then asked if he could add anything. "Well, officer, I don't know if it's important, but she was in front of me at the snack bar register buying a couple burritos." He pointed out the location. "She left the counter and I ordered my food."

Missing

"Did she seem nervous, scared?"

"No, Officer, she seemed -- well, normal."

"Anything else you noticed?" Detective Gonzales thought that her questioning sounded quite experienced but would be more impressive if she could shed the uniform that made people call her officer.

"Yes, Officer, I saw her again when I left. She stood by the door, eating a burrito, and looking outside like she was waiting for someone. Also, I forgot -- she was wearing large dark glasses, but her nose and chin sure looked like the picture I saw, and she was tall, almost as tall as I am. Not that I'm that tall -- I'm 5-10, but she must have been 5-8. She had dark glasses on -- oh, I told you that -- and she had a pretty smile."

Thanking the fifty-ish man for being observant and assuring him his information could really help, Detective Gonzales took down his name and number in case further questioning might be needed. She asked each store employee if they remembered seeing the missing woman. Not one remembered her. The cashier at the snack bar, a young man with multiple arm tattoos, explained, "Lady, I mean Officer Lady, 11:00 in the morning to 2:00 is our busiest time of the day. Lots of people buy burritos. I don't remember anyone in that crowd."

Returning to the station, Maria noted another possibly valid caller. A motel desk clerk named Brenda Ellis. She reported a woman matching the missing doctor's description had checked in Monday afternoon at the Liberty Motel. The detective called the motel but Brenda had left for the day. The clerk on duty asked if he could help, but she explained to the man, named Lupe, that she needed to talk to the day clerk.

She phoned Cielo Vista and asked Dr. Ronyl Brooks if the missing doctor was partial to burritos and if she ever ate the ones at Stripes. The doctor replied, "If this weren't so serious that would be laughable. Rhonda loved Tex-Mex food, but I can't imagine her eating at Stripes."

He handed the phone to Linda, who had come in his office to discuss how they could help find Rhonda. Linda collaborated what Dr. Brooks had said in an icy voice, "That seems totally unlikely. My friend wasn't in the habit of shopping or eating at gas stations."

Maria asked her if the doctor ever wore a black hoodie. Linda thought and finally said, "I know she carried one in her gym bag. We worked out together twice a week at the Y."

Linda insisted on knowing why the detective asked these questions. Because of the ongoing investigation, Maria couldn't tell her. Linda didn't believe her. Contradicting her reputation for being a sweet gentle woman, Linda barked, "Don't think you can keep anything about my friend from me!" and slammed down the receiver.

Maria went into the property room and saw a plastic bag marked "Rhonda Collins". *So Belkin didn't really quit the case.* Then Marie read a cryptic note, not from Belkin but from one of the clerks, saying: "Dr. Linda Hernandez brought in a hairbrush. Said belongs to missing woman. Bagged by V. Lucero, dated 5:48, Monday afternoon". *Okay, so we have her DNA. Is it worth looking for a match at the Stripes store? Not too likely since I imagine the store was cleaned and sanitized Monday night.*

A quick call to Stripes confirmed that custodians cleaned the bathrooms three times a day, the snack bar twice and the rest of the store at night. The manager then added, "The only note added to the cleaning log is that the afternoon custodian found a smart phone in the waste paper basket in the women's restroom."

Gonzales' face lit up. "Do you still have it?"

"No, the custodian noted it was soaking wet and couldn't get it to work so tossed it."

"Could I talk to the custodian?"

"No, she's gone for the day. Try back tomorrow around 2:00."

"Do you have a home phone for her?"

I can't give it out because of privacy issues."

Maria wished privacy laws didn't exist. Using a kindly tone to say she understood, Maria knew Belkin would have growled, "We'll see about that. I can get a warrant." She sighed. *I have to get tougher if I'm to be credible.*

No time for pity. Maria called Dr. Ron's number again to see if he knew what kind of cell phone Rhonda carried. He didn't but said he'd ask around. "Dr. Linda already has left. She'd probably know. I'll let you know tomorrow. Right now there's a reporter here, and I want this case to receive the publicity it deserves."

Maria shook off the news of the reporter. *Okay, now I have two calls to follow-up tomorrow.* Leaving a report on the case on the Chief's desk, Maria left for the day, long after Belkin and most others on the day shift.

First Maria called her parents, brother and boyfriend to boast a bit about her promotion. Then she took a bus to the glittering La Palmera Mall to buy some togs befitting a detective. Thinking about the classy clothing ascribed to the missing woman, she knew they wouldn't be affordable. As it was, her credit card took a hit with three pairs of tailored pants, two jackets and four tops.

Shopping finished, she took a bus to the apartment she shared with her best friend, Sydney. The apartment was dark, which meant her housemate had left for her night-school classes. At the sound of a key in the lock, Big Boy, an oversized striped marmalade cat, bounded to the door in a manner usually reserved for dogs. Maria picked up the heavy cat, purring like a locomotive, and lugged him into the kitchenette. She opened a can of Fancy Feast for him and put a

Lean Cuisine in the microwave for her own dinner. Big Boy decided not to tell Maria that Sydney had already fed him.

Instead of turning on the television or checking Facebook, Maria found a large piece of poster board and covered the kitchen table with it. With a black marking pen she put DISAPPEARANCE OF DR. RHONDA COLLINS at the top. She divided the paper into two halves. At the top of one side, she wrote ABDUCTED; on the other RAN AWAY. Under ABDUCTED she wrote "based on fears of all who know her"; under RAN AWAY she started to write "reported being seen in a Stripes store eating burritos" but there was no evidence that the doctor was the one that had been seen. Belkin had maintained there was no hard evidence that she had been abducted; Maria could find no evidence that said she'd run away. Hearing her housemate come home, Maria slipped the board behind the refrigerator.

Together the young women watched the late news while Big Boy went from lap to lap for attention. The first news item urged residents to get out hammer, nails and plywood; time to board up windows as Leo might pay a call. Neither of the women showed interest as that was the responsibility of their landlord. Both focused on the second news item: an anchor showed a clip of his interview with Dr. Ronyl Brooks at the Cielo Vista Clinic. The anchor asked many of the questions posed by the police including the possibility that the doctor had left town on her own. Brooks answered carefully, "Here we've ruled out the slightest possibility that a person as caring and responsible as Rhonda would do that." In a choked voice, he added, "We're all afraid something bad happened to her to prevent her from returning to the office as scheduled."

"What do you think could have happened to her?" asked Sydney, who wouldn't know until the case had ended that her best friend had been assigned to it. Maria just put her palms up, shrugged and looked non-committal, wondering not for the first time that day if she'd made a wrong career choice. She would postpone telling Sydney about her promotion, or she might figure it out and would assail her with questions that shouldn't be discussed. Maria wouldn't do anything to compromise the case, the case she hoped to crack.

CHAPTER EIGHT

Body in the BMW

Maria rode the bus to work through more pouring rain Wednesday morning. The good news: the hurricane watch had been canceled. According to the newspaper headlines, LEO'S ROAR BECOMES PURR. The hurricane everyone thought would make landfall suddenly pulled in its claws and curled up kittenlike some place out in the Gulf of Mexico.

In Corpus Christi, weather, especially during Hurricane Season, drove conversation. This Wednesday at SCCPD was no different. Maria heard snippets of chatter as she made her way to her miniscule office.

"We dodged the bullet this time," commented the head clerk, voicing the remark heard throughout the city.

"I sure wouldn't want to live through Celia again! Have I told you how we'd wait in front of the HEB grocery with handfuls of dollar bills and mob the bread truck drivers before they could deliver the bread to the store?" The soon to be retired Hank shared again his oft told hurricane memories.

"We're going to grow webbed feet if this rain doesn't stop," giggled one of new clerical staff.

"This is nothing. Did you hear a big tropical is headed for Houston? Glad I'm not planning to fly out of there today," rejoiced one of the lab techs.

Not stopping to chat with anyone, Detective Maria Gonzales called the Liberty Motel to talk to the day clerk, Brenda Ellis. Brenda, in her mid-forties, held the record for the longest employment, ten years, at the infamous hotel. She loved her job, mixing with all sorts of characters needing to rent a room. Brenda was smart and had developed skills of observing and sizing up customers. She delighted her friends with descriptions -- without names, of course -- of some of the more interesting people she met.

As talkative as she was observant, Brenda Ellis told Maria about the lady who had checked in around the middle of the afternoon. "Quite frankly, she looked too classy to be a place like this. Nice make-up, expensive looking clothing, big designer sunglasses and a really sharp black hoodie that sure didn't look like it came from Wal-Mart. She had blonde hair showing under the hood, and she was tall and thin, thirty-something, just like the description on TV, and I saw the ruffled collar of her ivory silk blouse that showed in a gap where the hoodie wasn't zipped all the way."

"Did you see her when she checked out?"

"No. She was gone before I came in this morning."

"Did she register her car?"

"Just a minute, I'll look. We require that each guest put down make, model and license number."

The officer waited as Brenda thumbed through the registration book. "Yes, here it is. Wait I have someone on the other line."

Again Maria waited and when Brenda returned to the line, she told her the woman she'd described drove a gray Ford Taurus. Maria's brain jolted. *That's the description of the stolen car. The detective in charge of that case had received dozens of calls about sightings of that car, but none had panned out. Surely there's no way the missing doctor ditched her car and stole another.*

"Ma'am? Are y'all there?" Brenda asked.

"Yes, could you please give me the license number?"

"It's kinda hard to read." Chuckling, Brenda added, "You know what they say about doctor's handwriting!"

The desk clerk made her want to laugh, too, but Maria stuck to her professional tone adding to the common belief that law officers have no sense of humor. "Just give me what you think it says," and Brenda read off what she believed were two or three possibilities for each numeral and letter.

Maria copied down all the variations and asked the clerk if there was anything else.

"Well, the doctor's name is Rhonda Something but this person signed in as 'Marsha Watkins' but that could be made up. People tend to use aliases here. I don't blame a high-class gal like the doctor not wanting to use her real name at a place like this."

The detective didn't comment but thanked the clerk.

"Will there be a reward if this leads you to her?" Brenda asked.

"Absolutely," replied Maria not wanting to discourage the hopeful tipster, but she knew in her heart that this information only told her that someone who may or may not have been the missing doctor had gone to a motel, and the person drove a gray Taurus, that may or may not have been stolen.

The latter information she would share with Lt. Vargas, the one who had posted alerts all over the state for the missing vehicle. As she left Vargas's office, the Chief hailed both her and Belkin. "Just got a call from a parking ramp attendant. Thinks he found the missing doctor's fancy car on the third floor of the Vega Building. He said he peeked in the window and saw a red parking tab, and red means it was issued on Monday. I want you both to check it out."

"Now we might be getting somewhere." Belkin put himself back on the case the Chief didn't know he had abandoned.

Maria asked Chief Ortiz, " Could we take Ralph?"

"Absolutely not. He and his partner are on another case. Besides neither of you took canine training."

Out of earshot of the Chief, Belkin railed, "You actually think we're going to find a body?"

"Not really, but I like Ralph, and he could be helpful." Maria realized how simple she sounded. *Why did she let Belkin bring out the worst in her? Make her say stupid things?*

Belkin couldn't believe his well-educated partner had said that. "Forget it, this case doesn't warrant a highly trained, expensive animal."

I disagree.

The rain had stopped as the two officers left SCCPD to drive about three miles to the Vega Building. There in ten minutes, they had no trouble finding the luxury car on the third floor of the parking ramp. Maria pulled out the red polka dot notebook to see if the license number she had gotten from Vehicle Registration matched. A perfect match!

"Good job, Gonzales!" conceded Stan Belkin. "I see you did your homework."

Maria showed no emotion but inwardly did a happy dance. She stood back as Belkin struggled with a device to open the car door. Maria noticed a ring of keys under the car. She crawled under the car to retrieve them and started to hand them to the other officer, whose back was to her. Instead Maria grinned as she hit the "unlock" button on the car remote.

Belkin jumped when the door unlocked itself. He glanced up at Gonzales with the key fob in her hand and an innocent look on her face. Not appreciating her besting him twice this morning, the superior tried to get even by saying "That's why you crawled under the car and got your pants dirty."

Maria, embarrassed, started dusting off the knees of her new burgundy pants as Belkin continued, "We need to have the car towed so the evidence techs can go over it. Except for DNA they'll get results in a hurry. You know that it's not like television when DNA tests are done during a commercial, don't you?"

Maria refused to acknowledge the last statement though she thought of several sarcastic comebacks. *Re-al-ly? They do them faster on crime shows? Are you kidding? They taught us in grad school that every detective carries a DNA kit and can get instant results. What's your favorite crime show?*

The tan purse and shoes on the front seat caught her attention and with gloved hands she put them in an evidence bag. To her this looked more and more like abduction. No woman leaves her purse and shoes behind. Belkin ignored her when she remarked, "The purse could be filled with important information."

Belkin called for the tow and checked the parking stub. The time stamp read 12:19. "That fits."

He looked towards the building and wondered out loud, "What's on the third floor? The missing woman may have had some business there. I'll check that out but first we need to look into the trunk."

"Do you think . . . her body . . .?" Maria's voice trailed off.

"It's the first place to look."

Time stood still for Maria as Belkin opened the trunk. A horrible stench smacked their nostrils.

They both peered inside. Maria covered her nose with one hand and mouth with the other but had little success in suppressing a scream.

"Take it easy, Gonzales. First dead body you've seen?"

Maria regained her composure. "Of course, not. I just didn't quite expect this." *I truly am not cut out for this.*

"Come on, Gonzales, if you're going to be a cop, you have to get used to worse than this. Maybe you're better suited to being a nursery school teacher."

Trying not to be cowed, Maria took a second look. "I believe it's a 'possum cadaver'."

"Very good, officer. One that's been dead for a long time." He slammed down the trunk door. "Obviously the doctor didn't have much need of her trunk and I suppose this car's so well built the smell didn't permeate the inside of the car."

"If it's that well-built, how did the animal get in there?"

"Who knows? They love to crawl into cars. This one made it his final resting place."

"Maybe the doctor left the door open while she was carrying in groceries and she didn't see the animal because it hid behind the spare tire."

"Good detective work!" kidded Belkin. "If anyone reports a missing possum we'll be obligated to give him the bad news but tell him his little critter died in a right fancy car."

Maria ignored his banter as a chill went up her back and she tried hard to retain her breakfast. With calmness she didn't feel she stated, "I suppose Forensics will take care of -- of this."

"Forensics? Bullsh! You don't think they're gonna autopsy it?"

Changing the subject, Maria speculated, "Maybe she has a receipt or something in her purse."

"Go ahead, Gonzales," Belkin sneered, "look in the purse like you're dying to do while I check out the third floor."

Maria sat in the patrol car and snapped open the purse. Belkin was wrong again; looking through another woman's purse somehow felt like a violation. *I have to stop being so sensitive or I'll never be good at this. I need to find the doctor's driver's license and cell phone.* Maria found the license and plenty of other identification for Rhonda Collins, M.D. There also was a receipt for cash withdrawn from the Gulf Bank at 12:13, and one hundred in tens in the wallet. No phone. *That doesn't mean it's the one found at Stripe's, but... Then again she could have her cell with her, but she hasn't contacted anyone so maybe her abductor -- that is, if she was abducted -- might have taken it away. I need to call her friend Dr. Linda to see if she could come down to headquarters during her lunch break to identify the purse and shoes, and I need to call that Stripes custodian but it's too early. I must remember to ask Linda about the cell phone.*

She dialed the clinic to leave a message for Dr. Linda Hernandez; but as soon as she identified herself, Carla, the receptionist, demanded, "Have you found Dr. Rhonda? Is she okay?"

Maria assured her they were doing everything they could, and the young woman immediately put her in touch with Dr. Linda. She was more co-operative and said she'd do anything to help and would be there as close to noon as possible. As she talked to her, Maria saw the tow truck arrive. She pointed out the car to him, and with fancy maneuvering he managed to tow the car from the ramp. She didn't see a photographer crouched between two cars photographing that scene,

In the meantime Sgt. Belkin found the Community Credit Union taking up most of the third floor. He also saw a clock repair shop and two other shops for lease. He decided to try the CU first. He told the first free teller that he needed to know if someone had been a customer there on Monday. She started to quote privacy laws, but he stopped her. "This is about the missing doctor. Surely, you've heard about her?"

"Why, yes, of course, all that's on the news is her and the hurricane that fizzled."

Belkin interrupted, "Is she a customer here?"

The clerk consulted the computer and finally revealed, "She is a member here but I see no activity on her account on Monday."

Another teller had been listening in and blurted, "Actually, I remember seeing her Monday and she had on the clothing described on TV. I've been worried about her. She's a really nice lady."

"She was here but didn't make a transaction?" Belkin asked.

"She might have gone to her safety deposit box; I'll check the log."

The log verified the doctor had visited her box. The person who had accompanied her had initialed the log.

"I want to talk with that person."

"She's not here today."

"When will she return?"

The tellers met the question with silence.

Belkin snapped, "Don't give me a hard time. We're trying to locate someone who might be the victim of a crime."

"But, privacy concerns..."

"Listen, I'm going to return with a warrant to search that box."

"Wait, let me see if I can reach her by phone." The second teller called, apologized to her colleague for waking her, explained the situation and handed the phone to the officer.

A congested voice punctuated her answer with raspy coughs. "Yes, I took her to her box and I remember she went on and on about how safe she felt putting things in the box during hurricane season, and she told me to take care of my cold. I've worried about her after what's been on television."

Seeing Belkin coming out of the building Maria called out, "Did you have any luck?"

"She was in the credit union during the noon hour, visited her safe deposit box."

"The key probably is on the ring I found. Should we go see if they'll open it for us?"

"We'll still have to have a warrant."

Gonzales examined the keys. "Here is a tiny key with a number on it, and this looks like a house key. We could get a warrant for that, too, and I have Dr. Hernandez --I'm going to call her Dr. Linda to make it simpler -- coming down at noon to identify the purse and shoes."

"Way to go, Ms. Detective!" Belkin, pumped with the info he'd gotten, had decided to play nice. "And what did you find in the purse?"

"Usual female stuff, lipstick, styling comb, Kleenex." She paused, took a deep breath and continued as nonchalantly as possible, "Tampax, birth control pills, a wallet with her I.D. and a receipt from the Gulf Bank. She took a hunk of money out of there."

"Just like I told you. The MP, you know that means 'missing person', don't you? The MP or in this case the MD -- get it, MD for missing doctor? -- gathered her assets and took off."

Officer Gonzales flared, "You don't know that. I think it's more likely someone grabbed her when she came out of the Credit Union and was getting in her car. That would explain her purse left behind."

"What about her shoes?"

"I doubt that she would run off barefoot on purpose. I'd guess they fell off when she was being dragged from her car."

"You don't lack imagination, Gonzales, so why can't you imagine she took a powder? I bet if you tried you could think up a reason for her being OTR, On The Run, in case you don't know that. I'm guessing she left the shoes and purse to make it look like she was abducted. This smells as bad as that stinkin' possum."

CHAPTER NINE

Detained by TSA

About 10:30 Wednesday morning, after a stroll to the lot where the Taurus was parked, Sandra caught the airport shuttle to the San Antonio Airport. She had called every airline the night before and not one would make a reservation without a credit card. Sandra learned the time of departure of the desired flight and arrived in plenty of time to buy a one-way ticket. She had no trouble paying cash and wouldn't have much of a wait until it departed.

She showed her driver's license I.D. and passport to the first TSA employee, removed her shoes and put them in one of the standard hard plastic containers. She placed it and the gym bag on the screening conveyer belt. Routine stuff. As she passed through the x-ray unit, a man with a badge beckoned her to come with him.

Oh, no, they've caught up with me. With terror making her voice shaky, Sandra asked, "Is there a problem?"

The man ignored her question and asked, "Do you have a carry-on?"

"Yes, right there." She started to grab the gym bag and her shoes. *What on earth do I have in the bag that must have set off the alarm?* Why had she been singled out? Before she could retrieve her belongings, another uniformed person with a badge, a towering plus-sized woman who never had learned how to smile, pushed between her and the conveyer belt. "I'll get them. Come with us."

Sandra did as told and wound up in a small Homeland Security interrogation room. It was cold in the room and she really wanted her shoes. The two Transportation Safety Agents dumped the contents of the bag on a table and went through the few items of clothing, the hand mirror, and the toiletries Sandra had purchased when she bought the hair color. The roll of cash and the much folded Last Will and Testament resided in her bra.

They didn't locate the scalpel, which puzzled Sandra, until she remembered where she had thrown it during the rainstorm. A knock on the door cleared up that. They admitted the screener. He had spotted and confiscated something, but hadn't been able to confront Sandra before the agents whisked her away. The female officer smirked as Sandra began to flush and perspire. *So they didn't stop me because of something they found in the bag. That can only mean I've been found out! Someone alerted the airlines.*

"What did you plan to do with these?" the screener, holding out the scissors, asked while the woman proceeded to destroy the gym bag by ripping off all the pockets and slitting every seam.

"Why are you doing that?" Sandra asked as steadily as possible.

"You don't ask the questions, we do," the man stated. "I repeat: what did you plan to do with those sharp-bladed scissors?"

"Nothing. I'd forgotten they were in my carry-on. I'm a hairdresser. I always carry them and a mirror." The man showed no reaction and left the room so that his partner could conduct a body search. Unaware that the TSA agents believed in employing any means to catch a targeted terrorist suspect, Sandra couldn't help herself and sobbed, "What have I done to deserve this indignity?"

The agent instructed, "Strip down to your underwear." And added for scare value, "I hope I won't have to search body cavities."

Sandra nearly hyperventilated hearing that order. *I'm freaking out! Who wouldn't? But I have to co-operate.* She removed her outer clothing. The woman first checked out the clothing as Sandra shivered. Next she examined Sandra. She spotted the money and document Sandra had put in her bra. *No big deal. Women do that all the time.* She gave the document, a will, a quick look and then wanded Sandra.

Her captor handed over her clothing and shoes. "That's it," she put the contents of the gym bag, minus the scissors and some over-sized toiletries ignored by the screener, into a thin see-through plastic garbage bag.

"As soon as you're dressed, I'll be back." She left, locking the door. *A little late to be concerned about my privacy,* Sandra thought with bitterness as she dressed and looked for any means of escape. Unless she could change herself into a midge, she couldn't fly out the air vent in the ceiling. She tried to comfort herself with the ironic thought that she was a suspected terrorist, not someone wanted by the Corpus Christi police.

Her interrogators returned. Though the person in their custody acted guilty and extremely nervous which might indicate she had something to hide, she definitely didn't act like a terrorist. They always were much more composed. Their searches of her and her belongings had produced nothing. Still the ticket purchase, about which they had been warned by someone at the reservation counter, fit the profile of suspicion: ticket bought the same day of the flight, bought only a one-way ticket, paid cash.

"We have found nothing to indicate you pose a threat to airline security," the male agent announced. Music to Sandra's ears, but then she heard, "But we still have to question you about your ticket. Why did you purchase a one-way ticket the day of the flight and pay cash?"

Sandra figured out from their more relaxed manner they couldn't detain her much longer and felt almost giddy. *I could tell the truth.* "*Gee, guys, I'm on the run and in a hurry to leave right away so that's why I bought the ticket today. I'm trying not to leave a paper trail so I paid cash, and since I'm on the run, I don't need a two-way ticket.*" Instead she formed what she hoped would be a plausible answer.

"It's all because I refuse to use credit cards. It's just not possible to make a reservation on-line or by phone without one so today I needed a ticket and came out and bought it. With cash."

"Why not a round-trip ticket?"

Sandra sighed, "This is embarrassing. I had a round-trip ticket to Texas, but I lost the return ticket. So, I just stayed here for much longer than I should have, and now I really need to go home so I bought another ticket."

"You are free to board your flight. Thank you for your co-operation." The officer handed her the plastic bag, her new carry-on.

I don't dare report this as a possible violation of my civil liberties, but I sure don't have to put up with this plastic bag. Sandra found the right concourse for her flight. On the way there she stopped at the first clothing store, where she bought a pricey new outfit. The clerk put it in the store's designer shopping bag, and Sandra emptied the plastic bag into the shopping bag and proceeded to her gate.

Her plane had just left.

CHAPTER TEN

Safety Deposit Box Opened

Maria fell into a funk. *No matter how hard I try not to let him, Belkin is getting to me again.* Detective Belkin had angered Detective Gonzales so much that she used all her will power to hold her tongue while they drove back to police headquarters. There a television reporter accosted them asking, "What did you discover when you found her car?"

Maria started to answer as Belkin growled in Maria's ear to walk on by the camera without commenting. Inside she stated coldly, "I'll take the purse, shoes and keys back to Evidence, and remind them that we already have a DNA source to match with samples they find in the car."

"What sample?" Belkin sounded dumbfounded.

Maria didn't hear him or at least didn't acknowledge the question. When she returned, she found Dr. Linda had arrived. "A patient canceled so I came right over."

Belkin joined them and checked out the doctor. *Looks like she could use a doctor herself. Her eyes show a lack of sleep and concern marks her face. A distraught look? Or, a look of guilt?*

They took her into the property room and as soon as she saw the purse and shoes, she broke down. "They're hers, but where is she?"

"We're doing everything we can. We **will** find her," Maria assured the doctor as she handed her tissues. When Dr.

Linda had composed herself, Maria asked, "Could you tell me if she carried a cell phone, what it looked like?"

"Rhonda always had one in her purse. It's a smart phone, she's had it a while. I don't know for certain what brand, probably from the Verizon store on Spid. It has a red and black case."

Belkin had to ask, "Has she called you from it since you last saw her?"

That brought fresh tears. "I wish."

Gonzales gave Belkin a look. She thanked the doctor for rushing down, and asked she wanted to rest a while before driving back to work.

"I'll be okay, but with each day that passes, I'm more worried."

After she left, Gonzales couldn't suppress her anger and confronted Belkin. "That last question wasn't necessary."

"Oh, come on. How do we know the 'best friend' isn't the one who staged this whole thing? I think she's over-acting. The worry about her best friend is over the top."

"Then you've never had a best friend disappear."

"Have **you**, Gonzales?"

"No, but I have a best friend and I know how I'd feel if Sydney was missing. Besides what reason would Dr. Linda have to do something to Rhonda?"

"Gee, Gonzales, you're the one with the imagination. Why would one doctor make another one disappear? Professional jealousy, perhaps? Resented her 'best friend' getting the award she thought she deserved more, or maybe Dr. Rhonda was fooling around with Dr. Linda's husband?"

Maria gritted her teeth as a clerk handed the arguing detectives the warrants, signed by the Chief. "He said I should tell you that he 'leaked' the found car to the media so they'd know we are taking this case seriously. He also asked anyone who might have seen the doctor leave the credit union to call the tip-line."

The two officers returned to the credit union. Due to lunch breaks, it took a half hour for them to find someone to help them with the safety deposit box. Belkin detested waiting around any time and now complained about wanting his own lunch before help came.

When finally given access to the box, Gonzales spoke under her breath. "I pray whatever she put in it will provide a clue to what happened,"

Without hesitation Officer Stan Belkin opened the box.

Not even a lint particle.

CHAPTER ELEVEN

Holding pattern

Sandra re-booked a flight for later on this Wednesday. She wanted to complain about the unnecessary security check that had detained her and made her miss the flight, but decided it wiser to keep her mouth shut. The agent disclosed, "The next flight to Houston won't leave for over three hours, and you'll have a longer wait for your connecting flight than before."

Smiling to hide her distress, Sandra thanked her for rebooking and headed to an Italian bistro in the food court for a sandwich. She also picked up a People magazine. *Better to read, than just twiddle my thumbs and worry. No one can possibly know I'm here but why do I keep feeling someone will come up behind me and drag me off to jail?*

She sat in one of the white rocking chairs that lined SA airport concourses. Neither the magazine nor the waiting room television tuned to Fox News held her attention. *I didn't know this running away could be so complicated. I should have been in Mexico on Monday. Everything has conspired against me. The weather, driving a car that probably was stolen, changing my mind about Mexico, deciding to fly and Homeland Security -- I'll never get over those TSA agents.*

She thought about the first time she'd run away, almost twenty years ago and recalled she hadn't reached her original destination then either. As Sandra watched heavy rain pelt the terminal windows, she remembered all about that first time. She still felt guilty that she'd left her little sisters behind. She told Lurene everything about running away except about her sisters in foster care. Lurene had accepted her reasons for running but Ronnie had feared she'd kick her out if she knew how selfish she had been for abandoning her baby sisters. Now as an adult, Sandra believed that Lurene of all people would have understood that Sandra wasn't old enough to be on her own let alone a caretaker for two young ones.

Still even now after what she'd just done, all the anguish caused others, Sandra considered the worst crime was leaving two little sisters in the foster home to wait for a mother who might never show up. The judge had placed the little Jackson girls in one home and Ronnie Lee Jackson in another. Why hadn't Ronnie pleaded with the judge not to separate them, that the little girls needed their big sister? Almost sixteen, Ronnie could have continued to care for them at their trailer home as she had for weeks until Child Protection found out. The big sister, Ronnie Lee, hadn't said anything when the judge made his decision to put them in foster care, didn't even try; and she never could forgive herself for that.

Ronnie Lee Jackson left the foster home the same day she was placed there. She was scared so she did what she had to do, exactly what the adult Sandra did now: ran. The foster parents could have worked out but they also fostered two teenage boys their newly placed daughter knew from school. These boys had teased and bullied Sandra since they all were in grade school. They called her nasty names and made fun of her at every opportunity. The one in her grade sat behind her and hid her books and pencils. Each time she got up to recite, he tripped her. That earned her the nickname "Paddle Foot". In junior high torment switched from her feet to her chest. Both boys loved to snap the back of her bra or poke her to see "if they're real". They added more nasty names and threatened to catch Ronnie Lee after school to make her do disgusting things to them and that they'd both rape her. Recently, not long before she had to quit school to care for her sisters, the boys broke into her locker and left a dead shrew with a note saying, "Hey, Trailer Trash, here's a treat for your lunch".

In retrospect they were two kids from homes as troubled as hers. Today she could forgive them, if not the teachers who turned a blind eye to bullying at the time.

However, all she wanted to do was put as much distance as possible between her and them. She'd always dreamed of going to Texas, a place that sounded so exciting with its big ranches and oil wells. She just knew everyone there, including her, would be rich.

Sandra smiled to herself. *"I almost made it, too. Instead wound up in Oklahoma, just a skinny panhandle away from my dream state. Now I'm running away from it."*

She returned in her thoughts to the first time she ran. Before anyone in the foster home knew she was missing, Ronnie went back to the trailer and scoured it for any cash and added it to the money she'd earned and hidden. She packed clothing and all the food she could find, some wrinkled apples and saltines, into a small metal suitcase.

Ronnie purchased a ticket at the Greyhound Station, but didn't have enough money for a ticket to Texas. She went as far as she could on a diagonal south and then started hitchhiking. Daddy always told her it was too dangerous for a girl to hitchhike, but what choice did she have? People who stopped for her had been very kind, taking her to the next town and often buying her a meal at McDonald's so she guessed Daddy was wrong about that, too. The only time she was scared was at night when, after she ate some crackers and apples, she slept in park picnic shelters. Between slapping mosquitoes and being terrified of nighttime noises, she slept little. When dawn came, she'd walk a while and then put her thumb out. One day she made the mistake of accepting a ride from a semi-truck driver, and in time knew why Daddy had warned her.

At first she thought the driver, Monte, was the nicest man she'd ever met. He had a black and white tomcat. "This here's Buster, my travelin' companion."

Ronnie loved animals and felt good about riding with someone who had a pet. When she asked if he was going to Texas, he smiled and said "Sure thing." She told him her parents had died and that she was trying to get to her grandma's house in Texas.

"Hey, kiddo, Texas is one big place. Where does your granny live?"

Ronnie named the only place she could remember, "Dallas."

"Well, darlin' I'm not going that far. Truth be told, I'm going straight across Oklahoma on my way to California. Why don't you go with me? California is sure better than Texas."

That tempted Ronnie. She liked the man, who had a friendly smile all the time and who told funny stories. She loved holding the warm, purring cat on her lap and listening to country western music on the truck stereo. But, she wanted to go to Texas, and she found herself crying. Monte stopped her tears by telling her that he would take a detour to Dallas, which he had no intention of doing because he didn't believe a word of what she'd told him. *Can't lie to an old liar.* He also mused, *Kid's not bad looking, probably will be a beauty when she grows up.*

Monte shared his large cache of snacks, including the girl's favorites, Cheese Puffs and Snickers bars. At lunchtime he bought them deli sandwiches at a filling station and for supper he bought her a roast beef meal with lots of real mashed potatoes at a truck stop restaurant. This was the best she had eaten, not just since she had been on the run but for a long time before. The potatoes were so good, not like ones Mama cooked out of a box. She blushed, remembering with embarrassment how she attempted to cook real mashed potatoes for her sisters after Mama left. She had just cooked them and mashed them with a fork, and they were lumpy and tasteless. Not smooth and creamy like the ones she ate at this restaurant.

Back in the truck, as night fell, Ronnie asked when they'd reach Dallas.

"Now, girlie, pretty soon we're coming to a rest stop and I have to sleep several hours before I can drive some more," expounded Monte, who added with emphasis, "It's the law." Of course, what he planned to suggest next would be against the law with a minor, but he continued to speak, now softly in a cajoling manner. "I've been awful nice to you..."

Ronnie, in all innocence since he had been so kind, thought the trucker meant she'd have to be nice and quiet while he slept just like she'd had to do when her daddy slept days and worked nights. Monte then described in detail what he had in mind.

The young girl panicked. As the truck slowed down to enter the rest stop, she jumped out. She hit the pavement hard, scraping her legs and arms and hurting her left ankle, but she limped as fast as she could to the Ladies Restroom. There were several women in there so she felt safe. It occurred to her that maybe Monte wouldn't even try to find her, and she felt sad because she doubted anyone had been looking for her from the time she left home. Then she realized her little suitcase with her few articles of clothing was in the truck.

She wound up spending the night curled up on the cold concrete restroom floor. When it was light, she couldn't see the truck she'd ridden in. She'd hoped with crowds of travelers around, she could approach the truck and ask Monte for her suitcase, but now it was gone forever.

Seeing a town ahead, she began a slow, painful walk. The town Modell, according to a road sign, wasn't as close as she'd thought and the pain in her ankle was agonizing. She approached several kids waiting by the side of the road and figured they waited for a school bus. She smiled and said "hi" to them. Though pain shot through her body with each step, she climbed up the bus stairs with them.

No one, not even the bus driver, paid any attention to her. Just like at her own school, Ronnie felt invisible. She got off the bus at the school with the rest but went the opposite direction and wound up at Smokey's Bar and Grill.

An announcement about the flight to Houston jarred Sandra from her reverie.

Due to the deteriorating weather in Houston, her flight had been delayed. An hour later another announcement: The Houston Airport has closed down for the night. "Re-book your flight for tomorrow morning."

Sandra swore under her breath and rebooked her flight. Using the hoodie for a pillow, she tried to find a comfortable way to sleep in a seat in the waiting room. It didn't seem possible. She finally had just dozed off when blindsided by abdominal cramps and the undeniable need to vomit. It must have been something she'd eaten in the airport, maybe even food poisoning. She spent hours in the restroom and then finally was able to return to the waiting area, where she fell asleep.

CHAPTER TWELVE

Two women in a restroom stall

Over a late lunch on Wednesday Belkin launched another discourse ending with "The empty safety deposit box and the withdrawal from the other bank gives my theory credibility. The saintly doctor grabbed her valuables and -- pouf! -- vanished."

"But that doesn't explain why she left her car, her purse, " countered Maria. "Maybe someone was blackmailing her and met her at the Credit Union for the money and whatever she took from the box."

"Then he -- or she -- knocked the doctor down in the parking ramp, she fell on her head, took off her shoes and is running around Corpus Christi barefoot in a designer outfit. "But," Belkin held up one finger, "no one has seen her because she is wearing an invisibility cloak just like Harry Potter."

Ignoring his last crack, Gonzales conceded, "Your theory of her running away is tidier. She disappeared on her own. We can quit looking."

"I've been trying to tell you that all along, Sherlock," mocked Belkin.

Maria didn't even bristle, just shook her head with sadness. She didn't know what to think. So many people, including the doctor's pastor, friends from church, and her neighbors had called voluntarily to vouch for Rhonda's sterling character. Staff and patients loved Dr. Rhonda. She had a great job, a nice car, and townhouse that Maria and Belkin would visit soon. Why would the loved doctor want to disappear? Of course, if she hadn't, what had happened to her? Like the doctor's friends, and unlike Belkin, Maria had to suspect foul play. She couldn't implicate Dr. Linda in the least. She felt sorry for her and pondered: *Which would be worse -- to lose a friend to a criminal act or to have someone you loved and trusted decide to abandon you?* Maria refused to consider that Linda's best friend and husband would have an affair as Belkin had suggested. The inexperienced detective chided herself for reacting to this with her emotions.

Belkin interrupted her thoughts. "You should already know that the more time that passes the less apt we are to find her dead or alive. The first 48 to 76 hours are the most crucial. I believe we are nearing that time limit and can put the 'Missing Doctor' case to rest."

Yes, yes, I learned in grad school that it is crucial to find a missing person as soon as possible

Observing those dark eyes reveal the spunkiness Maria tried to suppress, Belkin waited for a response. Detective Gonzales was too busy thinking about what she would do next. *I have to follow up the leads from the Stripes Store. Did the run-away doctor buy lunch –burritos -- there? It's about six blocks from the Vega Building. It's logical she changed shoes to walk that distance. Did she wait for someone there, who aided her in getting away? Did she leave the car behind because she knew soon someone would be looking for her in that car? Did she spend the night at a motel? Or at a friend's, a friend who isn't talking? Where did she go from there?*

Maria wasn't ready to share any of this with Belkin. She should tell a partner, but he was no partner. They had stopped back at SCCPD to pick up a lab technician to accompany them to dust for fingerprints. While they waited for her, Maria called the Stripes Store and reached the custodian.

"Like the manager told you, I found a phone in the trash in the 'Ladies'."

"Can you describe it?"

"It was one of them smart phones, Verizon. Had a two-tone cover."

Maria heart skipped a beat. "What colors?"

"Black and red. It looked wet and sure glad I always wear gloves cause I wondered if it had taken a swim in the toilet!"

"What did you do with it?"

"Well, tried turning it on, but nothing. Then I took it home to dry out overnight. My kid told me to submerge it in rice to fix it. Not so I could keep it, you know, but to find the owner. I never meant keeping it, you understand. Anyways, it still didn't work and my kid, you know how they know everything about modern techno-ol-ogy stuff, he told me it was toast so I pitched it."

Her son was a whiz at electronics and had the phone working again, at least for a short time. Most of the data had been erased but there were some recent text messages that survived:

One from a Dave in the middle of the morning: *Sweetheart, can we meet for lunch?*

Sweetheart didn't respond until noon. *No. Meet me at Vega Building, third floor parking lot 12:30.*

With his mom's permission, the son decided to keep the phone to work on it some more, and any info on it they agreed to keep to themselves.

"Uh, where did you throw it?" asked Detective Gonzales. "I mean, is it possible to find it again?"

The woman again lied, "No, tossed it in the trash, and Waste Management come this morning."

Maria, making the mistake of believing the custodian, thanked her; and in frustration she put her head down on her desk in the tiny office she also shared with three recent academy graduates. *Timing is everything. Could well have been the doctor's phone but not worth digging in the landfill for a phone with no data.*

Belkin came to find her. "No time for napping!" She started to contradict him, but he continued, "There's a little lady here who claims she saw the doctor and another woman in a restroom outside the credit union before 1:00 PM on Monday."

Belkin introduced Maria to a determined-looking senior citizen named Muriel Martin, sitting primly in his office. She fit the old saw about being as broad as she was tall with tight ringlets in an unnatural orange shade, lots of blue eye shadow and enough blush for a cheer leading squad. A hibiscus blossom wilted in her hair. As the woman looked her up and down, Maria asked. "So, Miss Muriel, you saw the doctor and another woman?"

The woman began talking a mile a minute, "No, Ah didn't see the other one but Ah saw that lady doctor in that fancy silk blouse they keep telling about on television and Ah heard her talking to the other woman. Oh, mercy me, Ah wish Ah'd never gone in that restroom because of those two women but my husband and I were at the clock shop -- we brought in our cuckoo, my husband got it in Germany when he was in the army, and it stopped cuckooing." A girlie giggle. "Anyway we had lunch early at the restaurant on the first floor and at my age I shouldn't have had the chili so my husband went to see if the clock was ready while I hustled to the 'powder room'. That's what ladies call a restroom, but it wasn't to powder my nose". A titter.

Belkin, looking amused, broke in, "Miss Muriel, could you tell us what you heard?"

"Do you all think Ah'm the kind that eavesdrops on others?" Muriel answered sharply.

"No, Ma'am," Belkin answered," but you indicated that you heard them."

"Of course, Ah heard them. Ah know a young pup like you doesn't think old people can hear but Art --he's my husband -- just yesterday he put new batteries in my 'ears', that's what us 'old kids' call 'hearin' aides, and we don't like to run out so we decided to buy more at the clock shop because they fix clocks and they sell batteries, too, which made it easy-peasy for us." Merry dimples showed on her wrinkled face as she laughed, "Art says they sell batteries to people if they don't find anything wrong with the sound of the clock they brought in! Y'all get it? The clock's fine they just can't hear it!" When she ceased laughing, she looked puzzled. "Ah was so upset when I met up with Art, Ah forgot to ask if he remembered the batteries."

"Miss Muriel, could you tell us why you were so upset?" Maria asked a little more loudly than she realized.

"Hold your horses, Missy. Ah was getting to that, and Ah can hear y'all just fine. When Ah came out of the stall to wash my hands -- do y'all know how many people don't wash their hands after they go to the toilet? Anyway, as Ah was sayin, Ah heard one woman talking and that disgusted me because Ah thought it was someone talking on a cell phone and I think that is so rude to talk on the phone in a restroom, don't you' all agree? Who wants to hear all that vulgar flushing and worse? Then I heard another woman."

The woman stopped for a breath and Maria plunged in, "Did you hear what she said? I know you weren't trying to listen but do you remember what the woman said?"

"No, I don't." She paused. "Wait. It was something about a dog, name of Pepper or maybe Peppy."

"Did she sound upset?" Maria asked.

"Maybe, maybe not since Ah don't know what her un-upset voice sounded like." Muriel sounded perplexed.

"Did you see the woman talking on the phone?" asked Belkin, trying to be patient while keeping himself from the laughs that threatened to bubble out.

"No, but in the mirror Ah saw her go into a stall before Ah heard her talking. That's when Ah knew it was the missing doctor. Ah just saw her back but Ah recognized the fancy blouse from television and the nut colored pants, hazelnut the anchor said. They could have said tan since they were tan and so were her shoes, but Ah guess a nut color is too plain, not fashionable. And the hair. Ah recognized the blonde hair tied back in a pony tail, which I think is just plain lazy and not in style at all, and honest to John, it was so long it looked like just like a real horse's tail. Ha ha!"

"Miss Muriel, you told me you heard two voices," summed up Belkin.

"Yes, Ah did but Ah was too mortified to listen to what they else said in that stall."

"Now let me see if I have this right," Belkin continued. "There already was one person in the stall the woman went into? Did you see her?"

"No because the first one must have gone in when I was in a stall, but isn't that disgusting? Two women doing who knows what unspeakable things. Ah certainly didn't care to know so left, without drying my hands and had to wipe them on my jacket, and Art said my face was as red as the redfish he's always catching in the bay, and Ah was mad as a wet hen when Ah met him at the clock shop. I know the television says how wonderful the doctor is, but I don't think much of women that do unnatural things with other women, but you know, my sister Vivian said Ah could be wrong about what they were doing because once she had me come in the same stall because she needed help getting her girdle up. That's okay and it was my sister but the Bible says…"

"Thank you, Miss Muriel," Sgt. Belkin uttered, taking the woman's arm "You've been very helpful."

"Just call in case y'all have any other questions. Ah really don't think there is anything to worry about. The doctor ran off with her lover, and probably none of her friends or patients even knew she was -- you know -- a girl ho-mo-sex-u-al. That's just what happened on my soap opera."

The woman kept on nattering away as she found her waiting husband. Belkin and Gonzales shared a laugh as they waited for the lab tech to join them to go to the townhouse.

The technician called to say she'd meet them there.

On the way to the townhouse address, Detective Gonzales expressed her thoughts on what the "witness" had told them. "This puts a different slant on things. I guess I thought a male overpowered her and abducted her. Now we have a possible female suspect."

"You mean you didn't buy the theory of lesbians doing 'unspeakable things' in the stall?" Belkin teased.

"Not really, but I can't explain why both were in the same stall."

"Actually," Belkin opined, "a same sex relationship also would support my theory; and you remember her alleged 'best friend' mentioned she didn't date men. Maybe someone was about to expose her preference and she was afraid of the fallout because this is Texas, after all, so she grabbed all her valuables and disappeared. To save face, she made it look like an abduction."

"You're both all wet," chimed in the technician, Jenna Black, who had overheard part of the conversation when she came up behind the two detectives, now on Dr. Rhonda's front porch. "She made her lover jealous and the lover killed her and ran off with all those valuables just like on NCSI."

Quoting her partner, Gonzales joked, "You watch too much television!"

"I do. Abby Sciuto is my hero!"

The only thing possibly valuable from the old lady is that another female may be involved, and I have an idea who that might be, was Belkin's thought as they entered Rhonda's home.

This place is just like out of a magazine, independently determined both of the women. The living room sported plush off-white carpeting, furnishings snatched from showroom displays, original paintings by Hispanic artists. Beside a stone fireplace that looked never used, stood built-in bookcases filled with bestsellers, books about Texas and pottery.

Jenna murmured, "She must have hired an expensive decorator." Everything shouted the superior taste of the missing occupant. No one would guess she once lived in a run-down mobile home that had nothing in common with the townhouse except being very close to the residence next door.

Gonzales and Belkin together entered the bedrooms to check closets to see if clothes and suitcases appeared to be missing. Three clothes closets, overly well organized by type and color of clothing, boasted only a couple of empty padded hangers. An assortment of suitcases had been placed together on shelves in one closet with no empty spaces to indicate missing luggage. Belkin scoffed at the mounds of showy pillows on the bed in each room, while Maria dreamed of having a bed decorated just as romantically, if she and her boyfriend Xavier married.

Continuing to the kitchen, Maria asked herself, *"Does the refrigerator hold clues of someone planning to return Monday for supper?"* Frozen dinners in the freezer indicated someone planned to eat for quite a while, and the organic Greek yogurt in the refrigerator looked as if it just had been opened. Not much else in the refrigerator but condiments, a carton of organic milk and two covered cans, half empty, breed specific for Chihuahuas. Maria decided, *"The doctor probably ate out often and the dog ate well."*

Jenna Black dusted for prints, even in each and every drawer. She marveled at the huge collection of fancy lingerie the doctor owned. Stan Belkin continued to look for clues of a premeditated disappearance while Maria Gonzales searched for an address book. She exclaimed when she found a thick expensive one with a leather cover in a vintage keyhole desk, probably a family antique. Maria quickly decided maybe not since people in Corpus tended to store their antiques where there were no hurricanes and bought other antiques without sentimental attachment at local stores. She opened the address book and read an inscription *"To Rhonda from your best friend. As long as you have my address, you really don't need any other! Love, L. H."*

A gift from Dr. Linda! Maria said to herself and turned to the "H's". Nothing was there. The book had no entries of addresses. " Never used!" Maria told the others. "Apparently she kept all information in her phone." To herself she thought, *"The useless one buried in the landfill. I need to tell Belkin about that and the witness from Stripes. I'm beginning to think he's right. She wanted to disappear. But someone had to be threatening her, blackmailing her. I need to know why Belkin asked Dr. Linda if she'd heard from Rhonda, why he's acting suspicious of her, of all people."*

Belkin bagged and carried Rhonda's computer from a small well-appointed office to headquarters, where their tekkie would go over it and find nothing untoward, just dozens and dozens of bookmarked current medical articles. Jenna told them she'd have the results for them from both the town home and the car tomorrow. All Maria and Stan wanted to do was forget about the case until then. It was poker night for Stan, and mid-week date night for Maria.

She and Xavier Galvan went to Applebee's. It was hard to ignore the case as the predominantly placed large television sets blared the latest about the missing doctor. "SCCPD followed up a lead and found the missing doctor's car in a Corpus Christi parking ramp. The PD didn't comment, but," the perky anchor added, "this seems to indicate the doctor had been taken against her will, which, of course, has been the opinion of her co-workers and friends."

Maria couldn't tell Xavier about the case, but she did tell him how her partner frustrated her, treating her as if she was incompetent just because of her gender.

"You know how I feel, Sweetie. I wish you hadn't gone into law enforcement. Too dangerous, especially for women."

Maria, whose temper had been near boil all day and whose tongue had loosened with the long neck Shiner Bock she'd been drinking, retorted, "Now you're sounding like as big a horse's rear as he is. This job could be just as dangerous for my male partner if he keeps being such a pain in the butt; I am armed."

Xavier couldn't help laughing at the bravado expressed by his feisty girlfriend. "Now, Maria. Don't let that temper of yours get the best of you! Want another beer?"

Maria, who didn't want to argue and spoil this evening with the man she loved, laughed, too. She accepted the second beer and reverted to her usually pleasant self while wishing she could share with Xavier the delight she'd taken in showing up Belkin. Instead she made up her mind to stop thinking about work and just enjoy the time with her man. After they left Applebee's and she had some alone time with Xavier, then she'd concentrate on her job.

At home Maria pulled the poster board out from under her bed, its permanent hiding place, to add all of today's information. Big Boy immediately jumped on the over-sized paper covering most of the bed. "You know, B. B., I managed to impress Hotshot a couple times today, but on second thought, maybe I just annoyed him and made life harder for me." She pushed the cat off the part where she needed to write. Big Boy rubbed against her. "It's great to have someone nice to me. Belkin thinks I'm an idiot, and Xavier thinks I should give up police work. Of course he's said that from the first because he thinks it's too hazardous, and I doubt myself because I get too emotionally involved. I wish I could talk to

Sydney but there's this thing on cases called confidentiality. At least, I know whatever I divulge is safe with you." The cat yawned and curled up on the part of the board his mistress wasn't working on.

Maria finished the chart, but something nagged at her. Something to be followed up. Maria finally figured it out. She needed to call the head doctor's wife and talk to both the wife and her aunt. It was too late now. Better wait until tomorrow. *If I could just crack this case, but to accomplish this, as hard as it is, I will have to accept Hotshot's theory that Dr. Rhonda left of her own volition.*

CHAPTER THIRTEEN

Guilt and Suspicion

Wednesday evening with the kids finally in bed Linda, who understood too well the truth of the adage "There will be a special place in Heaven for mothers of three sons", retired early. With little rest the night before and the rough day she'd had, she expected to go right to sleep. When Dave was gone, it was hard to sleep but overwhelming fatigue would triumph tonight. Instead with everything on her mind, she couldn't sleep at all. Deserting her bed, she curled up on the couch with Poppy on her lap. "You're not so awful, little guy, you just miss your mom, but whatever could have happened to Rhonda?"

The dog pricked up his ears at the sound of his mistress' name and Linda figured he knew as much about Rhonda's whereabouts as the SCCPD. That entity had played a most disturbing part in her day, which rolled through her mind like a movie.

Dr. Ron had called all the patients Rhonda had seen Monday but none offered any insights. He'd heard over and over, "She was same as always, so caring and concerned and never mentioned anything upsetting." Such sentiments always were followed by "What can I do?"

The head doctor, revealing his lack of faith in the police, told everyone if SCCPD hadn't come up with something by the end of the week, he and his wife Melanie planned to hire their own investigator

The staff decided to hold a candlelight prayer vigil on Friday night and to distribute "Have you seen?" posters with Rhonda's photo. All the doctors were sharing Rhonda's caseload. In spite of the extra patients in her care Linda found time to design the poster, which she dropped off at a printer after work. Staff, patients and other volunteers would receive stacks of them at the vigil, which Linda had taken the responsibility for arranging with her church, the Episcopal Church Rhonda also had attended.

Before reliving her unpleasant trip to the SCCPD, Linda took time out to count her blessings. The weather looked favorable, no visit from Leo and no rain in the forecast for Friday, since they planned an outside vigil in the Cielo Vista parking lot, which seemed significant since that was the last place anyone had seen Rhonda. And thank heavens, Dave would return tomorrow so he could help her Friday evening and on Saturday, when the staff and their families and other volunteers would put up the posters in all the small towns surrounding Corpus Christi.

At the PD, identifying Rhonda's purse and pumps had been upsetting enough, but to have Sgt. Belkin ask her if she and Rhonda had been in contact seemed outrageous. How could he suspect her of withholding anything like that when she'd been doing everything a best friend could do?

Of course, she hadn't been completely forthright when he and the other detective interviewed her about what she knew about Rhonda's past. Did the officer sense Linda was hiding something? She was. Could he already know what she hadn't shared? Rhonda didn't like to talk about her past, but while they vacationed in Mazatlan, she had confided something to Linda.

To think about Matzalan provided Linda welcome relief from today. When Rhonda had proposed a week's trip, Linda didn't know how she could leave her children that long. In the end they had compromised and gone for half a week. Dave was okay with this since he said he didn't have to travel that week (so wouldn't be able to be with Rhonda anyway), and his mom would watch the kids during the day.

Until meeting Rhonda, Linda had been so busy with first her schooling and then her career and family that there had been no time to have close friends. Linda loved having this relationship with Rhonda, even though there were things she didn't understand about her friend. A bit naïve, Linda accepted Rhonda's unwillingness to share about herself as, perhaps, a result of not growing up in the Hispanic culture. In her close-knit family Linda had learned to chatter with sisters and cousins in intimate detail. Now Linda lamented she hadn't asked her friend more relevant questions.

Linda pictured the night Rhonda had confided in her. Sitting on green and white striped chairs, the two friends watched the sunset from the beach outside the hotel. Earlier Linda had gone in for a swim, but Rhonda had admitted that she came from a poor family and never had been able to take lessons. "I can't swim, at all" she divulged, "but I'll round up two chairs while you swim and then we'll both watch another breathtaking sunset." When Linda returned from her swim she found Rhonda had gotten her a tropical mango-colored cocktail with its requisite umbrella. She sipped it while, as always, Rhonda drank a Diet Coke. Linda had once asked her why she never imbibed. Rhonda had answered, "It's a long story, not worth telling." Since Rhonda never discoursed like a recovering alcoholic, Linda had decided there was a history of alcohol abuse by someone in Rhonda' past and let it go. This wasn't what Rhonda confided that evening, but maybe there was a connection. Linda had thought it a little odd that she wouldn't speak to her, as another doctor, about alcohol abuse.

They were enjoying such a wonderful vacation, but as the sky turned from orange and carmine to fuchsia and rose, Rhonda shed a few tears and commented that she wished they could go on being friends forever.

"Why wouldn't we be?"

"Gee, what a killjoy I am. First I admit I can't swim, and now I'm about to make a 'true confession'." She hesitated as if waiting for Linda to say it wasn't necessary.

Linda said nothing, and Rhonda persevered. "There's a secret in my past, and if that ever comes to light, I might have to do something you will find very uncharacteristic. I might have to sacrifice countless things, and what bothers me most is our friendship."

Rhonda had a look of fear in her eyes, and Linda, truly alarmed and more than a little curious, thought it might help her friend to talk more about it and pressed for details. Rhonda brightened up, "No time to be morose here. Let's get dressed up and go have another amazing seafood dinner."

Her friend loved seafood and meat, Linda remembered, but never ate poultry. She'd never thought to ask her why even when she spent Thanksgivings with them but avoided the turkey while filling up on sides. So many things she didn't know about Rhonda.

Returning her thoughts to Mazatlan, Linda asked herself the same question that first occurred to her on Monday. On the beach that beautiful evening had Rhonda referred to running away, disappearing? Linda never believed her friend could have done anything as terrible as she seemed to indicate. *I want to think Rhonda broke a man's heart before she came to Corpus Christi, and now he's caught up with her. Maybe all along she had feared retribution from this man. If the man appeared, she'd have to flee to save her life. But this theory had a flaw. Except for the fear Rhonda had shown when she inferred a problem in her past, her best friend seemed so normal and well adjusted, serene and happy with her life.*

Rhonda certainly was fine the last time I saw her on Monday morning.

I told the police she never dated, and I've wondered if that is because she'd had a bad experience with men in her past. It suddenly occurs to me that perhaps Rhonda is married and came to Corpus to escape an abusive husband, maybe an alcoholic. Monday morning, after we saw each other, somehow she found out he was in town so had to disappear. That thought sounds logical. I might share this if I'm forced to tell the police department more to convince them of the seriousness of the disappearance.

All anyone talked about at the clinic was Rhonda, and Linda had heard many times about Melanie Brooks' aunt calling Rhonda a different name. Tuesday night Linda had contacted Mel to ask how Rhonda had reacted. Melanie said that even though her aunt has a voice like foghorn, she wasn't sure Rhonda had heard everything Auntie Fe said because Rhonda just gave them a puzzled look as she rushed by to her car. As the clock struck 2:00 AM, Linda wondered out loud. "Is it possible the aunt HAD recognized her?" Poppy stirred in her sleep as Linda spoke. "Was Rhonda forced into a name change when she came to Corpus because of feared discovery? Was Rhonda once Sandra 'Something', the aunt's hairdresser, as Mellie's Auntie Fe maintains? Melanie and everyone else had scoffed at that, but what if Rhonda had worked her way through medical school as a hairdresser like I earned tuition money as a Pampered Chef representative? That's nothing to be ashamed of doing. But it didn't make sense because Rhonda had gone to med school in the east, not Oklahoma. And the timing was wrong. To go through college, med school, internship and residency, Rhonda wouldn't have had time to be the aunt's hair stylist for as many years as the woman said."

Linda heard small footsteps and Frankie, her youngest, appeared. "Mama, when does Auntie Rhonda come back?"

"Oh, darling son," Linda soothed, putting her son on her lap, "I don't know for certain."

"She won't be back forever," Frankie stated as if he knew the answer to his own question.

To have her own fear expressed by a four-year disturbed Linda, who tried to reassure mother and child. "Of course, she'll come back."

"I miss her."

"I do, too, Frankie."

"Can we keep Poppy?"

Linda recognized the child's inner conflict. Rhonda versus Poppy. "We'll take care of Poppy as long as he needs us."

A victorious solution came to Frankie. "Auntie Rhonda will come back and give him to us!"

How easily children's problems could be solved. Giving her youngest a hug, Linda smiled at him and said in her sweet but firm mom voice, "Okay, now that's settled, it's back to bed for you."

Frankie went back to sleep while Linda, still restless, continued to worry what she might have said to make the detective suspect her. Hadn't she done everything a devoted friend could do? When she saw the shoes and purse, hadn't she'd broken down because it looked as if Rhonda really could be a crime victim? Linda had done everything to prove her loyalty.

What Linda hadn't volunteered was the information that Rhonda always had her gym bag with athletic shoes in the car and if she had left on her own, she would have changed into better walking shoes. Linda hadn't mentioned the gym bag at all, but she guessed it wouldn't be found in the car because if Rhonda had run away, she probably would have taken it.

Linda smiled as thoughts turned to early Monday when Rhonda came to Linda's office. Rhonda had come in to show off her new blouse and accessories, bought to match her pants and jacket. "Look at my purse and shoes. They were much too expensive but the leather is soft as butter. You really must feel them."

Linda had fingered the purse and then made a big deal of kneeling at Rhonda's feet to touch the shoes all over. They both roared with laughter. It was silly, but the two friends, professional women to the world, often acted like kids when they were alone together. Of course, she hadn't mentioned something this ridiculous to the officers. She also hadn't mentioned that Rhonda never drank, but why would she have volunteered that? A doctor's definition of an alcoholic was someone who drank more than the doctor did, but surely only she had wondered if Rhonda's abstinence had something to do with her secret.

The distraught friend kept coming back to what she might have said to make Belkin suspect her, to act like she knew about the disappearance in advance. At least he hadn't asked if she'd harmed her. They couldn't link her to aiding, even covertly, in her escape, could they?

Suddenly Linda felt as deflated as a punctured tire. She didn't want to admit it, but maybe, the friend she loved and thought she had known so well, she hadn't known at all. She went to bed, and the competent medical professional, wife and mother, sobbed like a child.

Cried out, Dr. Linda Hernandez summarized her reasons for wanting the police to continue to think Rhonda was the victim of foul play. Besides hoping to protect her friend she'd convinced herself that if the police thought something had happened to Rhonda, they'd look for her. Why share her theory (and after all, it was just a theory that Rhonda had run) with Officers Belkin and Gonzales? She fell asleep about 4:00

with the thought of doing anything for her friend. Linda had no idea what she had chosen might cost her, including her own freedom.

CHAPTER FOURTEEN

Terror in the Night

About the time Linda fell asleep, Gloria Bennett heard the ring of the phone on her bedside table. A glance at the clock showed 4:00. She trembled as she wondered who could be calling then. Her mind raced as she inventoried her loved ones. Her husband slept beside her, it was a school night so her sixteen-year-old son had been in bed, at least quiet in his room, for hours. Something must have happened to one of her parents. Shaking, she answered.

A nurse from Spohn South Hospital gave her a message that no mother ever wants to receive. "An ambulance brought your son to the hospital. He suffered a drug overdose."

"That's impossible. He's been a asleep for hours!" Gloria shrieked.

Though Bill Bennett had slept through the ringing of the phone, his wife's hysterical voice awakened him.

"Quick! Check Austin's room!!" she demanded.

He did as told while Gloria explained, "My husband is checking his room. I can't believe he sneaked out, he's never done anything like that before."

Gloria heard simultaneously "Ma'am, I suggest you get here as quickly as possible..." and "He's not in his bed!"

"Is he going to be okay?" Gloria asked the caller.

"We don't know. You must come now."

On the way to the hospital neither spoke. A silence-shattering word would awaken the other from what each hoped was only a nightmare.

Less than a week ago Bill and Gloria had been enjoying the time of their lives on a fourteen-day Mediterranean cruise, a gift to each other for their thirtieth anniversary. They had no qualms about leaving their responsible sixteen-year old son home alone. Their only child, who was born to them long after they'd accepted not being able to have children, never had given them any trouble. Drug involvement didn't enter the minds of the couple, whose son excelled at school and athletics, a nice kid with many friends from school and his church youth group.

As soon as they returned home from the cruise, their big bubble of happiness broke. Many would comment on the irony of their homecoming in the following days. First they discovered their car had been stolen from the garage. The robbery must have happened while Austin was at school because he wasn't even aware of it. A hurricane watch further threatened their peace of mind; Austin had helped his dad with the labor-intensive job of putting up shutters they wound up not needing. That was a good thing. Something else that didn't affect the Bennetts directly worried them because a doctor who worked at a clinic near their neighborhood had gone missing.

Little traffic at this time of morning. Out of nowhere a speeding car ran a red light near the hospital and caused Bill to swerve. He swore out loud and muttered something about a drunk. Gloria began sobbing, "Or a kid, like ours, on drugs. Oh, Bill, what kind of parents are we that we didn't know?"

Bill couldn't answer.

The nurse on duty directed them to the intensive care unit, where they found their son. The nightmare persisted with a scene that any parent would find unbearable. White as death, attached by tubes to an array of monitors with incessant beeps and chirps, Austin lay lifeless.

"Is he going to make it?" Bill whispered.

"His life signs are better than when they brought him in. We had to pump his stomach. Now it's just a matter of wait and see what or if any permanent damage was done. Make yourselves as comfortable as possible."

Gloria took her son's hand and breathed, "It's okay, Austin, Mom and Dad are here. You know we love you, no matter what."

Austin's eyes opened briefly but he couldn't focus. He closed them with a grimace. The nurse offered encouragement. "That's the first time he's opened his eyes. Please keep talking to him. Your son can hear you."

Austin's parents talked to him for hours. Gloria told stories of his childhood while Bill rehashed the most recent soccer games. One of the many medical personnel, who had checked on the youth through seemingly endless hours, said they soon would move Austin to a regular room. He explained the improvement in their son's vital signs. "He's a tough kid. Why don't you find a cup of coffee during the transfer?"

Alone in a small waiting area on the floor where Austin would be, all they could say to each other is, "Nothing matters as long as he pulls through."

As soon as a nurse found them, they went to their son's room. Austin had awakened. They saw him crying for the first time since he was a little kid. In a weak voice he managed, "Mom, Dad, I'm sorry."

"It's okay, son. As long as you're...."

"No, it's not okay. I sold . . ." He couldn't finish.

"The car?" whispered his dad, voicing a possibility he hadn't even mentioned to his wife while they were beating themselves up earlier.

Austin nodded "yes" and fell back to sleep.

The nurse assured the parents that this was normal.

While Gloria's eyes were glued to her son, Bill excused himself. "I need to call the police department."

CHAPTER FIFTEEN

Key Witness

Maria continued her conversation with Big Boy, her best confidante, the next morning in the kitchen. "I thought about my partner all night, at least until I finally fell asleep about 2:00. Just sayin', Sir Cat, this isn't the way it's supposed to be. Belkin and I behave like adversaries, not partners. I'm as much to blame as he is. He always needs to remind me how inexperienced I am, and I resent the fact that I have more education than he does and I delight in showing him up. Down deep, Big Boy, I want to solve this case all on my own. Today I vow that I shall be the perfect cooperative partner."

Sydney joined her housemate and their cat. "Who are you talking to, Mar? I thought you were on your cell."

"Just taking to Big Boy. I hope I didn't wake you."

"No, my alarm did, I have to go in early. My possible new boyfriend Brad is giving me a ride."

After roll call, Maria wanted to get started on the phone calls, but first a written report demanded by the Chief, who again had voiced the opinion to all that the two detectives were pursuing a hopeless case. She was documenting the inspection of the missing doctor's car and residence when her cell rang. The day clerk from the Liberty Motel.

"I thought of something else. The woman who checked in was carrying a blue gym bag."

"Thank you for that. I planned to call you to ask a couple more things."

"Shoot! Oops, I shouldn't say that to someone armed," she guffawed.

"You were so detailed in your description, but I forgot to ask if you noticed any jewelry."

With her nearly photographic memory Brenda brought back the image of the tall, thin thirtyish woman with blonde hair escaping from the hood of her sweatshirt, and the ruffled collar of an ivory silk blouse seen where the jacket wasn't zipped, oversized sunglasses, expensive tan pants and exercise shoes. "No, I don't remember any jewelry at all, but did I tell you she wore exercise shoes? She must have changed out of those tan leather pumps the television said she was wearing."

"Thank you, again, and one more question. Could you give me the name of the clerk on duty when the woman in question left the motel?"

"Oh, sure, that would be Lupe. You can get a hold of him when he comes in at 9: 00 -- that's 9:00 tonight. He works the long night shift from 9:00 PM until 6:00 AM, when I come in. I work until 4:00 and then we have Lana come in when I leave until he gets here. That's the short shift.

Patiently waiting until Brenda finished reciting the motel staffing schedule, Maria asked, "Could you give me Lupe's personal phone number?"

"No can do, privacy you know."

"I understand. Again, I thank you for all your help, and I'll call Lupe. In fact, I think I talked to him once while trying to reach you." Maria sighed. *That means I have even more follow-up calls. I'll have to get touch with the witness from Stripes to see if he remembers the gym bag.*

Maria returned to the report as her "partner" wandered into her cubicle. Belkin's right jaw looked swollen, and Maria wondered if the hothead, with whom she had vowed to cooperate, had been in a fight.

His voice was stern. "Detective Gonzalez, we're supposed to be partners. I know you're new at this but you've been working against me. I think you're holding out on me. In fact I know you are because I had to hear from the lab that they sent DNA samples from the car, the residence and the hairbrush to Dallas. I had to pretend I knew about all that, which doesn't please me. What else are you keeping to yourself?"

He expected an argument, but heard, "Detective Belkin, you're absolutely right. I haven't felt we're working as partners either. Let's sit down together and go over everything we've both discovered."

I can't believe it was so easy to convince her! "Sounds good. That's what partners should do."

Stan put his hand to his jaw and winced.

"Are you okay?"

"Toothache. Hurts like hell."

"You should call Apple Dental. I go there and I'm sure you could get in for an emergency appointment."

"It's not that bad," Stan grumbled as he winced again. "Let's git 'er done."

Maria paused as she thought. *Men try to be so tough when they obviously hurt badly. Xavier was the same way when he fell and broke his ankle surfing, and her dad would do anything to avoid seeing a doctor.*

"Gonzales?" Belkin prodded and Maria began, "Okay, let's start at the beginning. Monday afternoon the department received the call about the missing doctor from the head doctor and later a call from Dr. Linda, as we've come to call her, who brought in the hairbrush and photo. Nothing was done on Monday so we missed possible evidence because every place the missing person had been seen had been cleaned by custodial staffs."

"Like what places?' Belkin asked and then went on. "Obviously the restroom by the credit union had been cleaned by the time our 'star witness' told us about seeing her, but where else?"

"Well, for one, the Stripes store near the credit union," Maria answered and elaborated. "When checking the calls on the tip-line (*that you said were a waste of time, but I won't remind you)* I came across a caller who was sure of seeing the doctor in that store about 1:15. I met this man at the store, where I also talked to another employee, a manager. The witness' description of the doctor fits the one that the media had and which we received from the interviews on Tuesday. That witness added she bought burritos and was eating her lunch standing by the door as if waiting for someone. The manager didn't remember our missing person. The only thing he remembered unusual from that day was the custodian said she found a cell phone in the ladies' restroom wastebasket. I contacted Dr. Linda to describe the doctor's phone; she said it was a smart phone in a red and black case. Later, I spoke with the custodian, and it was confirmed she'd found a very wet phone in a black and red case. She admitted taking the phone home, but it didn't work so threw it out with the trash, already picked up earlier that day.

"Did you believe all that?"

"I imagine the woman wouldn't have said anything if the phone had worked; she said a teen-age son assessed the damage and insisted it wouldn't work."

Belkin huffed. "Okay, where else?'

"A desk clerk from the Liberty Motel..."

With just the reaction Sandra had wanted when she picked the unlikely motel, Belkin looked aghast. "That sleazy place? Surely our fancy-smancy doctor didn't go there!"

"The day desk clerk recognized her from the photo and called back this morning because she remembered the person of interest carried a blue gym bag. I plan to call the man from

Stripes to see if he noticed a gym bag, and I need to talk to the night clerk because the woman described left before the day clerk was back on duty. Oh, yes, she said the woman came mid-afternoon, which would fit the time-line of the sighting after Stripes. Also, the desk clerk gave me the license of her car, and, guess what, she drove a gray Taurus."

"There must be a hundred of gray Tau*r-i* in Corpus Christi."

"Taur...what?" puzzled Maria.

"You mean with all your larnin', you didn't have Latin? I did back in Catholic high school in Iowa. Plural of words that end in *'us'* end in *'i'*."

He's smarter than I thought was her first reaction but then she ruffled at another insult. She hadn't studied Latin but stated with all the superiority she could muster, "Of course, we learned considerable Latin in criminal justice classes, like *habeas corpus, pro bono, ad hoc, corpus delecti, facil leg...*"

Belkin had stopped listening and interrupted with a brusque, "We need to see if the license numbers match."

Gonzalez smiled. "Actually, I've already given the license number to Officer Vargas, but he hasn't gotten back to me. Probably because I gave him three possibilities for some symbols. The desk clerk had trouble reading the handwriting."

Belkin began slow, exaggerated applause. It could have been considered sarcastic praise but his smile seemed sincere. "You are quite the little detective, Gonzales. Say, since we're partners, may I call you 'Maria' and how 'bout you call me 'Stan'."

Maria, ignoring the "little" reference grinned, "Sure, Stan."

"So, even though you want to believe the doctor is a victim of foul play, you've discovered what appears to support my theory?" Stan Belkin asked.

"Yes," Maria answered, "it looks that way, but I still want to know why. If she was coerced, we have a crime."

"Maria, we may never know why but if we have enough evidence, we can prove she was NOT abducted. For sure, we could have expected a request for a ransom long before now if she had been."

"It troubles me about the 'other woman' in the stall."

"I doubt the credibility of that particular witness." Belkin sounded serious but then joked, "No one has reported finding a body in that particular restroom so I don't think the 'other woman' did her in. My own theory is another woman helped her with the get-away."

Belkin noted the puzzled look that he had prompted in his partner's expressive "Cocker Spaniel eyes", but before he could say something Officer Vargas joined the reconciled-for-the-moment partners. "I just heard from the husband whose car was stolen while he and his wife were on a cruise. The car wasn't stolen so my case is closed but this might be relevant to yours."

An audible intake of breath from Marie. "Really?"

"Their son almost died of a drug overdose last night and when he woke up and saw his parents, he confessed selling their car for drug money."

"Oh, how awful for them," Maria interjected, with true concern. With a grim look on his face, Belkin shook his head, but not because of this kid and his parents but because of his long-ago first experience with an overdosing kid when he was a newbie like Maria. *The years have hardened me, and Maria needs to start toughening up. Yet, the compassion Gonzales has shown throughout this case has its appeal. Regardless, we'll both be better off when she isn't so emotionally involved.*

Vargas added, "I finally decoded all those license numbers you gave me, Maria, and it's a likely match between the car he sold and the one driven to the motel."

Maria's eyes changed from sad to excited.

Officer Vargas suggested, "You might want to interview the kid when he's up to it. He sold the car at a Stripes store. Could your missing doctor have bought a get-away car?"

Belkin shrugged while Maria could barely contain herself. Things were falling in place. Maybe the night clerk would have some idea where the driver of the Taurus went next.

"I'll set up that appointment for us at the hospital, partner," Belkin stated as he left.

"And you should make one with the dentist."

"Don't worry about me. Just make those phone calls."

Maria reached the man from Stripes, who admitted he had blue-green color blindness so wasn't certain of the color, but he did see the woman take money out of a gym bag when paying for lunch. *We'll have to ask that kid who almost died, too, about the gym bag.*

When Dr. Brooks' wife answered, she was very cooperative. Melanie Brooks repeated the story that her auntie had mistaken Dr. Rhonda for her former hairdresser, but said the aunt couldn't talk to Maria because Felicity already had gone back to Oklahoma. Melanie gave the law officer the aunt's number, and Maria called several times but could not reach the elderly woman. Melanie had forgotten to tell her that Auntie Fe always had her hair done on Thursday mornings. Maria wouldn't have another chance to call until Thursday night by which time it would turn out to be too late.

The Chief blustered in and demanded the report that should have been on his desk an hour ago. Belkin overheard this and returned to intervene, "So many things have been breaking in this case this morning that she hasn't had time to finish it."

In one way, Maria felt happy that Stan stood up for her, but in another, she wanted to handle the Chief on her own.

"I'm just adding what has happened today and will finish in a couple minutes."

The Chief went off muttering that they needed to wrap up this case yesterday. Then he looked back and asked, "Someone take a punch at you, Belkin?" He continued to his office without waiting for an answer.

Shortly after delivering the report to him, Maria called Dr. Linda and asked if Dr. Rhonda might have had a blue gym bag in her car.

"Why do you ask?"

"I'm sorry, I can't tell you that."

Linda's voice showed the terror she felt. "Did you find someone with a gym bag that you think belongs to Rhonda?"

"Dr. Linda, I wish I could tell you we have found your friend and that she's okay, but we haven't."

Linda gave in, "She did have a blue gym bag which she kept in her car. After work we often went in her car to the "Y" gym for a quick workout. We also went Sunday afternoon the day before she …"

The doctor choked up and couldn't go on.

"I know this is hard, but I have one more question. Did she have work-out shoes in her bag?"

"Yes." *Was this proof Rhonda had changed shoes before she ran? Oh, Rhonda, where did you go and why?* The young officer's voice interrupted her thoughts.

"Thank you. We don't think anything bad has happened to your friend."

They don't think anyone has harmed her, and I'm glad except I know something bad happened to make her run. Linda hung up the phone and returned to the next patient.

Maria's extension rang again. "I'm Frank Krause, family attorney. I haven't paid much attention to the news lately but I saw a photo of client of mine in the paper, the missing doctor, and the dispatcher referred me to you."

"Do you have information?"

"Only this. About six months ago Dr. Collins contacted me to make out her will."

When I kidded her why someone her age was making a will, she said something a bit strange. She said she'd been having premonitions of something happening to her and didn't want to leave loose ends."

"Did she seem frightened?"

"No, just matter of fact."

"Can you tell me her beneficiaries?"

"No, I shouldn't have told you this much, but I will tell you she had only one beneficiary."

Two thoughts slammed Maria simultaneously. *The beneficiary wanted the money right away and the doctor feared for her life*

"Thank you. We'll keep you in the loop." Maria hung up and saw Jenna, the lab tech, standing by her desk. "We have the lab results from the townhouse and car," Jenna told her.

"Thanks, Abby," Maria teased.

"I'm going to get Stan so I can go over it with both of you."

Stan had taken time off to go to the emergency dental appointment for what turned out to be a badly abscessed tooth. It wasn't until late afternoon that they had a chance to look over the evidence report.

CHAPTER SIXTEEN

Memories

Sandra awakened Thursday feeling weak and hungry but much better than expected, strangely peaceful and refreshed. Her first thought was that she did the right thing by leaving her sisters behind. They were too little to hitchhike. They'd been better off staying where they were. Maybe their mom had gone some place to dry out and came back. How she yearned to see them, even her mom. Sandra fantasized that she'd forgive her mother, who didn't drink anymore, and become her devoted caretaker as she aged. And her sisters, all grown up now, no doubt with their own little kids, would make her an auntie. *Rhonda loved being an "auntie" to Linda and Dave's boys.*

Stretching to ease the kinks inflicted by the hard plastic chair, Sandra moved to an empty rocking chair. A small child soon asked if she could rock, and Sandra would have loved to hold the child on her lap and rock both of them but knew the dangers of that. She sure didn't want to be arrested for child enticement so gave up the rocker. All those popular white rockers were occupied from then on during the still long wait for the Houston plane. In the restroom, Sandra washed her face, combed her hair and changed into her over-priced new outfit. Stomach grumbling she returned to the food court in search of breakfast.

She channeled all her thoughts to Brian in Chicago.

She met a young man, not much older than her but so much more worldly, when she tended bar at Smokey's. A

Missing

Saturday night with Patsy Cline, singing "Crazy" on the jukebox, few customers. A drop-dead handsome stranger sat down at the bar and ordered a martini. High roller! Most of her customers drank tap beer. The "perfect martini" she made brought raves, and he ordered another while flirting with her.

"What's a gal like you doing in a place like this?"

Sandra flirted right back. "Come on, you can do better than that or I'll make your next drink not-so-perfect."

"Okay, you're beautiful. I can tell by the way you speak that you're one smart gal. I bet you're a college girl working your way though college."

"Don't I wish!" How often Sandra had thought about being able to go to college to better herself! "But here's the problem. I'm on my own and can't afford to go to college without working; but if I work enough to pay tuition, I won't have enough time to go to classes and study."

"That doesn't have to be a problem."

"What do you mean?" Sandra asked as she made another drink for the alluring man with the dark brown tousled hair.

"How did you do in high school?"

Sandra saw no reason to tell him that she never attended. Instead she gave him a half-truth, "I was in the very top percentile."

"That doesn't surprise me. When do you get off work?"

"I close, so not until 1:00."

"I need to go back to my motel to do paperwork, but I'll stop back for you and tell you how I can solve your college predicament."

Sandra didn't really think the slick-talking stranger would return, even though she wished he would for both his looks and his promises. She naturally wondered if he really could make it possible for her to go to college, to be someone. At closing time, as she cleaned up the grill, her heart beat faster when he came through the door. "How about coming back to my motel, and I'll share my ideas with you. By the way, I'm Brian Cavendish."

Sandra bristled. Lurene had warned Sandra about men like that. "No thanks, Brian Cavendish. I need to get home to check on the woman who owns this place. I live with her, and I've been running Smokey's because she's not well."

"I'll come with you, and after you check on her, I can explain my program to you right at the kitchen table."

He told her later that he knew she showed character because of her caring for the sick woman and because she refused to come to his motel room. "I know, even if you hadn't had to check on your friend, you wouldn't have come to the motel. You're just not that kind of girl."

How I lapped up any compliment! He said he wasn't surprised I'd done so well in school so I must have seemed smart. Then he said I showed character! Maybe "Paddle Foot Trailer Trash" could become someone special.

Lurene didn't awaken when Sandra checked on her, straightened the covers and kissed her dry cheek. The painkillers prescribed for her cancer sometimes kept her awake, but tonight they provided a welcomed escape.

As they sat on Lurene's saggy flowered sofa, Brian explained what he did. "You're just the kind of person my program is designed for. You're smart and you'd be good at whatever career you chose but it's obvious you've had some bad breaks and it's going to take you forever to get a college degree."

He paused and said he was thirsty. Sandra bought them both Cokes from the refrigerator, and Brian asked if she had anything to put in it. The girl explained neither of them drank so they didn't keep anything at home. Lurene said she had seen enough of the heartache liquor could cause, and wanted no part of it after hours. Sandra agreed as she shared the disturbing memories about her parents' alcohol abuse.

"That's okay. " Brian responded. "Now the service I offer. To a few select people like you who are smart and well-motivated, I can secure a college degree for you without you having to step foot into college."

"You mean by correspondence courses?"

"No, easier than that."

Sandra eyes were big with wonder as Brian continued, "For a commission fee, I provide documentation that will get you the job you want. By the way, what do you want to be?"

Off the top of her head, Sandra said, "I want to be a teacher. I had a teacher in third grade who said I could do anything I made up my mind to do."

"I'd say she was a prophetess. If you want to be a teacher, I will provide you with a degree, a transcript and a teacher's license. Voila! A teacher! The only thing I ask is that you never tell a soul about me, about what I'm doing for you."

Sandra heard as if sweet Lurene whispered in her ear, something she often said, "Things that sound too good to be true usually are. Be careful."

The girl seemed to be thinking through her options. "What's to think about? You're good at tending bar but you don't want to do that forever. You want to teach, and I can make that happen." Brian had moved close and put his arm around her.

Sandra had avoided contact with men since the truck driver, but she found herself fitting so well against Brian's shoulder. She breathed his spicy cologne and felt herself drawn to him. They exchanged several kisses, and he put his hand inside her t-shirt. It felt so good she tingled all over but suddenly he stopped.

"I don't know what got into me. I guess it's because you're so beautiful -- your hair, your eyes, your smile. You'll think I've explained how I can help you just because I want to seduce you."

Sandra backed away, relieved that this ended before she made a big mistake, "I'm sorry. You're right, I'm not that kind of girl. I guess I caved in because I've been under too much pressure lately with Lurene's illness. I'm happy to run Smokey's for her, but if she dies, I won't be able to do that because her brother from Iowa will take over. He told me he wouldn't need me because he plans to have his wife and children as his only employees. I don't know what I'll do then, and that's why I considered your offer even for a minute."

Sandra sounded so forlorn that Brian took her in his arms, this time to comfort her.

Soon they were all over each other. While the woman who'd been her savior slept in the next room, Sandra lost her virginity on Lurene's saggy sofa to the man who'd promised her the moon.

Things continued to happen fast. Lurene died ten days later. All she could leave Sandra was her old red Chevy pickup. Her house and business went to her brother. Sandra and Brian found a loft apartment in town, moved into together. Soon he convinced her that it would be better for both of them if they moved to Tulsa. More teaching opportunities for her, more business opportunities for him. It really shouldn't make any difference with an Internet business where he worked but frankly he wanted to leave this little town in the dust. They found an apartment in a northern suburb of Tulsa.

Sandra checked the board. Still another hour. She thumbed through the magazine, but her thoughts returned to life with the man who solved her problems. Sandra found a job as a third grade teacher, chosen because of her own third grade teacher and because she remembered the important things she had learned in that grade, penmanship and multiplication. Having no idea how hard teaching would be, she worked to keep a lesson ahead of her students. She loved the kids and showed such empathy towards those having problems at school or home. The parents and kids idolized this first-year teacher, who looked more like a high school girl. Sandra Dee Lewis felt as if she had been elevated to a respected, worthwhile person.

What a happy time this was for her and Brian. Not only were they in love but they also enjoyed doing everything together: cooking, decorating their place, day trips. They both told each other about their pasts. Sandra explained about being bullied in school and having little self-esteem. She cried when she told him about her father, who went to prison, and her mother, who couldn't take it and deserted her children. How Sandra ran away and the guilt she felt for leaving the little girls behind. Brian said, "You are the bravest person I've even known. It's miraculous how you have risen above the childhood you had."

Brian's early life was much different. He grew up in Des Moines, where his dad worked at a bank and his mom was a nurse's aide. They didn't have money to spare, but they owned their own home in the suburbs with a fireplace, a fenced yard and a dog. The youngest of three brothers, Brian suffered considerable teasing from his older brothers just because he couldn't run as fast as they did. He empathized with Sandra about bullying. Otherwise he'd had a happy childhood in a loving family. His two brothers went to college on athletic scholarships. Brian, missing all the jock genes, worked his way though two years of college and learned just how hard it was to hold a job and study. So many students were in the same boat. Worse, after graduation they'd have to pay off student loans for years. That's when he hit on a way to make success available quicker and more affordable. He left college and Des Monies. He started up his own little business via computer with a little traveling thrown in.

He and Sandra made great business partners. He said she didn't have to pay his commission, but she did. It really didn't matter since her paychecks and the money he collected from his clients went into a joint account. She graded papers in the evenings and if they didn't take up the whole time, helped him research requirements for different careers to expand his client base. She kept the books just as Lurene had taught her at Smokey's. With the anonymity of the Internet, none of Brian's clients even knew his name. They mailed their fees to a risky business Brian and Sandra had named, "Dreams Come True."

The school district offered Sandra a contract for the next year, but she didn't sign it. Teaching was too demanding and teachers received too little respect from the world in general. She needed a career change but hadn't decided what.

After school was out, Brian got sick of Sandra sitting around reading magazines and watching daytime television. "Come on, Sandra, you can't sit on your butt forever! You need to decide what you want to be, and I'll make it happen. How much easier could it be?"

"Actually I like having the summer off. The best part of being a teacher, as everyone knows, is June, July, August!"

"But you're not a teacher anymore, remember?"

"True!" Sandra gave Brian her engaging smile. "My love, I have decided what credentials I want. I remembered my mom saying that I'm good with hair. I used to play beauty shop with my little sisters and did a good job."

"You have to be kidding. Surely with your brains you aspire to more than being a beautician?"

"Hair stylist, Brian. I could start out working for someone, learn and then buy my own shop. I'd be both a hairstylist and a businesswoman. Who could ask for more?" Brian tried to talk her out of it, but eventually relented. As soon as Sandra had her manufactured license she applied to an ad for a salon needing a new colorist. She read up on hair color but someone else already had taken the job. Sandra said she actually preferred doing cuts and perms, and the salon took her on as an extra. In no time, customers clamored for her.

From Lurene she knew what questions encouraged customers to talk and Sandra was lavish with compliments. The clientele loved her. Among the older set she gained a wide reputation as a stylist and as one who listened to all their complaints about aging bodies. She gave them excellent advice.

Sandra took out a loan her second year as a stylist and bought her own shop, which she named "Sandra's Cut, Curl and Color". For several more years she enjoyed running the business and had several working under her. Some customers, including a brazen woman, a compulsive talker, named Felicity Ritter, wanted only Sandra for her weekly standing appointment.

They had a history as she'd known Felicity in Modell, and at first Sandra loved talking to someone who also had known Lurene. She remembered Mrs. Ritter and her husband used to come in every Saturday night, and all they did was argue. Mr. Ritter died shortly after Lurene. By chance both the Widow Ritter and Sandra wound up in Tulsa.

Felicity loved to tell anyone who'd listen that "I WENT TO LITTLE SANDRA'S GRADUATION PARTY." She remembered every detail including the piggy bank gift she had given the graduate. Fe, as many knew her, asked why Sandra didn't use it for tips, which Fe never bothered to give. Sandra didn't have the heart to tell her the ugly spotted black and white thing looked more like a cow than a pig so she left it behind when she moved.

When Sandra did Felicity's hair, always to her exact specifications, the hairdresser gave all her attention to the client as she complained about her ailments and her kids and how mistreated and misunderstood she was. Sandra listened as Felicity, who never tipped nor gave her a tacky "Hairdressers are a Cut above the Rest" coffee mug, discoursed about celebrities, her dog and her husband, Mr. Ritter, now elevated to sainthood by the widow. Sandra tried to appear interested as her disagreeable patron shared her biased opinion on any given topic. Today Sandra was surprised that with all her babbling, Mrs. Ritter never once mentioned having a connection to Corpus Christi!

Sandra's own interest in that South Texas city came years later. Reliving an old sorrow, she now thought of the worst thing that happened during her hairdressing career.

Brian came home one night with news. "We're off to Chicago. Another guy who does the same thing offered to help me expand what I'm doing for more money."

"But what about my shop?"

"Oh, we'll sell it."

Sandra snapped her fingers. "Just like that, sell it? That business means the world to me. I'm not about to give it up."

"What are you trying to say?"

"That we should stay right here. Maybe you could commute to Chicago?"

"Absolutely not. Flying is a pain these days, Sandra. I'm going to Chicago, and I want you to go with me."

Years later on this Thursday morning in the San Antonio airport Sandra had a thought. Having gone through what she had with TSA, Sandra now wondered if Brian didn't want to commute because he was afraid something would tip off security to the nature of his business. He and his wife never flew to Corpus Christi to see her even though she raved about the climate, Tex-Mex food and beauty of the bay that led to the Gulf of Mexico. Sandra shifted to find a more comfortable position for her long legs. Somehow she felt better about the decision he made; he just wouldn't commute by plane. *At least he sure was right, then and now -- flying is indeed a pain.*

She continued to think about that first and fatal disagreement and how to his plan for her to move to Chicago, she had screamed, "NO!"

Brian moved out. It broke Sandra's heart, and thinking about it now added to her current miseries. *It was awful. I didn't know anything could affect me like that. Abandoned again. I felt as if I was losing my mind, as if I'd become a different person and this was happening to someone else. I don't think I've ever been quite the same.*

At the time Sandra feared a complete breakdown but persevered in running Cut, Curl and Color, all she had. It wasn't long before she realized that she was wrong to choose her business over Brian, but his indifference to her love of the business pushed her into staying. Males had caused all her problems -- her father, the boys at school, the judge who put her in the foster home, the truck driver and Brian. She decided men would not be a significant part of her life. In the case of Brian, she loved him and losing him had almost destroyed her. She had never dreamed he'd choose his job over her; she'd been so sure he wouldn't abandon her but he had.

From his perspective, Sandra wouldn't give up her job for him. Eventually they would reconcile, but they had hurt each other so much, they couldn't share the same relationship.

CHAPTER SEVENTEEN

Captive witness

When Maria returned from lunch, Belkin was still at the dentist. He had gotten word to Maria that she should go alone to interview the kid who'd sold his parents' car. He cautioned her that this could be tough. He didn't have to tell her. Her family had experienced something similar a few years ago when Maria's older brother almost died from a drug overdose.

Arriving at Austin Bennett's hospital room, Detective Gonzales first saw the suffering parents, despair etched on their faces. They stood close to him and each other as they kept watch over their only child.

"Excuse me, I'm Detective Gonzales from the South Corpus Christi Police Department.

"He's sleeping now." Gloria's voice was nearly inaudible.

Maria could have said, "I'll come back later," but instead she put her hands on a tense shoulder of each of the couple. "This is so hard. We went through this with my older brother. Would you like to talk about it? We could go to some place private."

They showed reluctance to leave their son's bedside, and Maria asked, "Have you eaten anything?"

"Just coffee."

"I'm going to the cafeteria to get us something for lunch, and I'll find a place where we can be alone."

When Maria returned with lunch, the Bennetts asked a nurse to notify them when their son awakened. Gloria nibbled at her sandwich while her husband remarked between large bites, "You are so kind."

"No one can know what you're going through but I do identify with what you must be feeling."

"We almost lost him, and nothing else is important except he'll be all right," Gloria murmured as her husband agreed.

"That's true and I'm so sorry I need to interview him."

"The one on the phone said it could help you find that missing doctor."

"Yes, or I wouldn't bother your son."

"We feel so damned responsible," Bill lamented. "We had no idea he did drugs."

"Please, don't blame yourself. I'm sure you're wonderful parents. Your son is smart. He made certain you didn't suspect anything."

Maria had said what they needed to hear, and both seemed more relaxed as they talked about going forward, finding the best rehab facility, joining a parent support group. They told Maria about their son being an honor student, only underclassman on the Double A soccer team, active in their church youth group.

"I can understand why this comes as such a shock. My brother wasn't quite like your son." Maria smiled as she continued, "He had to be dragged to Mass and sure wasn't an honor student. But he played high school soccer, too, just kept his grades up enough to stay on the team. He was a good athlete but was kicked off for violation of the pledge to abstain from alcohol and drugs."

"I dread that. It'll be so hard on Austin not to be able to play." Mr. Bennett's expression showed this would be equally hard on son and father.

Maria knew that could be the least of their problems but tried to keep Dad hopeful, "Maybe after he's clean, he'll be able to play again. It depends on the school district. *Though I know most have Zero Tolerance, I have to offer a grain of hope.* No matter how hard, you have to keep positive that all will turn out well. We didn't give my brother much hope, but he's a success story. Once he got his head back on straight, he brought up his grades, went to college, and is a drug counselor now."

A nurse interrupted their conversation to tell them Austin had awakened and was alert.

"Now, son, this police officer wants to talk to you, but don't be scared because she's a real peach," Bill said to his only child, his coloring better, his manner more subdued.

Maria grinned at the father. "Austin, this won't take long; and please don't worry, this has nothing to do with you taking illegal drugs. *Though there may be a police investigation into that, especially if he was dealing or can help us implicate a dealer but I'm not telling him that now.*

Austin looked relieved when she said that. "This has to do with a doctor who is missing. Have you heard about her on the news?

Austin shook his head "no".

"On Monday she didn't return to her clinic after her lunch break and hasn't been seen or heard from since. She may have bought a car from you. Can you tell me where you sold the car?"

"It was at Stripes."

"How did you arrange to meet someone there?"

With a furtive look of guilt and remorse directed towards his parents, he answered, "I advertised in the newspaper, right after my parents left on the cruise. This was the only call for the car I got. The lady said she was at the Vega Building, and I told her to meet me at the Stripes near there."

"When was this?"

"I don't know for sure. Afternoon, I guess."

"Closer to noon or sunset?"

"Noon."

Austin's eyes looked downward all the time he answered. The young detective guessed he'd done the same thing when he sold the car so she didn't expect much when she asked, "Can you describe her?"

"Not really except she was taller than me, and I noticed we both had on black hoodies."

"How about her age?"

"Not real old, younger than my mom."

I guess to a teen-ager someone in her thirties probably would be considered old but not real old. "Anything else?"

"She had a blue bag."

"Do you mean purse?"

"No, she paid me with money from a gym-type bag."

"Can you tell me how much you paid for the car?"

Austin hedged. He didn't want his parents to know how little he'd settled for on their car. "I don't remember, but it was cash, hundred dollar bills."

"Thank you, Austin, you've been very co-operative and I will be certain to tell everyone at headquarters that. One more thing, I'm going to tell my brother about you. He had a similar experience and if you ever want to talk to him, he helps mentor kids with drug problems." Austin grimaced at being "a kid with a drug problem" but seemed interested when Maria added, "He knows all about soccer, too. I'll give his number to your folks."

Detective Gonzales hugged the parents as she handed them her brother Johnny's business card.

CHAPTER EIGHTEEN

More airport reminiscing

Sandra could still be found Thursday afternoon thinking about her days as a hair stylist as the waiting time for the flight to Houston lengthened, due to some mechanical delay. *Don't want to be on a plane that isn't working right but sure hoped this delay won't make me miss the plane to Chicago. I'm so sick of waiting. Not that I am alone in feeling that. Some passengers are so rude to the counter people who have no control of the flights; others take it as it comes and read, talk, watch T.V., snack. Only children are oblivious to delays and continue to play and eat goodies from the vending machines.*

Years after the break-up with Brian, Sandra started thinking more and more about her family in Arkansas. She tried without success to find her younger sisters and an older half-sister, Sue-Ella. As it turned out, Sue-Ella found her. It had proved difficult because both had changed their names, but with the miracle of social media, they did connect. Sandra was overjoyed because she hoped that her half-sister would have news of their mom and sisters and Sandra immediately phoned Sue-Ella.

Sue-Ella now went by Rhonda Lee. As she told Sandra, she thought Sue-Ella was a "hick name" so in honor of her half-sister changed it to a more grown-up form of Ronnie. "I mean, what was our mother thinking? Sue-Ella, Ronnie Lee?"

Sandra thought, *I like the name Rhonda but now the only way I could change my name to Rhonda would be to become my half-sister!* She answered, "Midge and Rainey weren't much better."

"Oh, you mean the little ones she had after I left. I heard about them."

Sandra's heart sunk. Maybe Rhonda/Sue-Ella knew nothing about the family.

Deep in thought, she almost missed hearing, "I have some vacation time, and I'd love to come to see you."

A week later she appeared at Sandra's shop. The two half-sisters looked enough alike to be twins, tall, thin, light blue eyes, chin-length natural blonde hair. The shop wasn't busy so Sandra put an employee in charge and took her big sister out to lunch. The first thing Sandra asked was news of their mother. Sandra was bitterly disappointed because her half-sister hadn't been in touch with their mother since the man she called her "real daddy" took her from the Jacksons' home, when Rhonda was a preschooler. As Sue-Ella made plain, "That means I haven't seen Mama since Daddy Jack (as she called Tim Jackson, Sandra/Ronnie's dad) lost his job for stealing, and all of us Jacksons had to move into that little trailer…"

"It was never proven that Daddy stole," Sandra quickly interjected.

"Regardless, my real daddy believed it and said no kid of his was going to grow up with a felon in a trailer park. So he called my mom -- your mom, too -- and Mama said this man I'd never met could take me because he was my real daddy. "It killed me that Mama didn't even care, but I always had hated your daddy because he never paid any attention to me. He just loved you, so I wasn't sorry to leave. My real daddy drove me to a town two hours away. I met my stepmother. She gave me lots of presents and we got along fine. We lived in a small but really nice house with my own room so I had it pretty good. I did miss you and asked if you could come to live with us, but

Daddy laughed it off. I also asked if I could visit you and Mama, but Daddy always said, 'Absolutely and *positutely* not'. The 'positutely' was a funny word he made up, I think."

Rhonda realized that Sandra still wanted to hear more about the Jackson family, and Rhonda repeated the same with a few more details. "The only other things I heard about your family -- that started out being my family -- is that Mama had two more baby girls, and Daddy made sure I knew about your dad going to prison for vehicular homicide while drunk because it justified taking me away from Mama, years earlier."

Tears had formed in Sandra's eyes as Rhonda returned to telling about herself, "My stepmother died and Daddy started bringing home girlfriends. I got sick of it, went to live with a friend's family. Then at sixteen I quit school and got married."

"Just like Mama!"

Rhonda gave Sandra a strange look. *She must not know the facts of her big sister's birth.* "Well, let's say I was sixteen and pregnant just like Mama."

Sandra missed the point her sister had just made as she concentrated on the pregnancy. "You have a child?"

"No, born too soon and didn't make it."

"Oh, Sue-Ella, that's so sad."

Her half-sister shrugged and her eyes teared up. After a while Sue-Ella/Rhonda continued, "My marriage didn't last much longer after that. Bobby and I lived with his parents. They gave us a room of our own and bought us a beautiful bedroom suite for a wedding present. They were great to me, but Bob and I were too young to make a go of it. Our marriage broke up. I went back home. By then Daddy had married one of his playmates, not much older than Me. We studied for our G.E.D.s together and afterwards went bar hopping. We both met guys we liked. She left Daddy, and he never remarried. We're still in touch but I haven't lived in Arkansas since I turned eighteen when I married the guy I met at the bar and went to California."

"And that's where you live now?" Sandra had to ask.

"No, the second husband was a loser so I divorced him and married a wealthy older man. We moved from L.A. to Missouri, right near Branson's."

"You've been married three times?"

"Yes, I told Daddy I had him beat."

"But, didn't you say he married twice after he married Mama?"

"What? You didn't know? He and Mama never married. She was pregnant with me when she married your daddy. The big scandal that rocked their little town."

"How -- how -- do you know all this?" Sandra faltered.

"My daddy. He didn't know I was his until after I was born. He told me your daddy, once his best friend, and my daddy were at a bar. Your daddy told my daddy your mama confessed about me the day I was born. Your daddy said he'd forgiven his wife and loved me like I was his own." Her voice dropped, "Maybe he did. Until they had you, their own child."

Rhonda ignored Sandra's look, mixed with shock, hurt and disbelief, and asked, "Have you been married?"

"No, couldn't take the heartbreak you've had," Sandra lied because her secret desire was to have a husband to love her even though she said repeatedly that she wanted nothing to do with men.

"I could write my own country western song about heart ache," Rhonda whined. "My third husband died and left me pretty well off, but the money started to run out so I had to go to work, nothing but boring minimum wage jobs."

"I can relate to that! But after jobs like that I taught a year and then became a hair stylist and bought my own place."

"You went to college?" Rhonda asked with a combination of amazement and envy in her voice.

Sandra hesitated. Lying had become a way of life so she answered, "Sure."

"Oh, you're so lucky. I know the only way I can better myself is going to college but I'm too old now."

"No, you're not. There are lots of 'older students'."

"I suppose but it would take me forever for what I want to be."

"What's that?"

"A doctor."

Sandra checked her watch and said it was time to go back to the shop. She asked her half-sister if she would like a complimentary hair styling. Rhonda didn't hesitate to say, "You don't have to ask twice!"

Sandra soon found she and Rhonda had little in common. Rhonda seemed more sophisticated and experienced than Sandra, undoubtedly because Rhonda had lived in so many different places. Soon Sandra realized her sister was not on vacation but "between jobs" and undoubtedly "between husbands". The things they both shared were their less-than-idyllic childhoods and the desire to make something of their lives. Rhonda declined Sandra's offer of a job as receptionist in her salon, but didn't refuse the free hair appointments, bread and board or money Sandra gave her. The younger, more successful sister wondered how long Rhonda might stay in Oklahoma. Suddenly her sister went back to California, but returned when broke.

After ten years, Sandra found she'd grown weary of her job and wondered why she had chosen it over Brian, the love of her life. Such hard work to run a business. The unreliability of her employees, who would stay home with a hangnail, gave her headaches. Not to mention some of her demanding customers, who felt they owned her, like Felicity. In spite of her faults, Rhonda seldom criticized but after Felicity came early for an appointment while Sandra cut her sister's hair, Rhonda whispered, "How do you endure that 'babbling old bag'?"

One day thumbing through the daily paper while waiting for a tardy customer, Sandra looked at employment ads and one jumped out at her: **New family medical clinic in Corpus Christi seeks general practitioners.**

With all the medical stuff I've learned from my clients and the super advice I've given them, I could be a doctor. I think it's time for me to pay a visit to Brian in Chicago.

Thursday evening, lost in her reminiscing, Sandra missed the announcement of her flight but saw the other now familiar looking passengers lining up and joined them. She had expected to be in Chicago on Wednesday.

CHAPTER NINETEEN

Conflicting information

On the way back to the station from the hospital four things kept running through Maria's head: *Vega Building, Stripes, black hoodie, blue gym bag*. In her mind the detective added all those clues under the "Run-away" column of her big chart. It seemed apparent, as much as Maria hadn't wanted Belkin to be right, that Rhonda had fled. Certainly, as she had thought so many times, if Rhonda had run away, the woman probably hadn't come to any harm. On the other hand, look what Rhonda had done to Dr. Linda and all those who believed in the missing woman? *I know my instructors told us students over and over again that police work would be hard but I'm struggling. So many people suffer while we try to solve crimes involving their loved ones.*

Stan had returned by the time Maria trudged in. By then it was almost quitting time, and Maria thought Stan should go home after his prolonged ordeal at the dentist office. Since his mouth was still numb, he said he felt fine. The two detectives agreed to stay as long as necessary and called for pizza delivery. They debated the evidence for hours and finally summarized it.

Munching pizza on one side of his mouth, Stan spoke between bites, "This is what this is what we've got. Proof that over the noon hour the doctor withdrew money from the Gulf Bank and cleaned out her safety deposit box at the Community Credit Union. We have a witness, the colorful Muriel Martin, who saw someone fitting her description in the restroom on the third floor of the Vega Building, shortly after the time recorded in the safety deposit log. Miss Muriel said she heard the doctor and another female."

"If," speculated Gonzales, "the other woman in the stall killed Rhonda, what would she have done with the body?" Remembering the possum, Maria colored and added, "Well, we know she didn't stuff it in the trunk."

"Come on, Maria, I think we're pretty damned sure there's no body."

"Okay, let me phrase it this way, if you and I believed there is a body, where would we look for it?"

"Whenever there's someone believed to be dead around here, we search the desert. The trouble with that is we usually don't find our person of interest but all sorts of other human remains. Interested in tackling that?"

"No, but I'd like any kind of proof of what happened for the sake of her friends."

"Maria, you are such a bleeding heart that you probably should become a social worker, get paid for your empathy."

I know, I know, but why can't a detective be empathetic?

Seeing the look of defeat on the face of the kid he hadn't completely won over, Belkin changed tactics. "I tease you relentlessly but, seriously, you can't get this emotionally involved with friends and family of the victim. I don't know how may times I have to say it, but I don't think anyone abducted or killed Dr. Rhonda."

"But we don't know."

"And maybe we'll never know, but there are standard assumptions we can make. Allegedly the last time the doctor was seen was in the restroom, where she and another woman occupied the same stall. If the mystery woman killed the doctor there, what would she have done with the body? The doctor was probably her size or not much smaller. How could she have hauled the doctor out of the building without being seen? Another possibility, she hid the body in the building. Where could the mystery woman have done that where it hasn't been discovered? Too big to put in a trash receptacle in the bathroom or a mail slot in the hall."

"But couldn't the woman have abducted the doctor, killed her or had someone else commit the murder elsewhere?"

"The fingerprints indicate two people. We'll know more if a third person was involved after…"

"We have the DNA results?" Maria interrupted.

"Exactly, but let's stay with what we do have."

Maria flipped open her non-issue polka dot notebook. "Okay, then I have one witness saying someone fitting the description in the news was at a Stripes around 1:15. This Stripes is very near the Vega Building, a quick walk for Dr. Rhonda. The witness described her as having a black hooded sweatshirt and a blue gym bag. A second witness confessed to selling a gray Taurus for cash at the same Stripes store to someone with a black hooded sweatshirt and blue gym bag. Unsure of time, but probably also early afternoon. The custodian at Stripes found a waterlogged cell phone when she cleaned the restroom in the afternoon. It fit the description of the one Rhonda carried, but didn't work so the custodian threw the phone away and the trash hauler picked it up before we heard about it. A woman fitting the same description checked in mid-afternoon at the Liberty Motel, and I am waiting to call the night manager later so I can find out when the missing doctor left and if this person indicated where she was going. Also, she paid cash for the car and the motel so there's no paper trail."

"If not, the trail ends at that 'illustrious' motel. I still think we have enough to say the doctor planned her departure."

"I've been trying to talk to the aunt who said she recognized the missing doctor to see what more "Auntie" might have to offer." Checking her notebook again, Maria added, "Rhonda's attorney called today. He said she had made out a will not long ago and named one beneficiary and an executor, but wouldn't give me the names."

"We could find out, but I think we know who it was, don't we?"

In disbelief Maria responded, "Her best friend? Dr. Linda?"

"Who else? And, I think now she had a motive to aid in the disappearance because she was the beneficiary." *Actually if I believed someone did her in, I'd finger Hernandez because she counted on no one suspecting the dearest friend,* Stan Belkin mused and then said, "Persons closest to the victim are considered 'first suspects'."

"I know that but I don't think so in this case. She seems sincere in thinking something happened to her," argued Maria.

"No, Maria. You have done an excellent job of tracking down every clue..." The new detective didn't have long to savor the compliment as Belkin continued, "but, in my considerable experience, 'the lady doth protest too much'. Also I've had a chance to study the fingerprint analysis. Have you?"

"Not yet."

"Here it is. Both Dr. Hernandez' and Dr. Collins' fingerprints were found in the car. They matched those in the national background check registry. Their fingerprints appeared on both the purse and shoes with a preponderance of Hernandez' prints on both, and why on earth would she have been fondling her friend's shoes?"

Maria blushed as he added, "Those two sets were the only prints found in the car or on the shoes and purse. Unless DNA proves otherwise, that pretty much rules out a third person, which means if two women were in the restroom, one could have been Dr. Linda."

"But, we don't know that and I can explain how Dr. Hernandez's prints would be in the BMW. She told me the day before she had ridden to the gym in her friend's car. That's when she told me Rhonda left a gym bag in her car with exercise shoes and a black hooded sweatshirt."

"This is what I think. Dr. Rhonda met Dr. Linda in the restroom. Dr. Rhonda gave Dr. Linda her keys, she retrieved the gym bag and Dr. Rhonda changed her shoes and put on the hoodie. Dr. Linda arranged the shoes and purse on the passenger side of the car to make it look as if her friend had been abducted from her car. Oh, yes, she also removed a hairbrush from her purse and brought that to us."

"But she said she bought that and the photo from the doctor's home."

"Bullsh! She lied. Jenna didn't find any of Dr. Linda's fingerprints at our missing doctor's house."

Maria's eyes widened, "She lied? But, but, that's hard to believe especially since she's ..." Maria paused and took a deep breath, "heading up the big prayer vigil tomorrow night."

"What prayer vigil?"

"It's been on the news. They're expecting a crowd. It's at Cielo Vis..."

Stan interrupted, "Maria, you are too damned trusting. Can't you see? It's all an elaborate smoke screen Dr. Linda has constructed to ward off any suspicion from her."

"I ... guess ... it's ... possible," Maria stammered.

"Damned straight, and we need authorization to arrest Dr. Linda Hernandez."

"For lying to us? You're kidding."

"No, for interfering with the investigation."

"I guess the fingerprints on the shoes and purse substantiate that."

"Well, maybe with your imagination you can come up with a theory of how her prints would have gotten all over the purse and shoes if it happened earlier in the day, at the clinic. I sure can't think of anything."

Maria shook her head.

"I know you've believed in Dr. Linda, but I'm afraid she suckered you in. The fingerprints link Dr. Linda Hernandez to the so-called crime scene."

Maria looked down at her own shoes. Silence, louder than words, hung between them.

Finally, Belkin said, "This is my theory and it's only an educated guess, based on many years of doing this. I think Dr. Rhonda and Dr. Linda made an agreement. Dr. Rhonda took off, leaving her home and car behind. They made it look like Dr. Rhonda was a victim of foul play. Once Dr. Rhonda is declared dead, they plan to split all the assets."

"That takes years."

"True, but they're just in their thirties."

"It doesn't explain why Dr. Rhonda left now and where she went."

"I'm sure Dr. Linda knows all that."

"But her affection for her friend seems authentic."

"It probably is. Regardless, we have enough evidence to ask for a warrant." Belkin departed to the office of the Assistant Chief, on duty that night, to sign the warrant.

Maria fell into deep thoughts. *I can't prove that the doctor bought and drove the gray Taurus unless we find the car and match DNA with that from the BMW. I won't know any more until -- wait, it's after 9:00. I'll call the aunt and the motel again.*

Still no answer at the aunt's home in Tulsa, but Lupe, night clerk at the motel, answered on the first ring.

"Sir, this is Detective Maria Gonzales from the South Corpus Christi Police Department. A woman who drove a gray Taurus left the motel on your shift, Monday night. Do you remember her?

"Certainly! She left about 10:00. I kidded her about being stood up."

"Could you describe her?"

"Sure. She was tall and had a cute short brown hair-do. She was quite a looker."

"Her name was -- let's see --," Lupe thumbed through Monday entries, "here it is -- Marsha Watkins. Definitely, I should let you in on a little secret, people who stay at this motel often use assumed monikers."

Maria kept from gasping, "Did you say 'short brown hair'?"

"That's right. Cute."

Brown, short hair? Hmmmm? She asked a few more questions, thanked Lupe and was hanging up as Belkin returned with the warrant, saying, "It's show time."

"Stan, I still have misgivings. But, we're partners so I'll support you 100%."

Dr. Hernandez's husband had expectations for the evening that wouldn't be met.

CHAPTER TWENTY

Thursday with Auntie Fe

Felicia Ritter had talked to her niece, her sister's girl, Wednesday night. That would be last night.

Melanie told her that the doctor was still was missing. "Of course, she's missing; I blew the whistle on her, and she skeedaddled." As she prepared her supper, Fe addressed Timmy, a parakeet, cocking his head as if intensely interested. "You are a better listener than most people I know, Timmy Boy."

Fe had purchased the green and yellow bird when she moved into her assisted living apartment. They allowed some animals but that didn't extend to her king-sized old black lab, Sampson, who now resided with her son Todd on the other side of Tulsa. At least she got to see both of them on occasion. And his wife, Angela, whom she didn't like one bit -- sniveling spoiled thing -- she got to see her, too.

"Even though I don't really belong here, Tim, I'm glad you're with me. I just moved here to make the kids happy, and that's why I have a stupid Medi-alert thing that I'm supposed to wear. There isn't a thing wrong with me except I don't hear so good and sometimes I'm a little absent-minded. That's really why my meddlesome son and daughter put me here. I left a pan on the stove and forgot it, but anyone can do that. They made such a big deal of all the smoke damage when the chicken and dumplings burned to a crisp, but it didn't take them long to scrub the walls after the firefighters left, and I needed a new stove anyway."

"But here I am. And as long as I take my blood pressure medicine, I'm just fine. I think I took it today, or did I? I sure hope I didn't leave my pills in Texas. Then I haven't taken it since Monday." Pouring a generous amount of oil in a skillet, she rambled, "Oh well, speaking of Texas, I missed you when I was gone, but I love visiting my niece, Melanie. She's always sweet and takes me to nice places to eat and this time she took me to see the medical clinic owned by her husband -- he's Ron and a bit of a stuffed shirt, in my opinion. Oh, yes, Melanie was taking me to the Botanical Gardens, but when I heard they might have a hurricane all I wanted to do was come home so I cut the trip short. I'm not one to take unnecessary chances."

"But, if I'd stayed, Timmy Bird, I think I would have called that new police department. I have half a mind to do it anyway. See, Timmy, before I moved to Tulsa, Clem and I lived in Modell, a little town in the Panhandle, and we knew everyone. Then, after Clemmie died on me, I moved to Tulsa to be closer to the kids, and one day a beauty shop opened right down the street. Who should own in but Sandra Lewis! She was a run-away teen-ager who wound up on Lurene Caldwell's doorstep in Modell. Lurene owned a bar and grill outside town. They had the best barbecue pork sandwiches there. Clem and I went there every Sunday night. No, that's not right. Sunday nights we always had popcorn and apples and Clemmie was always so proud of hisself because that was the one meal of the whole week he cooked. Saturday we went to Smokey's. That was the name of Lurene's place, and Sandra helped out there."

"Anyway, here in Tulsa was little Sandra, all grown up. The last time I seen her Lurene had a big graduation party for her. Then I guess she went to Beauty School and moved to Tulsa. She had an old red pick-up just like Lurene used to have. Anyhow, Timmy, I started going to Sandra and she was my hairdresser for ten years. She was really good at hair and I loved to talk over old days with her. Then, without even telling me, her very best customer, that woman put up a "For Sale" sign, and that's the last I ever saw her."

"That is, until Monday," continued Fe without ever stopping for a breath. Busy with frying some sausage and hashed browns, she hadn't noticed the little bird ignored her now and looked at himself in his mirror. Anyone could figure out what he pondered. *"I can say 'pretty bird' and 'pizza'. I wish I knew how to say 'shut up'."*

"Anyway, Mellie took me to visit her husband's clinic and who should I see but my old beautician. She acted like she'd never seen me in her life. The nerve of the woman and this is what I mean about you being a better listener than some people. I told Mellie everything about Sandra but she ignored what I said. Mellie said she was a doctor named Rhonda, who'd been there for eight years. And, when I got home, I figured out that's how long Sandra had been gone. I just looked at all the cancelled checks my kids ask me why I save, and I found the last check I wrote to her. How dare she act like she didn't even know me after all those years of doing my hair? I used to pour out my heart to her, and I was a great tipper."

Turning off the skillet, Fe boasted, "There's not a thing wrong with my brain and not my eyes either since I had cataract surgery. I see clear as an owl now. I know who I saw, and it was Sandra. She sure wasn't a doctor, and she didn't work her way through medical school or anything like that when she was my beautician. Melanie said last night that Ron -- he's her husband, Timmy -- suggested she did work her way through medical school doing hair. Let me tell you, Tim Birdie, I'm convinced she was just pretended to be a doctor, and I bet that's against the law because she could have misdiagnosed someone and caused them to die. I think I will call the police and tell them I recognized her and that's why she ran away. They should catch her and put her in jail or tell her she has to go back to being a hairdresser, but I sure wouldn't go to her after the way she treated me."

Felicia Ritter started to call directory assistance for the number of the new police department in Corpus Christi. With her Medi-alert device left on a dresser, she collapsed.

CHAPTER TWENTY-ONE

Thursday night arrest

As they sat on the couch with glasses of Merlot Thursday evening, Linda filled in her husband with everything that had happened during the time he'd been away. She suddenly had a thought. *I didn't want to betray a confidence but...* She shared what she was thinking. "I may still have the phone number Rhonda gave me for her friend in Chicago. I could call her to see if she's there." Linda didn't want to tell her husband yet that she had doubts about the abduction so quickly added, "Since the police are convinced Rhonda left her own, I might be able to prove them wrong."

It took a while to find the old address book where Linda had recorded the number. She'd never thought to put it on her cell phone contact list. She pressed in the numbers on that phone, and a woman answered. *Just as I told the police, Rhonda went to visit another woman.*

"I'm Linda Hernandez, a friend of Dr. Rhonda Collins from Corpus Christi. Dr. Collins gave me this number for an emergency contact because occasionally she flew from Corpus Christi to visit a friend. By any chance is Rhonda visiting you now?"

"I'm sorry I don't know anyone by that name," Grace Cavendish proclaimed in her usual chirpy voice. Grace, wife of Brian Cavendish, the man who once had a lover named Sandra Lewis, asked, "Did you say she's a doctor?" Without waiting for an answer, she offered, "Maybe my husband knows her."

"May I talk to him?"

"He's out of town right now and I'm not supposed to give out his cell number."

"That's okay, but when he returns or whenever you talk to him, will you give him my number? It's really important that I get it touch with Rhonda."

"Certainly, and may I ask you this, did you say you're from Corpus Christi?"

"Yes, both my friend and I live there."

"First I thought you had the wrong number, but then this struck me. We have a friend from there, and she has visited us a few times. She's an old friend of my husband and we've become friends, too, in the last five or six years. But her name isn't Rhonda, it's Sandy. Oops! That's what I call her. It's really Sandra."

"Sandra!" Linda felt panicky. *That's the name Melanie's aunt called Rhonda.*

"Yes, Sandra -- Sandra Lewis, only I probably shouldn't have told a stranger her name," the woman giggled.

Dazed, Linda thanked her and hung up. She turned to her husband. "This is so strange. I called the number Rhonda gave me. The woman I talked to doesn't know Rhonda but said a 'Sandra' from Corpus Christi sometimes visits them."

"Sandra?" Dave questioned. "Isn't that the name Melanie Brooks' aunt called Rhonda?" He barely could hear his wife's muted reply of "Yes"

She sat there stunned, and then finally said, "I need to call Mel to see if she'll give me her aunt's phone number."

Dave couldn't show his wife how this shocked him but covered, "Hey, Babe, I can think of something we can do to get our minds off this."

She caressed her husband's cheek. "That sounds just wonderful to me, but let me make this call first." Again she pressed in numbers on her phone. Dr. Ron answered and she asked to speak to Melanie. He commented, "Oh, I bet this is about the Prayer Vigil tomorrow night."

Linda didn't disagree. Soon she heard Melanie's voice, serious instead of her usual cheery greeting, "Hi, Linda."

"Mel, did you ever remember the last name of the woman your aunt mistook for Rhonda?"

"No, I didn't. Why?"

"Well, I'm as disgusted as everyone else about the police not doing enough to find Rhonda."

"I know. Ron says they're convinced she disappeared on her own, but we don't believe that especially since they found her car."

"I thought somehow I could prove your aunt is mistaken and let the police know that. Then maybe . . . anyway, could I have her number?"

"She probably isn't up now, but here's her number. I'd suggest you call her in the morning."

As Linda wrote down the number, the doorbell rang and Poppy went into a barking spasm. Dave answered the door to a man and a woman who showed law enforcement badges. He could barely hear them over the ruckus made by the little dog they had acquired because of Rhonda's absence.

"Are you Mr. Hernandez?"

"I am."

"Is your wife, Dr. Linda Hernandez, here?"

Linda had come to the door to grab Poppy but stopped when she saw Detective Belkin, looking surly as always, and the young female detective, who seemed very uncomfortable. Only one thing occurred to her, "Did you find her?"

"No, Ma'am. That's not why we're here. You, Linda Hernandez, are under arrest for giving false information and withholding information in an attempt to mislead this investigation." Belkin proceeded to put cuffs on the horrified doctor while Gonzales, reluctance in her eyes, Miranda-ed Linda, to the beat of the dog's staccato barking.

Dave picked up Poppy, who didn't stop his clamor, and Linda's husband lost it. "This is ludicrous." He then addressed Linda, "Honey, don't say a word. I'll call Tom, and I know he'll come right over to the police station and straighten this out. I'll be down as soon as I can ask Mama to come look after the kids," He gently touched his wife's shoulder, "It'll be all right, my sweetheart. This has to be one stupid, unbelievable mistake."

By the time the squad car bearing Linda reached the station, Thomas Cantu, an attorney and her sister's husband, already had arrived. Belkin stiffened when he recognized the attorney. They shared a history of conflict because each was belligerent about never being wrong.

"What are the charges?" Cantu demanded.

"We have reason to believe Dr. Linda Hernandez has aided the missing Dr. Rhonda Collins in her disappearance, and we need to question her after she is booked," Belkin stated.

In time the two detectives, the attorney, and Linda sat at a scarred wooden table that nearly filled a small examination room.

Belkin had a page of notes in front of him, "First Dr. Hernandez, you told us that you went to your friend's town home on Monday, right after work."

Tom smiled at Linda to encourage her. She stated simply, "I did."

"Then why didn't we find any of your fingerprints in the residence?"

Emboldened as a clerk ushered Dave into the room, Linda snapped, "I could tell you in truth that Rhonda's housekeeper comes on Tuesday morning and cleaned everything, but the housekeeper wouldn't have found my prints either."

Detective Gonzales looked up from writing down each question and answer as Belkin continued his inquisition.

"And how do you explain that?"

"I put on surgical gloves and booties before I entered her home."

Belkin's eyebrows shot up, "And WHY did you do that?"

"I worried that the person who might have harmed Rhonda had gone to her home, and I didn't want to destroy any evidence if that was the case."

Belkin rolled his eyes. "What proof can you give us that you were there?"

"I brought you a photo and a hairbrush."

"Are you sure you got those from the doctor's home? We think you could have taken the photo from your own home or office since it has both of you in it, and could you have pulled the hairbrush out of your friend's purse when you helped her stage an abduction?"

"Absolutely not!" Linda looked over at her husband as he asked if he could substantiate that she was at Rhonda' house. Belkin agreed only because the attorney insisted. He muttered under his breath, "The husband shouldn't even be here. For that matter they should have a different non-related attorney."

"You couldn't have helped seeing and hearing the Chihuahua at our house," David Hernandez said in a high voice bordering on the panic-stricken.

The detectives nodded as he continued, "Do I look like the kind of man who'd have an obnoxious dog like that?"

Turning to Maria, Belkin scowled and saw she tried to suppress a smile. With all the sarcasm he could muster, he asked his partner, "Why I'd say he's a lab or a golden retriever type, wouldn't you, Detective?" Turning back to Hernandez, he snarled, "Your point?"

"That dog belongs to Rhonda. My wife found the dog unattended at Rhonda's home Monday and brought him, his bed, food, etc. to our house."

Cantu interjected, "That seems proof that my client was at the townhouse."

Belkin ignored him and first addressed Mr. Hernandez, "You've had your say and I won't let you stay if you say anything else." To Linda, "Is this true?"

"Yes, Rhonda adores that dog. I can't believe she would have left him willingly. Of course I took him home with me."

"Okay, so you have established that you were at the residence and that you wore gloves, shoe covers. Now, tell us this. Can you explain away just as easily why were your fingerprints all over the shoes and purse in the missing doctor's car?"

Linda bowed her head as she spoke while her husband looked bewildered. "This is really personal but I can explain. Rhonda and I were very close friends, and sometimes we acted silly. On Monday morning Rhonda came in my office to show off her new outfit. She'd worn the pants before but they looked so good with the blouse I've told you about that she purchased shoes and purse to..." Linda paused and a tear ran down her cheek. "Rhonda told me they were as soft as butter and encouraged me to feel them. So I felt the purse and then I made a big deal of bowing in front of her and asked if I really could 'touch Milady's shoes'." Spreading out both hands in demonstration, "I put my hands all over them."

Belkin shook his head and then hit her with what he needed to know. "Are you sure that's what happened or did you leave fingerprints all over Dr. Collins' shoes when you aided your friend's escape by putting her shoes and purse in her car, left them there to make it look like an abduction, to throw off law enforcement?"

"Absolutely not! Why are you so certain that she ... she ran away?"

Dave, with a panicked look on his face, listened intently to what Belkin had to say.

"We have plenty of evidence to back that up. Now answer the question."

"No, I did NOT help her! The paper said they found the car in a parking ramp during the noon hour. There are plenty of people at the clinic who know I didn't leave there from early morning until I went to Rhonda's home after work."

"Your prints were found in the car."

"Not surprising. Sunday afternoon Rhonda picked me up to go to the gym."

Cantu intervened, "We're done here. My client has answered your questions satisfactorily."

Belkin glowered at the attorney, "Keep your shirt on, Cantu, I have a few more for your client." Belkin turned to Linda. "Dr. Hernandez, you and everyone at your clinic maintains that Dr. Rhonda Collins must be a victim of foul play. Yet I suspect you aren't telling us everything. Are you?"

Am I withholding anything? I'm glad I didn't reach the aunt because I would have to admit that it's possible Rhonda did leave on her own if the name the woman in Chicago gave me is the same. And I did withhold the phone number but Rhonda asked me not to share it. Of course, she asked me not to say anything about her "dark secret" and I never have, but I've only supposed that might have something to do with her disappearance. I don't know if it does so I shouldn't mention ..."

"Dr. Hernandez, do you want me to rephrase the question?"

"No, I heard the question. I was just going over in my mind if there was anything that I haven't told you, and I can't think of a thing."

"Only two more questions. You have indicated how much you love the missing woman. Were you and Dr. Rhonda Collins lovers?"

It was hard to tell which of the Hernandez couple looked more stricken. Dave stared at his wife with a mixture of confusion and sudden doubt. *They can't be lovers. Did she find out about our affair? Did Rhonda throw me over for my wife? NO! That can't be!*

Cantu addressed his sister-in-law while slinging a look of sheer hatred toward Belkin, "Linda, don't even dignify that with an answer."

Not receiving an answer, Belkin asked another, "Dr. Linda Hernandez, did you kill Dr. Collins?"

Linda answered this time. "Why can't you believe that I would never harm my best friend in any way?"

Her husband continued to muse: *Did Linda find out about the affair? I couldn't find Rhonda when I was supposed to meet her Monday at the Vega Building. Did my wife do something to Rhonda? No! Linda won't swat a fly.*

"BELKIN! Cantu roared, "You're out of line. You CAN'T accuse someone of murder without some proof. Release my client immediately or I will press charges for false arrest."

Belkin took a deep breath as he looked with disdain at one of the most powerful attorneys in Corpus. The officer turned to Linda. "You are free to go, but we may have further questions."

Cantu and the Hernandez couple wasted no time in leaving. After calling home to make sure everything was okay with Grandma and the kids, Linda and Dave went out to a restaurant to discuss just what had gone on that evening though both husband and wife kept to themselves many of their personal thoughts.

When they left, Officer Gonzales' eyes shrieked outrage. "Stan, I said I would support you 100%, but why on earth did you ask those questions? We've compiled evidence that Dr. Rhonda did disappear on her own and discussed Dr. Linda as possibly the one who would have aided her. We aren't even considering murder."

Belkin shrugged, "I just wanted to see if I could upset the doctor enough so she'd confess. It's a common enough technique."

"I believe her when she says she didn't harm her friend."

"Bullsh. I still think she knows more than she's telling."

"But, why did you suggest they were lovers? Don't you believe women -- or men for that matter--could have a strong bond of friendship without sex?"

"Again I wanted to rattle her cage. Something's not right here. Did you watch her husband's reactions? Let's forget about it now, partner, and go out for a well-earned beer."

"No, thank you." Her eyes shot fire again. "I'm going home. I prefer the company of my cat."

They both exited the main door. With neither of them saying a word, Belkin propelled her through a horde of gobbling reporters.

CHAPTER TWENTY-TWO

Thursday late

Late Thursday night Sandra, vowing never to fly again, reached Houston and barely made her flight to Chicago. As she dashed to the right concourse, Melanie Brooks, waiting for her own flight, noticed the fast-moving tall, slender woman in the stylish clothing. Except for the woman's short brown hair, she looked so much like the missing Rhonda. Too tired and upset about her aunt's stroke to chase down the woman, Melanie convinced herself she was imaging things.

Melanie had taken the last flight from Corpus Christi to Houston. As Melanie waited to hear the magical words "Now boarding for the Tulsa flight", it hit her. *Lewis! Sandra Lewis! That's what Auntie Fe had called Rhonda.* She'd have to tell Ron.

As Sandra's flight took off, doubts began to torture her. What if Brian wouldn't help her? The last time she asked for a career change, he refused. She remembered the conversation well. They were in a cocktail lounge in Chicago. She'd flown from Corpus to Chicago just to ask for his help.

They hadn't seen each other for a long time but had kept in touch through Sandra's visits to Chicago. She'd had no real relationship with a man since she and Brian parted and hoped secretly that someday they'd be together. Though neither of them would have believed it could happen, the one-time couple had become good friends. Sandra knew Brian had many lovers since their break-up, but wanted to keep Brian in her life so badly she had settled for friendship. Eight years ago, she needed his help.

As that time they sat across from each other on tall high-backed chairs at a small mahogany table, Sandra had stated simply, "Brian, it's time for a career change."

"Isn't your salon doing well?"

"Very well, but I'm tired of it."

Their eyes met as both thought the same thing. If she had decided that long ago, they'd still be together.

Though Sandra had never ceased loving Brian, she felt certain only she regretted that they had parted. Brian had moved on and was engaged to a little beauty with the name Grace Foss. Grace and Brian now saved up for their wedding and honeymoon. With a start she saw he still stared at her, and she could see longing in his eyes.

As Brian gazed at Sandra, he knew he still was in love with her. *She is such an amazing woman and we were so happy together.* Brian wanted to tell Sandra how much he still loved her, but he'd hurt Sandra once and he couldn't show his love without hurting Grace. *All I can do is use my resources to help her again.* "What do you have in mind? Maybe real estate? Accounting? You always were good at keeping books."

"I want to be a doctor."

With raised voice and finality in his tone, he said, "Absolutely NOT!" Others looked their way as it became clear to Sandra that although Brian had said he'd help her, this he wouldn't do. "Name something else, anything else," he pleaded.

"But, Brian, that's what I want." Sandra smiled her most beguiling smile and began humming "Whatever Lola wants, Lola gets".

Brain wouldn't budge.

"Come on, Brian. I've been diagnosing my old women customers for years. I'll be a good, understanding doctor. I read an ad wanting doctors in Texas."

"No, Sandra, I care too much about you. It's too risky. You could be found out just during the interview process. In Texas they'd probably put you on death row for impersonating a doctor and possibly harming a patient. At the very least, they'd send you to prison if you were found out."

Sandra ignored all that. "Have you ever created a doctor?"

"Yes, but it's complicated with med school, internship, residency, and it's costly."

"Are you worried things will go wrong and I'll implicate you?" Sandra asked, fury in her voice and the feeling the sense of craziness she'd had when they'd broken up.

"Of course not, I accepted your promise when I made you a teacher and beautician ... I mean, hair stylist."

"I remember you told me that you got me my teacher's and stylist's licenses as a special favor and that you usually provided credentials to people without them knowing they were dealing with you."

"That's right. I trusted you not to tell anyone about my involvement if you got into trouble with false records, but how could I trust strangers? That's why we set up the "Dreams Come True" corporation and all checks are written to that for my services. I never know the customer; the customer never knows me. Safer that way."

An idea struck Sandra. "Well, since you refuse to make me a doctor, will you do it for my big sister since you don't know her?" Of course, she hadn't discussed any of this with Sue-Ella aka Rhonda Lee but she knew how much her sister wanted a better life. Besides Rhonda had mentioned wanting to be a doctor. *I could work this out. I'm not sure where Rhonda Lee is right now as she bounces back and forth between Tulsa and other places she's lived with her serial husbands, but I probably would be able to track her down if necessary.*

"What big sister? Come on, Sandra. You never mentioned a big sister, just the little rug rats. Did you just make her up on the spot?"

Sandra voice showed indignation. Unfortunately Brian knew her too well. "No, I didn't make her up but I did come up with this option just now." She pulled a recent photo from her purse.

"Wow! You two could be twins."

"Actually she's my half-sister; we have the same mom. But she lived with her dad. We found each other on Facebook and she came to Tulsa and has been living off me ever since. Make her into a doctor, and she can support me for a while. We'll move to Texas and Rhonda will be the breadwinner."

"What about your career?"

Sandra ignored this. "If you will do this, I'll pay well for it. I'll sell my shop and give you half the proceeds. That is if you can sell it for me because I'm giving up the business to go wherever my sis goes."

A business proposition flawed Brian couldn't resist.

CHAPTER TWENTY-THREE

Eight years earlier

Six weeks after Rhonda L. Collins had received what she needed from Brian, she began practicing as a doctor at the Cielo Vista Family Clinic in Corpus Christi, Texas. This clinic had posted the ad that Sandra had noticed two months earlier.

The new doctor made a promise to herself that Dr. Collins would become the best possible doctor and that the woman would remake herself into the type of person she'd always dreamed of becoming.

Rhonda found she enjoyed being a doctor more than she ever could have imagined. Salary and benefits great! The automatic respect given doctors rewarding! She transformed herself from an Arkansas peasant to a real lady. Rhonda liked herself! With the charm of the mom shared by Rhonda and Sandra, she made friends quickly with the rest of the medical staff. The new doctor believed, based on her own history, that every person and job had dignity including the office staff and the cleaning crew. They loved her, too.

Rhonda got along very well with the head doctor, Ronyl Brooks, and frequently asked his opinion, which pleased him. She admitted to herself being attracted to him and regretted he was married and, more to the point, her boss. Except for an on-again and off-again relationship with another married man and a close friendship with a good friend, a doctor colleague and her family, Rhonda devoted herself to her career, spending time on the Internet reading up on the latest in the medical field.

Most of her patients were children or menopausal women. She knew that all the latter needed was to be able to talk to someone who cared. As for the little ones, generally their illnesses weren't serious. Her job was to reassure the parents that their children would live and that they were good parents; she prescribed a common antibiotic for their ills. For patients with more serious ailments she never hesitated to make referrals to specialists, and they respected her for that. She talked to Dr. Ron if she wasn't certain about a diagnosis and he appreciated her thoroughness. She gained in seniority, just behind Dr. Ron and Dr. Linda, after one older male doctor retired and Ron hired two more young doctors.

All the staff liked Dr. Rhonda because she was so cheerful and caring. She remembered each one's birthday and brought a gift. One day she and Dr. Linda Hernandez realized they both were reading the same medieval fantasy series, featuring, "King Bewilliam", by South Texas author, Devorah Fox. From then on they felt destined to become special friends. Linda invited Rhonda to her church. Though religion never had been part of her life, Rhonda became very involved and made many friends. She enjoyed holidays with the extended Hernandez family, many relatives of Linda and Dave and their three sons, whom Rhonda thought of as her nephews. The only complication to her relationship with the family was that she and Dave became lovers.

Unaware of this, Linda felt blessed to have Rhonda in her life and taught her too-conscientious friend to have a good time. On weekends they shopped at Gratitude and other boutiques and clothing stores in Port Aransas. After lunch at one of the many fine restaurants and a walk on the beach determined to burn up the calories, they'd end up at Miss K's for a decadent dessert. Because they enjoyed their friendship so much their day trips expanded to overnight trips to Austin and San Antonio, both fabulous cities. They even managed a trip to Mexico during Spring Break.

Though always appearing upbeat, Rhonda carried the dread the wonderful life she had created could evaporate. She feared that someone would "mistake" her for sister Sandra and everyone would know the truth. Until then, she, like her favorite old movie heroine, Scarlet, intended to live in the moment and deal with life later. That also was the only way she could reconcile that the man with whom she had the sometimes affair was the husband of her best friend. They both had tried to break it off many times. This affair had begun before Linda and Rhonda's friendship blossomed. Rhonda enjoyed sex with Dave, who liked the variety, and the calm of Rhonda's beautiful townhouse.

Early in 2012 Ron announced to the staff that an accreditation team would be on site the next week. "They will examine records and observe staff-patient interactions. They may interview you. All routine stuff, no worries." Rhonda's blood ran cold when she heard this. Linda sensed her friend felt nervous about it but reasoned with her, "I've been through once before. It's nothing to get worked up over."

Rhonda tried to joke, "What if I do something to bring shame on the whole clinic?"

"Rhonda, you won't. You're the best!" promised her true friend.

Regardless, Rhonda felt anxious and went to an attorney to make out a will.

Almost a month later, after Linda and Rhonda had returned home from their vacation in Mexico, Ron told the staff he had the results of the accreditation visit and joked that everyone could relax. At the end of the meeting, Ron called Rhonda into his office. It made her uneasy to talk to the man who had hired her, the first person she'd deceived in Texas.

"Well, doctor, it seems you really impressed the accreditation team."

"I did?" Rhonda was incredulous.

"Yes, they observed you with a little boy screaming his head off. You did you horse act with all the whinnying and ponytail swinging. You won him over completely and went ahead with the exam. One of them recommended you to a panel in charge of the National Distinguished Young Doctor Recognition Award; you are one of the national winners."

"You have to be kidding!"

"No way! I need your signature on an acceptance form and here's a press release for you to sign. You might want to have a formal photo for that, and there is a very handsome cash acknowledgment attached to this, which will be presented to you next month in Columbus, Ohio.

Rhonda couldn't contain her joy and hugged Dr. Ron. Nothing had been said about her fake records. She had won the honor and the sizeable cash award money based on her performance. No one would know that they went to a doctor who had only a G.E.D. Though the G.E.D. program had been comprehensive, most people would hope their doctor to have graduated from a prestigious private high school or academy, college and medical school. In July as she stood with the other winning doctors on a stage in Columbus, she thought, *Life doesn't get any better than this.*

Less than two months later, the walls Rhonda had built for her new life would come tumbling down.

CHAPTER TWENTY-FOUR

Off the Record

Maria came to work early Friday. She still was livid with her partner, but had decided to let it go. That is, after calling Dr. Hernandez, which she knew was something she shouldn't do. So what! If Stan found out about it and reported her to the Chief, Maria could reciprocate and rat him out for bullying Dr. Hernandez. Of course, partners don't to that. She justified making a call to mend fences with Dr. Linda because they still might need her assistance. It had been stupid of Stan to antagonize someone who could be of real help, and Maria yearned to fix that.

As she hit the number for the clinic on her cell, she wondered if the doctor would even speak to her. She wasn't available. Maria left a message for her to call back, not blaming Dr, Linda if she didn't.

Not too much later Linda, always hopeful there would be news of Rhonda, called back. The young detective surprised her when she asked if Linda had any time that she wanted to take her out for a cup of coffee. The doctor's unforgiving frosty tone didn't match Maria's warm one, "With the vigil tonight, I don't have any spare time today."

"I plan to come tonight, and guess I can do this on the phone." Maria paused to figure out just what to say. She apologized, "I'm so sorry for what we put you through last night. I can only imagine how terrible you feel about your friend."

Linda sensed an ally. "I know you're doing your job, but it hurts so much that the police think I did something to harm her and that our relationship was inappropriate."

Maria didn't answer. She knew that she had become too emotionally involved, just as Stan said, because she felt too much empathy with Linda. As much as she wanted to tell Linda that Belkin could be a jerk, she couldn't go that far. Fortunately Linda filled the silence with a question.

"Do you think she ran away?' Linda asked softly.

"It looks that way, but we're still trying to find out for sure. I have a couple more leads to follow."

"I may..." Linda faltered, " have some information for you. If I do, I'll give it to you tonight at the vigil but please don't say anything to anyone about this."

Maria's eyes lit up. What kind of information could Dr. Linda have? Maybe she'd show up Belkin yet. Being his loyal partner certainly hadn't worked for her.

Another phone call to make. She called Felicity Ritter again. A woman answered but sounded very young. "I'm not Miss Felicity; her phone calls are being routed to the front desk of our assisted living facility. She had a stroke and she's in the hospital and can't talk." Maria wanted to scream in frustration mixed with compassion. She had lost an important lead but could have spent all day trying to reach Mrs. Ritter. She was glad the one who answered didn't abide by privacy issues.

Belkin reported to work. The same covey of reporters hung around that had accosted his partner and him when they left the night before. News vultures from television, radio and newspaper continued the harassment from the previous night. They pounced on the detective asking if the police considered Dr. Hernandez a suspect. The media hadn't been there when they brought her in so someone -- probably Cantu -- had tipped them off. Last night Belkin answered, "Nothing to tell you." Today he'd take a different approach to discredit anything they'd heard.

The barrage of questions came hard and fast.

An ever-persistent face yelled, "A neighbor of Linda. Hernandez e-mailed us that you took her away in cuffs last night. Can you comment?"

"The neighbor better have her eyes checked. In truth Dr. Hernandez has been very helpful to the case, and we drove her to the department to have her assist us."

The reporters continued to hurl questions like missiles, "Is it true? "Did you?" "Do you have?" raged the queries. "Listen up!" shouted Belkin, "Do me a favor and back off, and I will give you a juicy tidbit. Several witnesses have spotted the missing woman carrying a blue gym bag. Add that to your description for the public. Also, encourage people to come tonight to the Vigil for the missing woman. Let me repeat that Dr. Hernandez has been invaluable help in helping solve this.

Once in his office his thoughts turned to his partner. He had made such progress with her yesterday, actually had convinced her that his theory was right, but had infuriated her last night when he asked Dr. H. if she had killed her "lover", neither of which he believed beyond the realm of possibility.

At the same time he and Maria heard the Chief summon her to his office. Concerned about damage control, Belkin decided he'd better join them. He strode into the Chief's office in time to hear him say, "Detective Gonzales, I received a call from the father of the kid who sold his parents' car. They said you were extremely helpful to them, and I wanted to share the compliment." The Chief gave her a rare mile.

"Thank you." Maria bubbled inside to think the Chief had praised her for her empathy, which she worried made her appear so weak. Smart, she grabbed the opportunity to bring up the case the Chief thought was senseless to pursue. "The parents couldn't have been more co-operative, and I think

Austin Bennett provided valuable information about the missing doctor."

"Oh?" The Chief's eyes narrowed. "I thought you'd be ready to drop the case by now." He wasn't smiling now.

Belkin cleared his throat at the door.

The Chief looked up, "As long as you're both here, tell me the latest."

Belkin began, "We have had multiple sightings of the doctor on Monday afternoon by reliable witnesses."

Gonzales interrupted, "That included Austin Bennett, who sold his parents' car for drug money. He admitted selling the car at a Stripes store to a tall woman with a blue gym bag. Two other witnesses, one at Stripes and one at a motel where allegedly the disappearing woman stayed also described the blue gym bag."

Belkin added, "We traced her from the Credit Union to the Stripes on the same street, where she bought the car, and then to the Liberty Motel where she registered a car just like the stolen one she bought. We don't know where she was between Stripes and the motel."

"Last night I called the night clerk because the woman in question left the same day she checked in." Maria turned to her partner. "I haven't had a chance to share that with you, Sgt. Belkin." Turning back from Belkin, who looked surprised at Gonzales' news, Maria continued, "Anyway, he said the woman who drove the missing Taurus checked out about 10:00 PM, He said she carried a blue gym bag and wore a black hooded sweatshirt with the hood down." Gonzales paused.

"And she had long," began Belkin. "Blonde hair," finished the Chief.

"No," Gonzales interjected. "The clerk said she had short brown hair."

Both men looked befuddled.

"My theory is the doctor stopped at the motel to cut and dye her hair."

"Are we talking about one woman or two?" the Chief grunted. "One could have registered but two shared a bed. Then the other checked out."

"But why would both carry the same, or identical gym bags? Instead of purses?"

Belkin grimaced. "Just because we didn't find a third set of prints in the car doesn't mean our doctor couldn't have met someone at the motel."

Maria still thought her cut and color theory was right, but said nothing. She had another phone call to repeat.

Belkin cautioned, "Before we go any further, we need to tell the Chief what happened last night."

"Yes. Sir, last night we felt we had enough proof to arrest the doctor's best friend, Dr. Hernandez. Assistant Chief Knox supplied us with a warrant."

"What proof?"

"Based entirely on the lab report," Belkin replied.

"However, she successfully explained away the evidence, and we released her."

"Officer Gonzales has simplified it. Everything that happened last night is in this report. Her lawyer, none other than Thomas J. Cantu, threatened to sue us for false arrest. We complied and released her."

Chief Ortiz shook his head. "He could still sue, but knowing my assistant, Knox, I'm sure you wouldn't have gotten the warrant if the evidence wasn't convincing."

"It was, sir," began Maria. "It convinced me, at least, last night, that Officer Belkin's theory was right, that the doctor disappeared on her own."

"Belkin's theory? I've said that from the get-go. You've wasted a week on this case."

"But, Sir, unless we find the missing car and get some DNA, we can't prove the doctor left on her own. She still could be a crime victim. Please give us more time."

The chief hated to be swayed by the earnest look on Maria's face, but answered, "Okay, I'll give you a few more days, but that includes this weekend. I want to get this case out of the way. We already put out statewide alert for the stolen car. I'll change that to a get-a-away car with a female driver with short, brown hair or should I make that two occupants in the car, one with long blonde hair and one with short brown?"

Belkin answered, "Just one and by the way, there's a vigil for the doctor who disappeared. A big crowd expected. We probably should have police presence."

"Sure, sure. I'll send a couple uniforms."

All Maria could think was how everything about Belkin bugged her. Just now he acted like he'd always known about the vigil. She had intended to ask Chief Ortiz for patrol officers to manage the traffic and for whatever might happen.

Belkin followed Maria back to her cubicle. She braced herself for another of his diatribes. "I want to clue you in on something, Gonzales. This disappearance is getting tons of publicity. That's why I told you to be quiet last night."

Tell me something I don't know.

He droned on. "The public loves mysteries, and I hear from my sources that this one has been elevated to celebrity status. Everyone in South Texas is talking about the missing glamorous, prominent doctor and wondering why we haven't found her. If the media asks you a question, there are two answers: 'No comment' or 'It's under investigation so we can't comment'. Any how, they can incriminate us whatever we answer."

"And," Maria commented. "If we don't tell them something, they make it up. Did you see the feature in the Wednesday paper?"

"That was typical sensationalized tripe. The media loves to speculate, and then people embrace their theories instead of the truth. Like Monday. One station had someone at the Clinic the night before we got there and they raised doubts that the police were doing anything, which we weren't because enough time hadn't elapsed."

"But they raised so much doubt that the Chief had us right on it."

"Sure, power of the press. Then Tuesday, right after we left the clinic, one of the TV vans showed up. They televised their interview with Dr. Ron, which led to the conclusion the doctor's life was endangered. Of course, we were receiving calls about sightings that cast doubt on that."

"I saw a TV interview with the desk clerk. How would they know about her?"

"She probably tipped them off herself. Lots of people crave media attention."

Maria, remembering her conversations with the clerk, thought that seemed likely.

Then feeling guilty, she admitted, "I didn't even see the photographer that shot the tow truck in the ramp." She referred to a front-page photo.

"Probably the same man who waited at the station and harassed us when we brought in the shoes and purse,"

"So far there's been nothing about our false arrest."

"It could happen yet. I tried to persuade them it didn't happen, but was surprised Cantu hadn't already called his own press conference. He could have paid them to keep quiet about his sister-in-law."

"I'm sure there will be lots of coverage of the Vigil tonight. Are you going?"

"In hopes the Doctor herself might show up? No way, I'm taking the wife to the movies tonight."

"I didn't know you're married." *Poor woman.*

"This is number three, but I'd be looking for number four if I gave up our date night for the Vigil."

"I plan to be there. My boyfriend is going with me instead of our regular Friday night date. I think it will help to show positive support from the Police Department." Maria didn't mention her conversation with Dr. Linda.

"Can't hurt. Often missing people have been known to show up at their own Memorial services so Rhonda might be there." Belkin waited for a reaction from his partner. She stood there impassive so he added a parting shot, "Don't stay out too late. Thanks to your persistence we're on tomorrow."

Maria, ignoring the professionalism taught in her college courses, pulled a face at his retreating figure.

CHAPTER TWENTY-FIVE

Tea and chatter in Chicago

The plane touched down at O'Hare shortly after midnight on Friday. Sandra had made it!! She'd had her share of bad breaks with the weather, the TSA, missing a flight because of it, having flights cancelled, spending the night in an airport and possibly suffering from food poisoning. Sandra also had phenomenal luck, and she was unaware of most of it. She had escaped from Corpus Christi mostly because people with whom she had to interact were distracted or just weren't paying attention. Timing played a big part. If Dave Hernandez and Sandra had crossed paths in the Vega Building, it could have ended there. Felicity's ill-timed stroke prevented her from alerting the police. Melanie could have blown the whistle in Houston if she had been more certain it was Rhonda she'd seen run by. If the flight Sandra had taken from San Antonio hadn't been late, she would have strolled down the concourse. Melanie would have recognized and approached the run-away.

Sandra breathed a great sigh of relief when the plane landed. She hailed a taxi to take her to the premiere downtown Hilton. This hotel was the polar opposite of the Liberty Motel and more elegant than the inexpensive chain where she usually stayed in Chicago, and they did have an available suite. A gal could stay here forever with living room, bedroom, Jacuzzi bath, all rooms tastefully decorated, and an exciting view of Michigan Street with its endless shopping opportunities.

Secure in the thought that Brian would help her this time if she offered him enough incentive, Sandra sank into the bubbles in the Jacuzzi. Fully relaxed, she crawled into a bed so soft and luxurious that she had no trouble finding sleep.

An energized Sandra arose early, ordered a room service breakfast. She left the hotel during rush hour and took the subway to the first bank that was open. Here she opened an account, deposited most of her stash, and signed on for a credit/debit card. Next stop, a phone store, where she was forced to spend way too much time and money to buy a new cell and pick out a plan for using it.

Having completed necessary business to make her a completely transformed American adult, she took a cab to Brian's. With confidence she made her way to the apartment complex where she had come many times beginning when Brian first lived there as a bachelor. Though totally unalike, she and Brian's wife had become friends. A couple years earlier Brian had beseeched Sandra not to tell his new wife about his business. " Grace thinks I'm in real estate," he admitted. Sandra had not betrayed that or any other confidence between the two.

"Sandy, what a surprise!" Grace enthused as she greeted the friend with a hug.

Grace was the only person who called her "Sandy".

"Obviously I can't get very close with the gargantuan child I'm carrying."

"I didn't even know you were pregnant," exclaimed Sandra, guessing her friend was in her last trimester.

"Yes, my dainty little baby girl must weight thirty pounds by now."

"You're not that big. Every pregnant woman thinks she's as big as a bus-- each one is wrong."

"But I still have six weeks to go! Now changing the subject, I'm sorry I haven't kept in touch better. I'm so happy to see you and I know Brian will be, too, but he's in the UK on business. He works for Crawford and Haynes now. New job and enough money so we will be able to buy a house AB."

"AB?"

"After Baby," Grace explained with a giggle. "We reckon all time that way: BB, Before Baby, WB, With Baby and AB."

"When will Brian, be back? Hopefully BB!"

"Sandy", pessimistically worrying that Brian might be gone months when she needed him now, was delighted with Grace's answer. "Late tonight. I'm so excited. He's been gone ten days." Then she became serious, as serious as Grace could be. "Where are my manners? Sometimes I think my brain vaporized when I got pregnant. Come into the kitchen and I'll make us some tea."

Sandra followed her nose into the cozy kitchen that smelled of something delicious. She praised the red gingham café curtains Grace boasted she'd sewn, and commented on two tuxedo cats dozing in the windowsill. "I didn't know you had kitties."

"Oh," Grace mused as if seeing the cats for the first time. "They're Clarence and Otis, brothers. I'm worried about how they'll be with the baby. We adopted them before I knew I was pregnant so we could practice being pet owners and someday we can have a dog. Brian didn't used to like cats, but he's crazy about those two lazy slugs and says they'll get along fine with a baby."

Thinking about Poppy, Sandra commented, "I love animals, and someday I plan to have a dog. Or a cat. I love them, too."

They visited at the table while waiting for the water to boil. Grace made tea in a white and pink flowered antique pot that had belonged to her great-grandmother. "The tea is ready!" she caroled.

Over green tea and homemade banana bread, the source of the wonderful aroma, Sandra made her point for coming, "I really need to talk to Brian."

"I know he handled the sale of your shop when you moved to Texas, but he isn't doing real estate anymore."

And never really was. "No, it's not about real estate. I just need some of his good advice."

Grace accepted that. She thought her husband brilliant and could understand why Sandy, who seemed a little tense to her, would come to him for advice; not that it bothered her a bit. After about an hour of catching up, she became very confidential. "Sandy, he told me about everything."

"About what?" Sandra dared to ask as several granny knots formed in her stomach.

"He told me that you lived together, and I'm not the least bit concerned because you two treat each other like brother and sister."

"Yes," sighed Sandra with drama, "Brian is the brother I never had. Tell him I'll call him tomorrow."

As they stood by the entrance waiting for Sandy's cab, Grace spied something on her mother's antique piecrust occasional table, set beneath the mail slot. "Oh, by the way, here's a letter for you. I noticed the return address is from a lawyer in Corpus Christi." A light bulb started to glow in her brain. *Maybe that's why Sandy needs to talk to Brian. I hope she isn't in trouble.* "It came quite a while ago," she added.

Sandra studied the return address and the March postmark. *My copy of the will naming me beneficiary. I want to show this to Brian. Maybe he'll know how I can have the money as soon as possible. Such a great plan Rhonda and I made!*

Grace didn't think Sandy appeared upset by the letter, and that calmed any fears about Sandy having gotten into some sort of bad trouble involving a lawyer. "Oh, I almost forgot. I told you about my brain deterioration with this pregnancy --

poor baby, destined to be born to an idiot mother. At least she has a smart father. Anyway, there's a woman who has been trying to reach you, a Dr. Hernandez."

"Oh, sure, I have her number. She's a doctor at the clinic where my sister works. I'll give her a call."

CHAPTER TWENTY-SIX

Unofficial detective

As Linda drove to work Friday, she knew she had to pretend the night before hadn't happened. Last night at the restaurant her brother-in-law had insisted that he would keep the unfortunate episode out of the media. Linda and Dave had talked long into the early morning hours. They both had secrets about Rhonda that neither was ready to confess,

The main thing on her mind this Friday morning had to be the vigil. She must go forward with it regardless of how Rhonda disappeared. Everyone, feeling helpless, still asked what each could do to help find Rhonda. This would be as positive an experience as possible for anyone who participated because they could help by putting up posters on Saturday.

Regardless, last night intruded on her thoughts. She hadn't caused the disappearance and it hurt that the police thought she, a doctor pledged to save lives, was capable of murdering anyone, let alone her dearest friend. Such a charge overshadowed that ruthless Belkin asking if she and Rhonda were lovers. A man like that probably had no friends so couldn't begin to understand a deep platonic relationship. After they left the police department last night she had told her husband, making a joke of it, that she was not bi-sexual and had not broken her marriage vows. Dave had hugged her, and both he and Tom said that Belkin had crossed a line. Dave said anyone who knew her would never believe she had a lesbian love affair nor killed her lover, with which Tom agreed. In spite of their support Linda sensed the detectives thought she was holding out on them. They were wrong since she had told them everything she knew -- for certain. Yet her conscience bothered her because she hadn't told the whole truth.

She mulled over the feelings she'd had since Rhonda's departure. At first her mind wouldn't let her believe her friend had come to harm. Then she figured out a plausible theory of why Rhonda had left on her own. She didn't share that theory because she didn't want the police to avoid looking for her in case she was wrong. Now it seemed quite certain that Rhonda had faked abduction; the police had accused Linda of helping Rhonda. She hadn't, but she had made every effort not to tell what she suspected because she still wanted the police to find her friend. She wanted to be able to see Rhonda and tell her that no matter what had happened, Linda believed in her and would stand by Rhonda just as she had all this week. One thing that kept her going was that someday they would laugh at how Linda almost went to jail because of loyalty to her friend!

On the way to the clinic she stopped at the printer to pick up several boxes of posters with Rhonda's photo. She looked at one of the copies before she met her first patient of the day. *She really isn't beautiful, as the media has said repeatedly. Her lips are too thin, her nose a little sharp, but she does have beautiful long natural blonde hair.* Linda ran her hand through her own glossy shoulder-length dark hair. She continued to study the photo. *And exquisite high cheekbones and she never worries about her weight like I do.* She thought about all the wings she shouldn't have eaten last night when Tom, Dave and she went to Chili's after the police station. She looked back at the photo. *What constitute her beauty are eyes that sparkle when she smiles, which is pretty much all the time. Beautiful eyes and smile constitute an inner beauty that attracts everyone to her.* Linda looked again. Remembering

Mazatlan, she wondered if the bright smile was only a façade, a way to mask a deep secret in her past, the darkness to which she had hinted that beautiful tropical night.

Addressing the photo, Linda spoke softly, "If only you'd get in touch with me. I don't want to believe our friendship means so little to you that you wouldn't tell me your plans. I know something terrible scared you and made you do what you did. I can't tell the police where I think you could be because I want you safe." Knocking on Linda's office door, a nurse faintly could hear the doctor's voice and thought she interrupted the doctor taking a phone call. "Patient ready in Room 1-B."

Later, between patients, Linda pressed Melanie's aunt's number again. For her own curiosity she had wanted to find out the last name Auntie Fe had attributed to the one she thought was Rhonda. There was no answer, but Ron quickly cleared that up when he came to Linda's office door.

"Linda, I have a message for you from Mel. She won't be able to help with the posters tonight at the vigil."

"What's happened?" Linda asked in alarm, the week's events causing her to expect the worst. We received a call from Aunt Fe's doctor. When she didn't show up for Bingo last night someone went to her apartment and found her on her kitchen floor. She had a stroke, and Melanie flew to Tulsa. Even though Mel had a long wait in Houston we're thankful she got on the last flight there from Corpus and one to Tulsa."

"I'm so sorry. Please tell her it won't be a problem to find someone else, and tell her I'll pray for her aunt."

"Thanks, I feel so damned guilty that I'm always commenting on Fe's compulsive talking. This has affected her speech, and for her I can't think of a less humane thing to happen. I just wish she had been wearing her Medi-alert."

When he left, Linda noticed a voicemail from the young detective Gonzales. What now? She didn't want to call back but she didn't want them to have anything to hold against her. More important maybe they had located Rhonda. Of course, that's what Linda had thought when the officers arrived at her doorstep last night. Linda did respond to the detective's message and was amazed that the young woman apologized. Detective Gonzales said she planned to come to the Vigil. Suddenly, Linda felt this woman was on her side and wanted to give her the phone number in Chicago. "I may have some information for you tonight, but please don't tell anyone yet," Linda confided to Maria. *Then maybe she'll be able to find Rhonda!* But first she wanted to call Grace Cavendish again to see if her husband had returned.

She didn't have a chance until the afternoon. Grace told her that her husband wasn't home yet, "But guess who came for a visit this morning? Sandy from Corpus Christi!"

Linda's heart skipped a few beats. *This has to be more than coincidence. Were Sandra and Rhonda acquainted? Or...?* Suddenly, Linda felt a mountain of anger towards her friend. *Why did you keep so much from me? What kind of friend shares nothing of herself?*

"Are you still there?'

"I am and I'm wondering if Sandra has a number where she can be reached?"

"Sure a brand-new cell number!"

Because she destroyed Rhonda's phone? Trying to stay calm, Linda asked in a quavering voice, "Would you please give it me the number so I could call her and ask if she might know my friend?"

"Wouldn't that be a hoot? Sure, here it is."

Linda called Sandra's new number. There was no answer. Praying Rhonda would return her call, Linda left a voicemail. "This is a long-shot, but Rhonda, is this you? I miss you so much; everyone is worried to death about you. Tonight there's a big candlelight vigil for you. Please come back, or just call me and tell me you're okay. I won't tell anyone else if that's what you want. If for some reason you did leave on your own, I understand that it was something you had to do. I'll do anything for you, you know that. I love you, Rhonda, my friend."

CHAPTER TWENTY-SEVEN

Enjoy limited bliss

After her visit with Grace, the loveable but somewhat ditzy Grace, Sandra did some serious wardrobe shopping. Nothing like retail therapy! First stop -- Nordstrom's, where she applied for a credit card. She would find both that and the bank's card within days in the mailbox she rented after setting up the bank account, but for now she had a temporary card at Nordstrom's.

She couldn't wait until Brian returned home so he could help her get a new start in life. After watching those kids playing in the airport terminal, unbothered by long waits, she had decided she wanted to try teaching again. It was certainly demanding, but now that she was older, she thought she could handle administrative woes better.

Because of her parents' stormy marriage and the truck driver with evil intentions, she had soured on the thought of ever marrying. Then Brian came along, and the two, who were only kids, were content to live together. She had thought, compared to a divorce, breaking up with a live-in wouldn't be so terrible. She was so wrong. Sandra never could put herself through that kind of pain again. Now she wanted children, even without marriage, and considered adoption, maybe a Chinese child.

Her phone chimed as she rode the down escalator and unfamiliar with her new device, she startled and nearly tripped as other shoppers gasped. She recognized Dr. Hernandez's number so didn't answer.

When she returned to her hotel, she saw Linda had left a voicemail. How had she found her number? Not too hard to figure out! *It had to be Grace as I stupidly gave her the number.* Sandra just wasn't up to listening to the message. Instead she bought a pay-for-view movie and had room service bring her a dinner of sirloin tips in brown gravy with tender asparagus spears. Friday night would bring more blissful sleep.

CHAPTER TWENTY-EIGHT

Another sighting

Late Friday afternoon Marlys Jensen clicked on the television to a local news station as soon as she arrived home from her job as a Wal-Mart cashier. She, like the majority of people in Corpus Christi, avidly followed the case of the missing doctor. The "classic ivory silk blouse" the doctor wore captivated the souls of everyone who discussed each detail of the all-consuming story. Young, beautiful doctor disappeared on Monday, never returned from her lunch break. Each day the media added tantalizing details, but by today, Friday, the police hadn't come close to solving the riddle of the doctor's disappearance. At the store, where Marlys worked, all the employees had divided themselves into two groups: the group that knew the doctor had been abducted and come to harm and the other group that delighted in saying she'd faked the abduction and probably now lived in a foreign country under an assumed name. Aligned with the first group, Marlys believed the worst.

The doctor's story eclipsed another one Marlys and her friends had been discussing. A Corpus Christi couple had returned from a cruise to find that their car had been stolen right out of the garage.

"Can you imagine? You just come home from a wonderful time and then find out something like that!" Marlys' friend Em had voiced what everyone in the area thought.

As Marlys waited for more news on the disappearance of Dr. Rhonda Collins, she watched the car crash de jour on S.P.I. D. and the all too frequent stories of a house fire, a drive-by shooting, a stabbing, more gang graffiti, and a drunk rounding a corner ending up with his car in someone's bedroom.

The woman ticked off on her fingers what she had learned from the media about the missing woman. One, on Monday, a young reporter on her favorite nighttime news program, stood out in the pouring rain in front of the Cielo Vista Clinic, where the doctor worked. He described her as in her thirties, tall, long blonde hair, wearing that beautiful silk blouse, nut-brown pants with matching shoes and purse. She drove a BMW. *Obviously a class act, my friends and I agreed.*

Tuesday, she watched an interview with the clinic's head doctor, a good looking and obviously distressed man. He explained that he and all of the other employees feared the worst because Rhonda was a well-loved responsible woman, who wouldn't leave on her own.

Wednesday her car was found in the Vega Building parking ramp, on the third floor. It had been there since the reported time of disappearance on Monday. A reporter who dogged the police station told how the police had found her purse and shoes in the car. The reporter had snapped a photo of the tow truck hauling off the car. "Pretty tricky maneuver in that ramp," he'd commented. The same day the newspaper had run a feature story on the doctor, who recently had won an outstanding achievement award. The staff writer said she'd interviewed the doctor at the time and stated what a caring, appealing woman she appeared to be.

The writer of the long feature had interviewed the missing woman's patients, colleagues, neighbors, and friends at her church. Everyone contacted held her in highest esteem. No one could believe she had disappeared on her own, yet didn't want to believe she'd come to harm.

She told how the missing doctor's best friend, another doctor, Linda Hernandez, had organized a prayer vigil for Friday evening. More learned from the feature was that the missing woman had lived alone in Corpus Christi for eight years and owned a little Chihuahua dog she adored. "There's no way she would have left him alone," agreed Marlys and her single lady friends, pet lovers all, when they discussed the article. And all said, "Praise the Lord" when they read that a friend had rescued him and had the little dog at her home.

The rest of the feature speculated on why someone like her might have disappeared (perhaps a psychotic episode) or why someone would have abducted her (ranging from a jilted lover to a sexual predator). The South Corpus Christi Police Department would not confirm these theories or anything else about the case.

Whatever news about he doctor they saw on nightly television was the topic of conversation with her friend Em, who also clerked at Wal-Mart, when they carpooled to work the next day. That day, Thursday, a TV reporter leaked the news that the car stolen earlier in the week might have been purchased by "The Run-away Doctor" and hinted that the police had been following her. *Imagine a connection between those two big stories!* Another announcement -- a prayer vigil would be held outside the Cielo Vista Clinic at 7:45 Friday night.

Oh, yes, she'd forgotten that one station had an interview with a desk clerk at that awful motel, the one she and Emily called "The No-Tell Motel", which they passed on their way to work. *The clerk said a woman fitting the doctor's description stayed there but I don't believe that for a minute*

Finally a teaser for a topic that interested Marlys. "Police have added something to the missing doctor's description. More after the break."

The story continued after an annoying local car sales commercial and several network ones, including the one for the hideous girl with the too red lipstick named Flo. "Police have reported witnesses allegedly sighted the missing doctor on Monday afternoon. According to them, she wore a black hooded sweatshirt over her 'classic ivory silk shirt' and exercise shoes. All said she carried a blue gym bag."

"*A blue gym bag*! Marlys had worked at Wal-Mart for ten years, ever since she and her now deceased husband, had retired from Winona, Minnesota to Corpus Christi. She figured she's waited on a couple million customers. When she heard the first description, she mused that she could have waited on the doctor that Monday and didn't even realize it. Now she definitely remembered a tall woman with a blue gym bag. Immediately she should have called security because a backpack or oversized purse indicates shoplifting. However, Marlys Hanson prided herself in being able to detect dishonest shoppers, and this woman didn't set off any alarms in her head. *As honest as the day is long.* She remembered she had teased the woman about her bag when she took money from it and told her she should look into a new invention called "purses". The shopper had laughed and said she'd remember that. *But, wait, I don't work on Mondays so it couldn't have been... Oh, yes, I did, I worked for Marjorie so I could have Saturday off. It could be the same woman.*

I need to pick up Emily for the vigil, but first I have to call the police station tip-line.

Her attention turned back to the news. A neighbor of Dr. Linda Hernandez (the missing woman's purported best friend) called to say she saw Dr. Hernandez being put into a police car. "We have tried repeatedly to reach **the only two officers** assigned to this case, and we finally contacted Lt. Stan Belkin, a police *defective*... excuse me, **detective** ... who denied this. He said they drove Dr. Hernandez to headquarters to ask her further questions because she had been so helpful to them this week. We earlier contacted Dr. Hernandez and she put to rest any possibility of being arrested as a suspect in the case and urged the public to come to the vigil tonight."

Marlys left her name and number on the tip-line along with the news about having the missing doctor as a customer on Monday afternoon.

CHAPTER TWENTY-NINE

Sorrow and Hope
Another sighting

A huge crowd assembled in the Cielo Vista parking lot Friday night. Dr. Ron's wife, with her aunt in Tulsa, was the only one connected to the clinic staff not in attendance. Linda finally had told her boys the truth about Auntie Rhonda being missing, and they stood with their dad trying hard to be brave. Receptionists Carla and Amy fought to keep from breaking down as they held on to each other.

Besides Rhonda's colleagues, neighbors and friends from church, several city officials and representatives from various churches attended. Emily and her friend Marlys were among the many who'd come because they had heard about the poor doctor from the media. Marlys had explained to her friend how certain she was that that the missing woman had been her customer Monday and that the police would probably call soon for an interview. Emily hugged her when Marlys told her that she'd called the police tip-line. It delighted Emily that her friend might be the one to help the police bring the lady doctor back to her friends.

The media was well represented, and two off-duty police directed traffic. They nodded at Maria, who stood close to her boyfriend. All listened to a guitar duo who played and sang Christian folk songs as the group grew in size.

The pastor took the guitarists' place. "God is our refuge and strength, always ready to help in times of trouble. This is from Psalm 461, Verse 1, and is as true today as when it was written so many centuries ago."

A rented electric organ had been placed near the clinic doors so it could be plugged into an outdoor outlet. The organist from Rhonda's and Linda's church played as the crowd of adults and children, which surpassed all the staff expectations, sang from song sheets the Isaac Watts hymn, "Oh, God our help in ages past, our hope for years to come."

The pastor continued with prayer. "Let us pray. Heavenly Father, we gather tonight in common concern for one who is missing, our friend, our neighbor, our colleague, our doctor, our beloved Rhonda. We do not know where she is but together we pray for her safe return to us. May we be comforted that wherever she is, Rhonda is in Your loving care. Amen."

Several people offered individual prayers for Rhonda, and over three hundred voices joined in a variety of hymns of praise and hope, including Rhonda's favorite, "Here I am, Lord."

Both Drs. Ron and Linda spoke about their wonderful colleague and friend.

Dr. Ron explained, "No matter what you have seen on television or read in the paper, none of us know what has become of our friend. We don't want to fear the worst so we must believe something unexplainable happened to make Rhonda leave. We beg the South Corpus Christi Police Department to continue to follow every clue, no matter how insignificant, so Rhonda may be returned to us. If she had her own reason for leaving, we will forgive her as God forgives us. We just want her back." His voice cracked and he turned the mike over to Linda.

"Rhonda, if by some miracle you are near enough to hear us..." (Everyone began looking around as they hoped the doctor would reappear.) "... please know that we love you, we miss you and we want you to return to us." Then Linda held up one of the posters and explained that after the vigil, the staff would distribute them so everyone could display posters in their neighborhoods and post them in neighboring towns.

The vigil had been timed so that at the beginning it was light enough to see the song sheets, and at the closing, dark enough for the glittering candles to represent hope. As darkness fell the clinic staff members passed out the candles, Linda lit her candle and from it lit the one held by the person nearest her, and so it continued until the last place where Rhonda had been seen glowed in her honor. Together strangers joined in shared compassion and concern as they sang, "Come back Rhonda Friend" to the tune of "Kum Ba Yah," and recited The Lord's Prayer.

As participants signed sheets and indicated where they would take posters, Linda spotted Officer Gonzales and slipped a piece of paper into her hand. Maria read it immediately. Linda had typed: **"Here's the emergency phone number Rhonda gave me once when she went to Chicago. I'd forgotten I still had it."**

CHAPTER THIRTY

Name game

The first thing in the morning Melanie called her husband to report on Felicity, who was doing incredibly well, bawling out the nurses with her left fist since the stroke had left her speechless and her right side paralyzed. Both conditions were expected to be temporary.

Ron told Melanie all about the Vigil, which reminded her of the Rhonda look-alike she'd seen at the Hobby terminal in Houston.

"But, I'm sure it really wasn't her or I would have stopped her, and by the way I remember the last name Auntie Fe called Rhonda. It's 'Lewis'. Remember I told you I thought it was a man's name."

When the conversation ended, Ron debated calling the PD with the last name. In the end he did decide to call, expecting only voicemail so early, but the woman detective answered.

Maria showed up for work much earlier than Stan. He'd chided her about staying up too late but where was he this morning? Xavier had suggested going some place after the Vigil, but Maria wasn't up to it. They had gone back to her apartment, where Xavier wanted to distract Maria from her job especially since Sydney was gone for the weekend and Big Boy, with his lack of scruples, certainly wouldn't judge. The romantic time they'd spent together included discussing their becoming engaged at Christmas time. She fixed breakfast for him this morning, and he'd dropped her off to at headquarters to make certain she arrived on time.

A note on her desk said to check the tip-line. She also wanted to call the number in Chicago which Linda had handed her last night. Before she could make a call, Dr. Ron called with more information, for which she thanked him profusely. She tapped in the number of the tipster, Marlys Jensen, who answered on the second ring.

"Ms. Jensen, this is Detective Gonzales from the South Corpus Christi Police Department. I found your message on he tip-line and wanted to ask you a few questions."

"Oh, good you called now, I was just about ready to leave for work."

"You said that you are a cashier at Wal-Mart. Which one is that?"

" The one in Portland."

"Thank you. You also said that when you heard about the blue gym bag, you thought the missing doctor may have been one of your customers on Monday afternoon."

"I'm sure she was. I'm not positive of the time but it was early to middle of the afternoon."

"What are the hours of your shift?"

"9:00 to 5:00, just like Dolly Parton," Marlys quipped.

"And you think you waited on her mid-afternoon but aren't sure when?"

"Well, let's see, let me think," Marlys answered and then remembered, "Okay, this is closer, I had just come back from my last break at 2:05, and I saw her standing first in line as soon I returned and turned on my light to say 'Open'. I noticed her because she carried a blue gym bag and she reached in it for cash to pay for her purchases."

Hoping the woman would say the customer bought a hair coloring kit and scissors, Marie asked if she remembered what the woman with the blue gym bag had purchased. Marlys laughed a loud, hearty laugh. "Ma'am. I wait on hundreds of people every day, and I sure don't remember what she bought but what I remember is kidding her about the gym bag, where she carried her money. I suggested she try one of the new-fangled things women carry called a purse."

"What did she say to that?"

"She just laughed, and she had the most beautiful smile." Marlys added, "I sure hope you find her. My friend Emily -- I call her Em, liked Auntie Em in the Wizard of Oz -- and I went to that vigil last night and I was so overwhelmed by all the wonderful things her friends said. They truly love her."

"It was a beautiful service, and I thank you for your tip. It could be very helpful."

"You're more than welcome. I am praying you will find her, and I don't want an award. Now I have to get back to Wal-Mart, where anything can happen and usually does." She laughed her contagious laugh again.

Maria indicated she might have future questions, and Marlys quickly gave her cell-phone number and her address before she hung up to go to work.

Halfway out the door, Marlys remembered she'd worked for Marjorie on Monday so had today off so she could help clean up her church's designated highway mile.

Maria now could fill in the gap between the time Rhonda left Stripes, where she seemed to have bought a car, and the time she found a motel, where she had stayed long enough to have cut and colored her hair. The change in hair color and style were implied by the desk clerks' differing descriptions of the woman. Rhonda drove the car that matched plates of the gray Taurus, thought stolen but actually sold by Austin Bennett to a tall woman in a black hoodie who carried cash in a blue gym bag.

Her next call Saturday was the number Linda had given her with the explanation that she just remembered she had it. *Stan would have considered that "just remembered" too convenient but I trust Linda and appreciate her finding the number.* Maria already had researched the phone number and found it listed to a Brian Cavendish in Chicago.

The call awakened Brian, who arrived home late Friday. He answered in a voice thick with sleep. "Cavendish Residence."

"I am Detective Gonzales with the South Corpus Christi Police Department, this number was given me as an emergency number for someone we are trying to locate."

"What?" In a fog Brian didn't recall that his wife had filled him in on the phone calls from Corpus and Sandra's visit.

"Sir, could you tell me if someone named Dr. Rhonda Collins has been in contact with you?"

Brian's answer was instinctive. "I'm afraid you have the wrong number. I don't know anyone by that name."

He hung up and went right back to sleep. He never remembered the call.

When Maria called Linda's cell, she reached her and family members in Victoria, where they distributed the Rhonda posters in business and residential areas.

"Dr. Hernandez, I wanted to ask you more about the number you gave me." Linda hesitated a minute and explained how she had just remembered she had it. "When Rhonda first bought Poppy from a breeder, she was nervous about leaving him with a pet sitting service while she was in Chicago. She asked me to drop by her home during the weekend to check on Poppy. If I sensed a problem, I was to call Rhonda at the Chicago number."

Then Linda, weary and feeling very betrayed by the best friend she'd ever had, spilled everything about the number, "I called the number yesterday and reached the Brian Cavendish residence. The wife said she didn't know a Rhonda, her husband might. However, he was out of town. Then she told me she knew someone in Corpus Christi. Her name is Sandra Lewis."

"Sandra? Isn't that what Dr. Brooks' aunt called Dr. Rhonda?" asked Maria.

Linda almost corrected the officer, but Maria caught herself. "I mean the aunt of the doctor's wife."

"Yes, she called her Sandra 'Something'. No one has been able to remember the last name, but it seemed like too much of a coincidence so I called the number again on Friday afternoon. The wife said Sandra Lewis had visited her that morning. I asked if the wife could give me Sandra's phone number. She gave me her cell number. I called but there's been no response."

Sandra Lewis, The same name the aunt had called Rhonda! Maria barely could believe what she'd heard and she needed to keep Dr. Hernandez talking. "I called the aunt but here was no response."

"She had a stroke and has lost her speech," Linda explained.

Maria murmured concern as she acted like she hadn't already known that in hopes the doctor might divulge more. "Do you remember anything else she said?"

"I didn't hear her but Melanie Brooks said her aunt insisted Rhonda had been her hairdresser."

BINGO! The doctor really could have cut off all that hair and given herself "a cute haircut" and colored it. Maria could barely contain herself, but asked, "Doctor, do you think Rhonda could be an assumed name?'

"It crossed my mind, but I don't know what to think. Here's Rhonda's cell number." Linda's voice trembled as she recited the numbers. Please call me if you learn anything." To that Maria answered, "I will."

CHAPTER THIRTY-ONE

In the bag

Members of a non-denominational, formerly Baptist church, had committed to cleaning up a mile of roadway outside Corpus Christi. With neon orange vests and disposable gloves, the volunteers divided into two teams to comb both sides of the highway. Empty plastic bags, playthings of the Gulf winds, distinguished themselves as the most prevalent source of litter.

Marlys Jensen and her church friend Leah Valdez, a retired teacher, volunteered with this important project the third Saturday of each month. Working beside the northbound lane with a huge black trash sack between them, Leah spotted a Wal-mart bag, tied at the top, which seemed to be quite full.

"I wonder what's in it?" Marlys mused as she started to open it. "Maybe a bag that originally I filled at my register!"

"Yuck! Just toss it into the sack," Leah admonished. "Probably a dirty diaper. You know how people leave them around."

Marlys started to toss it in the sack with all the other litter they'd picked up but something made her pause. "Just a peek to satisfy my curiosity." She began tugging on the ties. "Rats! It's impossible to open with these gloves."

"Oh, all right, I'll help you," Leah offered, suddenly curious herself.

Both women tugged on opposite sides of the knotted tie until the bag ripped, spilling out contents that made them both turn pale. Blonde hair. Lots of blonde hair! And an ivory silk blouse stained with blood.

"Oh, no, is it possible? Do these have something to do with the missing doctor?" Marlys was near tears.

"Don't even go there," Leah, trying to hide her fear, responded with the tired saying.

"Leah, I wasn't going to tell anyone, but I'll tell you. I think I waited on her. This is too much of a coincidence. Maybe even a Message from God told me to open it. We have to take it to the police department right away!"

"Which one? Downtown or the new one?"

"The new one. Haven't you been following this story?"

"Of course, I have. I know all about that poor woman. Emily called me last night and said she went to the vigil and it was very touching."

"I took her to the Vigil." Marlys was short with Leah.

"Then I don't need to tell you how lovely it was." Leah sounded a little snippy."

"Come on, Leah. We're both upset over this. Let's go tell the team captain we have to go now." They carefully gathered together the halves of the torn bag.

The captain accepted their urgent need to leave and used his cell phone to put the news on Facebook. On the way to SCCPD the two volunteers discussed all they had heard about the case with Marlys trumping her friend by telling her she already had talked to a detective this morning.

They agreed they had crucial evidence in the bag.

CHAPTER THIRTY-TWO

One bloodied ivory blouse

Almost 11:00. Belkin sauntered into headquarters. "Well, have you solved the case yet?"

"Closer than you'd think."

At that precise moment two women burst in with a Wal-Mart bag.

One spoke, "I'm Marlys and I called on the tip-line and spoke to someone but this is even bigger." The woman talked so fast she was almost breathless. "This is my friend, Leah, and we were cleaning up our church's mile of highway and found something that we think has to do with the missing doctor. We found it near our church's volunteer highway sign. "We are responsible for a mile clean-up."

"And where is that?"

"Right out of town. The highway goes to San Antonio, but it's not the freeway."

Belkin and Gonzales put on gloves. Maria gulped as she pulled out an ivory silk blouse with reddish-brown stains on the front. Belkin reached in and kept pulling out long, blonde hair. The bag seemed bottomless.

"Thank you, ladies. Did you touch anything in the bag?"

"No, just the outside, and we wore gloves," said Marlys

"Give the clerk your names and numbers in case we need anymore information, or decide we need fingerprints to match any on the outside. We'll take all this to the lab for testing."

After the women left, Maria observed, "There's no one in the lab."

"They just come in on weekends as needed. I know enough to check out the stain on the blouse. I'm quite sure it's not human blood."

Maria, her face ashen didn't even hear Belkin's last comment. She concentrated on not upchucking the bile in her throat. Her classes in evidence and crime scenes hadn't prepared her for this. Trying to seem more professional than she felt, Maria stated, "This looks like she was abducted and whoever did it threw this bag out his or her car window."

"Bullsh!" exploded Belkin. "If this crap belongs to the doctor, she threw it out herself, very conveniently by a sign where it was bound to be noticed."

Maria narrowed her eyes. "I'm going to call Linda Hernandez to see if she can identify the blouse and hair."

"Oh, sure, I bet she'll run right down after what we put her through Thursday night."

Maria answered evenly, "I've already talked to her this morning. She and her family are in Victoria distributing posters with Rhonda's photo."

"My, my, you two have gotten quite chummy since yesterday."

Maria ignored him, called Linda. "We have received some things which appear to belong to Dr. Rhonda." She paused. "We need you to identify them."

"We're on our way home and just crossed the harbor bridge. We'll there soon," Linda choked out, frantic from the news. *Forgive me, Rhonda, for thinking you left on your own.*

Linda and Dave arrived. Belkin, showed Linda the blouse, and Dave had to hold up his wife to keep her from keeling over.

"Don't panic," admonished Belkin. "We don't know for certain it's a bloodstain. Probably food. Can you identify this?"

"Yes, murmured Linda. That's the blouse and it looks like her ..." She couldn't continue. *She was abducted and, oh, I can't think the worst. Rhonda and Sandra weren't the same person.* She looked at her husband who had the strangest look on his face. She sobbed, "Who has her? Who chopped off her ... Where is she?"

Maria, who had time to study the stain and agreed it wasn't blood, spoke softly, "Dr. Hernandez, please don't give up hope."

"Not until we have a body," added Belkin, which brought more tears.

Belkin went to the lab, and Maria urged Mr. Hernandez to take his wife home. When Belkin came back, Maria tore into her superior. "Why did you have to say that?"

"Gonzales, without a body, we have no proof that Dr. Rhonda is a victim of a crime."

"But, couldn't we still search for her. After all it seems she committed a couple crimes herself."

"Like littering?" he joked.

"Obstructing justice and fraud and probably ..."

"Let it go, Maria. The doc, for reasons we will never know, ran off. That's not a crime and we have wasted a whole week on this. I'll let the Chief know the case is closed."

"But, we have no proof she ran away. We have no proof she bought the car. We have no proof at all."

"Maria. I appreciate how hard you've worked on this NON-case, but it's a beautiful day. I could get in some golf and maybe you and your fellow could go to Port Aransas and watch dolphins."

Watch dolphins NOW? You condescending ... "But what about the lab work?"

"Okay, okay, I'll run a quick test but if you just get a whiff of the stain, it smells faintly like hot sauce."

Maria had turned on the computer and was beginning to google when Stan returned. "Yup! Type B Positive hot sauce. I'm outta here."

Relief poured over Maria but quickly was replaced by her unshakeable need to do more to solve the case. "Do what you want. I have something more I want to check out. The Chief gave us more time and I plan to make use of it. I still might be able to prove…"

"Suit yourself," interrupted her brash partner, "but I have all I need to know that this is a damned soap opera not a criminal case. Definitely not worth pursuing further."

"I disagree."

"Bulsh."

Maria jumped out of her chair, stood up as tall as she could at 5'3" to look her partner in the eye, "Detective Belkin, I think you're the one full of bulsh."

Stan backed off. As soon as he left the PD, he broke into a grin.

After he left, Maria checked the national criminal database to see if there was anyone who had been chopping off the hair of victims. She worked for hours but found nothing. She checked social media for anything relevant and though the missing doctor still was a major topic of conversation, the detective wasted time on bizarre tips and theories while learning nothing helpful. When she returned home, she planned to check over her big chart and look for anything she might have forgotten or overlooked.

Before leaving she sat at her PD desk and deliberated if she should check out one theory that cropped up repeatedly: Linda's husband and the missing doctor were having an affair but she wanted to break it off and confess all to her best friend so he had to do away with her. Maria thought about how Mr. Hernandez had seemed the night they'd brought his wife in. *Highly upset, but no more so than a man whose wife had been arrested. At the vigil he was the picture of a loving father and supportive spouse. Today he seemed drained of any reactions. Still, there was something that didn't seem quite right with him but what did they have to go on? Nothing. Except according to Dr. Linda, Rhonda didn't date and Dave was the only man she seemed to know outside the office.*

Suddenly Maria remembered the birth control pills she had found in Rhonda's purse. *Why didn't I think of this before? We already should have talked to him alone and now I think we need to do that to find out about his wife's possible involvement and then we ask about his suspected affair with Rhonda. We might have to beg for an extension. I need to reach Stan about this.*

Maria called Stan, but he didn't answer. It was too complicated to leave on voicemail so she hung up. Too tired to do anything more, the detective quit for the day. Her watch showed 6:45 PM. A long Saturday.

CHAPTER THIRTY-THREE

Denied

Even though exhausted, Brian agreed to meet Sandra Saturday afternoon. Friends of his wife were having a baby shower for her so they couldn't be together anyway. Besides he always was glad to see his first love. Though he had dated many women after he and Sandra broke up, it took a long time until he found Gracie, someone else he could love as he had Sandra. It pleased him that Grace and Sandra had become friends during the course of his marriage.

Brian figured that Sandra hadn't visited Grace and him for two/three years. Sandra had called a few months ago to tell them she was having some mail sent there, which she had done for years, and not to forward it as that would be a good reason to come visit.

Because he no longer drank, he waited for Sandra at a coffee shop. Brian thought about how he'd changed since he first met Sandra behind the bar in a little Oklahoma town. Though at the time he thought himself clever and above the law, he was a criminal and he continued with his illegal career until a few months ago. He went with Grace to her
O.B. check-up and together they viewed their own unborn daughter. Touched beyond belief, Brian knew the little one deserved a better father than the man he'd been so long, the man who drank too much and made his living illegally. He had been extremely fortunate not to be found out, which was reason enough to quit while he was ahead. Before he wound

up in prison. But now because of his own child he couldn't continue his criminal ways. He always had told Grace he was a realtor, and explained he needed a change when he found a job with an international financial company. She wasn't too happy with his overseas trips though conceded the money was better. Brian decided he should tell Sandra, about all this and she appeared, smiling broadly.

Sandra loved coffee shops, the aromas and the sounds. Robust coffee, which always smelled better than it tasted, gentle steamed milk, spicy teas and the hiss of the specialty machines, the happy chatter of patrons, who paid outrageous prices for the beverages but no cover charge for the incredible ambiance. Sandra felt confident that everything would go right in such a pleasant, comfort-giving place.

"Sandra!"

Sandra heard Brian's voice before she saw him.

"I hardly recognized you. I've never seen you with such short hair, not to mention a different color."

"Do you like it?'

"Sure, what's not to like? It's classy, really suits you."

"You're looking good yourself."

"Thanks, but I know I look sleep deprived after that trip to UK."

"Just practice for when the baby comes."

"Pul-leese, don't say that. Now, what is it you want to talk about? And, first, I need to tell you I'm not in the business anymore. By the way, how's your half-sister? Still a successful a physician in Texas?"

Sandra ignored the last two questions and focused on the bombshell he'd dropped.

"What do you mean you're not in the business?"

"Sandra, I'm going to be a father. I want to be the kind of father my little girl can look up to, and from what you told me about your dad, you can understand that."

"I do understand, but Brian, I really need your help."

"I'm sorry, I can't. I'm completely legit now, work for a big international finance company, and make a better salary.

"But you still have all that knowledge, don't you?"

"Your point?"

"Couldn't you just provide some documentation for teacher re-licensure in Oklahoma?"

"No, Sandra,"

"What will I do?"

"Sandra, you're smart. If you want to teach, go to college and work hard like everyone else."

"But I've worked hard and done well at all my jobs."

"Sure, but I enabled you to take short-cuts to get those jobs. Now you'll be able to get them on your own. We both got what we wanted by dishonesty. I no longer want any part of that and you shouldn't either."

"You won't help me?" Sandra asked in complete disbelief.

"My company could loan you money for tuition."

Sandra stood up, with ice in her eyes and voice, rejecting him and his offer. "That won't be necessary." She turned away but looked back, and in a defeated tone said, "Congratulation in advance on the arrival of the baby. I won't bother you again."

As she walked towards the door, Brian jumped up. "Now, Sandra, don't be that way. You're still a terrific person. Both Grace and I want your friendship."

Sandra shook her head and continued walking.

Brian followed. "Sandra, please, I'm sorry." His voice turned gruffer, "I trust you won't take this out on me."

"Brian," Sandra spoke softly, " I promised long ago that if I got in trouble, I wouldn't reveal who had produced false documents for me, and I won't now. Good-bye."

Brian believed her but regretted the way this was turning out. All the way home he thought about the relationship he had with Sandra. *Why do I still care so much about her? I do trust her and I haven't kept on good terms with her just so she wouldn't disclose my illegal activities. I have Grace and soon our baby, but I can't help having feeling for Sandra. She never answered how the sister that was supporting her is doing. Did they have a falling-out? Is that why she wants to teach!* Then it struck him. The phone calls. *Grace mentioned someone looking for her. Could Sandra -- or her sister -- be in trouble?*

Sandra went back to her hotel room feeling completely dejected. She had never gotten over her first love, but also had kept in touch with Brian because she could depend on his help. What a blow.

The distraught woman picked up her cell phone from the chiffonier and saw several voicemails. One came from Linda. The others came from the PD in Corpus. She couldn't listen to any of them, too upset. A text came in from Brian.

Please don't leave things this way.

Come over tomorrow and we'll have a cookout.

Her immediate text response, which said "No thank you," she deleted as she pondered whether Brian might have had a change of heart. She brightened up as she thought, *Maybe Brian truly feels sorry for turning me down.* She hadn't even explained why she wanted the change. Maybe he would help her after all if she told him everything. She texted back to ask what time to come.

Sandra seldom had felt so lonely in her life. Her impulse was to pick up the phone to call Linda, to tell her the truth, but Sandra lacked the courage. How had Linda tracked her to Chicago? Sandra remembered. Once Rhonda had given Linda the Cavendish home phone number as an emergency contact in case she couldn't reach her by cell. Sandra recalled that at the time Rhonda worried excessively about the new pet-sitting service she'd contracted to care for Poppy when she went out of town. She wished Rhonda hadn't given out the number, but too late now. It complicated things.

She hoped Linda would accept that Rhonda was never coming back, but apparently Dr. Linda wanted to know what had happened to her friend. It had moved Sandra that Linda would do anything for her friend. Sandra felt terrible that Rhonda's best friend, by her words and the sound of her voice, missed her and worried about her. Rhonda had thought the world of Linda, for good reason.

So unless he had changed his mind, Brian couldn't and wouldn't help her anymore. What was she going to do now? What were her options? Sandra wished everything hadn't conspired against her going to Mexico. She could have been happy there and could still go there if she bought a ticket a couple weeks in advance and put it on her card. One option. Sandra shuddered. No, she'd never step foot into another airport after the degradation she'd endured.

She could go back to Corpus Christi. It didn't mean confessing. As the missing Rhonda's sister, perhaps she'd be able to take over Rhonda's home, car, and Poppy.

She googled restaurants on her phone. She'd decided to make a dinner reservation at some five-star restaurant to cushion her disappointment; a $100 steak would help. She saw even more voicemails on the phone. She listened to the ones from the police department. They said basically the same thing: "A message for Sandra Lewis. Are you acquainted with Dr. Rhonda Collins? Please return this call."

No way! I don't plan to share any information with them about Rhonda. They can look all they want but they'll never find her or her body. I alone know she no longer exists, period.

Then she listened again to the one from. Linda. She didn't intend to respond, especially when she had realized that Linda had called her Rhonda.

CHAPTER THIRTY-FOUR

Not over yet

Maria had gone to sleep thinking that the first thing in the morning she would call Stan and see if he'd agree to summon Dave Hernandez for questioning but a phone call awakened Maria and postponed that plan. It was the SCCPD. The police in San Antonio had arranged for a tow for a gray Taurus with keys on the seat, abandoned in an office parking lot where Sandra had left it forever when she took a taxi to the airport. A contractor planned to resurface the parking some time during the weekend, or the car could have sat there for months. The car and license matched that of the description and license of the alert sent out by the SCCPD. Fingerprints and hair samples had been taken from the car and would be sent to Corpus.

Maria felt elated. If the DNA matched, they would know for certain the driver of the Taurus and the BMW was the same person. Perhaps the doctor had left the car, taken a cab to the airport and flown to Chicago. Excited about bringing the case to an end, Maria had a brilliant thought and asked if she could pick up the samples and the car today to speed things up. The Sunday dispatcher, who didn't realize she couldn't authorize this, agreed with the plan. Maria awakened her soon-to-be fiancé with a call.

"How would you like a road trip to San Antonio?" she asked and added urgently, "We need to leave immediately."

After grousing that this was his only day to sleep in, Xavier surrendered and soon he and Maria were on their way. They didn't look forward to having to drive home separately, with Maria driving the now-famous Taurus, but, at least, Maria felt certain the SCCPD would pay for the gas for both vehicles. She called the SCCPD to let them know she was on her way to San Antonio to collect the car and samples; the dispatcher assumed she had received authorization to do this.

When they reached the downtown SA police station they learned samples already had been sent, and the desk clerk had no idea where the car was. Maria realized that in her extreme enthusiasm, she had screwed up, overlooking correct protocol to obtain either the samples or the car. *No need to tell Xavier.*

Xavier and Maria looked at each other. Feeling pretty subdued by her mistake, Maria agreed with Xavier that just so the day wasn't a total bust they'd go to River Walk for a drink, then to El Mercado for a late lunch at Mi Tierra. As they sipped their margaritas, Maria was lost in thought about the evidence in the hands of the San Antonio PD, but she tried to focus on the moment. It was San Antonio, after all. They did a bit of shopping and walked through the beautiful grounds of the Alamo, which both had visited many times before, always with a feeling of true Texan pride.

The case never was far from Maria's mind. While Xavier went to look for a pottery flowerpot for his mother, Maria called the number for Sandra Lewis, given her by Linda. She didn't gain much from the call except she thought Sandra sounded more frantic than truthful. Sandra had given her no information about the missing woman. She seemed genuinely concerned about her sister, but it could have been an act.

On the way home, Maria called the chief to admit to him the trip had been wasted but didn't explain her part in the debacle. Fortunately for her, he didn't seem to care. All day reporters had hounded him to death about the stained shirt and shorn hair. Even though it was Sunday, which should have been "MY day of rest", he planned to issue a statement that it all was a hoax, case closed.

Maria sighed. Stan would be happy, but for her it wasn't over. There was more she needed to check out.

CHAPTER THIRTY-FIVE

Same Sunday in Chicago

Sunday morning Sandra found a church service, as Rhonda would have done. The pastor preached on forgiveness, and the run-away from Corpus Christ felt comforted to know that not only had God forgiven what Sandra had done but already had forgotten about it. Sandra clung to the pastor's message to help her deal with all the deceit she had felt necessary. Forgiveness was on her mind as she rode on the subway to her hotel.

Would the people Rhonda had hurt, her colleagues, patients, best friends, forgive her that easily? Could she forgive Felicity Ritter for ruining the good thing she and Rhonda had going? No. What about her parents? Her alcoholic mom gave in to hopelessness, and Sandra could forgive her. Her alcoholic dad? He'd had some tough breaks or maybe he wouldn't have become an abusive drunk. Yes, she'd begun to forgive him. The pastor had said we should be forgiving towards people who hurt us especially those who suffer from illnesses like alcoholism, mental problems.

She went back to the hotel. Lonely and bored, she listened to voicemails. The most recent began, "Rhonda, this is Linda. There was a huge vigil for you Friday night. There were over three hundred people in the Cielo Vista parking lot, all praying for your safe return. Then on Saturday many of the same people distributed posters of you all around Corpus and the surrounding towns, as far north as Victoria and as far south as Kingsville."

Sandra was dumbfounded. *All those people wanting Rhonda to return. I guess except for fooling around with her best friend's husband, something no one knew but me, she appeared to be a stellar person. Of course, if they knew how Rhonda deceived them, would they be praying and putting up posters?* Another voicemail from Linda: "Please come back. We'll make you sure you have police protection so whoever it was that caused you to leave won't be able to hurt you. I miss you so, my friend."

Linda had been such a good friend to Rhonda. Her love obvious, the best friend's calls made tough Sandra break down in tears. It occurred to her that Linda must have given the police her number, the one she had to have gotten from that sweet but ditzy Grace. *I never should have given that to her. I have no on but myself to blame for this development but myself.* Sandra listened to an earlier call from Linda,

"Rhonda, I am so worried about you. No matter what has happened, you know I will stand by you."

The phone chimed and startled Sandra. She answered without checking Caller I.D.

"Is this Sandra Lewis?"

"It is." She could hear car sounds and panicked when she heard, "This is Officer Maria Gonzales with the Corpus Christi South Police Department." Sandra paled. *Have they found out where I am? Are they coming after me? Dear God, please help me."*

"We have been trying to reach you. Are you acquainted with Dr. Rhonda Collins?"

"Yes, she's my sister. Actually, half-sister. Same mother."

"When's the last time you saw her?"

Sandra swallowed and starting making things up, easy enough for a pathological liar. "It's been a while because I live in Chicago, but we keep in touch."

"When last did you speak with her?"

"It's been two, three weeks."

"Do you know where she is today?"

"What do you mean, is something wrong?"

"We just want to know if you'd have any idea where she is today?"

Sandra felt trapped. Perspiration stained a new Nordstrom shirt. "She's a doctor. I suppose she's at her clinic. Oh, wait, today's Sunday. Duh, I went to church, I should know what day it is! I know they aren't open weekends. She loves to go to the beach on her days off. Please tell me what this is about."

"Dr. Collins left her job at noon on Monday and hasn't been seen since.

Sandra didn't have to pretend to be scared, as shown in her voice. "What happened to Rhonda? What happened to my sister?"

"That's what we want to know. Is there any other number where we can reach you and what is your address?"

"This is the only phone number I have, and..." Grabbing a phone book, she gave her a false address, which Maria would later verify did not belong to her.

"Thank you and please call if she gets in touch with you."

"I will." Sandra was on the brink of hysteria, and it showed her voice.

She pressed "end" on the phone. How she wished she could press "end" to all police phone calls.

Why did Grace have to make my new number available to Linda and the Police Department? I have to change the number. I suppose that will cost another fortune.

She barely had time to compose herself before Brian called her on his cell to say he'd be there within minutes. She'd told him she could get a cab, but he had insisted. *Maybe he wanted time alone with her to talk more? Perhaps he's softening?*

No time to shower. She sponged off and changed her shirt.

On the way he asked, "Are you sure you want to teach? I remember so well how sick you got of everything about teaching."

"That's true, except for the kids. Now I'm more mature, I think I could handle it better."

"Sandra, I'm sorry the timing is wrong for me to help you, but let me tell you how much better I feel about myself since I found an honest job. I know you'll feel the same way."

Her response was not what he'd expected from the headstrong woman he once had loved. "Brian, I understand why you won't help me. I've decided to take your advice and go to college."

"Sandra, you're as incredible as ever. You can do it."

They had reached Brian's apartment. He said, almost pleadingly, "You won't tell Grace any of this, will you?"

Sandra smiled. "Just because you're a rat doesn't mean I'm not still crazy about your wife. She informed me you're out of the 'real estate business'. I didn't mention anything then and won't now. Oh, yes, she said she knows about us."

Brian acted embarrassed. " I thought with the baby coming, Grace and I shouldn't have any secrets about our past love lives."

"It's okay." Sandra sounded sad and resigned. *Don't worry. I know better than to become involved with a married man.*

As they enjoyed the hamburgers Brian had grilled, Grace asked, "Sandy, did that woman from Corpus Christi ever get a hold of you? She thought you might know the whereabouts of her friend Rhonda."

"Yes, she called me, I haven't gotten back to her yet, but the only Rhonda I know is my sister who lives in Oklahoma."

"Hon, Is that the same woman who you said I was supposed to call back?" Brian asked Grace.

"Yes, a Dr. Hernandez. I told her I didn't know Rhonda but you might."

"I forgot to call her, but I don't know a Rhonda either."

Brian and Sandra exchanged a wry smile and a shrug about the woman neither of them knew. "How easily he lies," thought Sandra, as if she weren't the queen of untruthfulness.

CHAPTER THIRTY-SIX

New tactic

A week had passed since Rhonda's disappearance. The public still gossiped about the "blood-stained blouse and the chopped off long blonde hair" when Sunday the Chief issued a statement to all reporters. "The Dr. Collins case is closed. False evidence was planted in her car and along the highway. No crime was committed. The doctor, for reasons known only to her left on her own." Though closed, further investigation would continue, but the public didn't need to know that.

Some believed the hoax; most didn't. Marlys and her friends certainly didn't. They knew that someday the Chief of Police would choke on his words when Rhonda's body was found or when her kidnapper finally demanded money for her release.

Maria had this Monday off, but nothing would have kept her from her job. She had been in close contact with Linda the rest of the weekend. Linda repeatedly had called the number Grace Cavendish had given for Sandra Lewis. Linda shared that she referred to Sandra on the phone as Rhonda because in her heart she believed they were one and the same. "Maybe I think that because," Linda, near tears said. "I just can't accept that she's -- I can hardly say it --dead. If only I could hear something from her."

How the young officer wished to confide that Sandra apparently had put her hairstylist skills to use in an attempt to leave every trace of Rhonda behind. Maria had decided last night, after the futile but fun day in San Antonio, that she owed it to the case to follow up on the whole hairstylist turned doctor angle and, for now, to drop suspicions about Linda's husband. Maria intended to go to the clinic and asks to examine Rhonda's credentials. If she could prove they were fraudulent, Maria would have Rhonda's motive for her need to disappear after Felicity Ritter confronted her.

CHAPTER THIRTY-SEVEN

Case closed

It was the usual harum-scarum Monday morning at the clinic with added drama from the announcement that after only one week Chief Ortiz had declared the Dr. Rhonda case closed. Carla and Amy, clinic receptionists, voiced their feelings about the "do nothing cops" and endlessly discussed the fate that poor Rhonda must have met. They hated not knowing.

Several staff members suggested that Dr. Ron find the private detective he'd talked about. Dr. Ron promised to do that after he interviewed applicants for a nurse practitioner job to ease the caseload for the doctors. Waiting for the time of the first interview, he looked up phone numbers under Private Investigators in the city's Dex book. With a rap on the door, Gonzales interrupted him.

"I thought the cased was closed," Ron growled and offered Maria a look that matched his tone.

"Unofficially, but there still are some loose ends that need tying up, and I need your help.

"All right."

"How carefully did you check Dr. Rhonda's records when you hired her?

"Why?"

"We have reason to believe her records aren't authentic."

"That's impossible!" Ron's voice rose with each sentence. "She was an excellent doctor. Remember, she won the Distinguished Doctor of the Year award. You don't believe what Felicity said, do you?"

"I should have asked how your wife's aunt is."

"Haven't talked to my wife today, but Felicity has been making amazing improvement. She had a left side stroke, and these things take time."

"I wish her well and now may I ask if you checked Dr. Collins' records and references?"

Dr. Ron had trouble understanding why the detective would ask that. His pride in his staff and his own ego made it difficult for him to think there could be anything about Dr Rhonda's records to raise suspicion. "Her medical school credentials were incredible, and she had terrific references from the hospitals where she interned and did her residency. That and her sparkling personality convinced me that I should hire her. I've never regretted it. She's been a fantastic doctor, an asset to this clinic."

"I need to examine her records."

He grabbed Rhonda's file from a cabinet and shoved it at her. "Suit yourself. I have to interview some applicants but can do that in Rhonda's office. Look them over but don't remove them from my office."

"I won't." (*At least for now and only if I don't need a warrant from the chief.*) "May I use your computer?"

"Go ahead."

Maria googled the med school in Pennsylvania from which Rhonda Collins had graduated. It either had closed or never had existed. She found the hospital where the graduate had interned and placed a call. An employee in the personnel officer could find no intern by that name in their well-kept records. Maria asked if they had an intern named Sandra Dee Lewis. They hadn't. The same proved true for the hospital where Rhonda claimed to have done residency.

Linda spotted Maria in Ron's office and decided to tell her she had received a return call from Brian Cavendish. "Like his wife, he denied knowing Rhonda."

"I guess this means Rhonda used an alias when she visited them."

Maria gave her a strange look. "I think Rhonda is the alias. I have something to tell both you and Dr. Brooks." Soon after, Ron returned to his office.

"I've checked the medical school from which Rhonda graduated and the hospitals where she trained. The school doesn't exist and there are no records for her in either hospital. Her records don't appear to be authentic."

Both doctors looked stricken.

"You may press charges for impersonation, false documentation. Law enforcement will have to reopen the case."

"No!" shouted Ron, as he slammed his office door. "The reputation of this clinic is too important. I DON'T want it to get out that Rhonda wasn't an MD." He paused, "If she had jeopardized a patient, naturally I would file charges but she didn't. We still don't know if she disappeared because of what Mel's aunt said. As far as we are concerned, she has just disappeared. What happened to her will remain a mystery. I don't want anyone else here to know about this."

As an after-thought, he added, "I'll put it on our website: 'Dr. Rhonda Collins no longer is affiliated with this clinic.' Let everyone guess what happened to her."

The phone rang. Dr. Ron answered with more calmness than he felt. He heard his wife's voice and asked, "How's Fe?"

"She's better. Still not able to talk and as I've told you, there's something she keeps trying to communicate. Today I thought she might be up to it so I handed her a piece of paper and a pen. With the hand that isn't paralyzed, her left, she scrawled slowly: "Doctor is Sandra Lewis.""

Ron shared the news with Officer Gonzales and Dr. Hernandez.

Felicity Ritter had recognized Rhonda. She had been her hairdresser. Dr. Rhonda Collins had been exposed as a fraud. Or had she?

CHAPTER THIRTY-EIGHT

Full disclosure

A week had passed since her disappearance. In an undisclosed location, Rhonda relived that day, at least until it became too distressing.

Monday mornings never failed to be busy at the clinic, and Rhonda didn't feel quite up to what she knew was ahead. She felt more than a little out of sorts because of something that happened during the weekend. That something was breaking up with her lover. In one way it was a relief because there was nothing right about this relationship, but, as lovers, he had made her feel special and cherished. Their relationship completed the joy she had in her new life. She knew she also provided a break for Dave, who couldn't relax in his home full of noisy little boys. Neither Rhonda nor the husband wanted to hurt Linda, but Rhonda and Dave tended to forget about that when they were in each other's arms.

It had started at a Cielo Vista picnic for staff and families on a beautiful late summer day but ended abruptly when it started to rain. Rhonda then discovered a flat tire on her sister's ancient red pick-up. Dave, husband of Dr. Linda Hernandez with whom Rhonda quickly had become acquainted, volunteered to help. He sent his family home and told them that he'd have Rhonda drop him off as soon as he put on a spare. Rhonda thanked her colleague for the help her husband was giving her, and Linda, not distrustful of her husband, said she was happy he could help.

Dave had been attracted to his wife's friend all afternoon and instead of having Rhonda drop him off, they went to Rhonda's townhouse and had sex. They both felt guilty afterwards and swore it would never happen again; but the attraction was too great. It became routine that whenever Dave had been out of town for work, he'd stop at Rhonda's for some extra-marital loving at her peaceful home before returning to the pandemonium at his.

Rhonda and Linda became close, and Rhonda often joined Linda and Dave and their boys for holidays and other activities. The lovers pretended they were nothing more than family friends. Dave helped Rhonda purchase her BMW; and with the help of Dave, who was an investment broker, Rhonda made many sound investments. All the time that the pair interacted as good friends, they continued their illicit passionate affair.

The many times they came together blurred -- up until last night. Coming home from a trip to Dallas, Dave stopped as planned. Rhonda was not waiting in a provocative negligee or costume with a martini in her hand and a meal in the oven.

"Dave, this can't continue. We've been lucky all this time that Linda hasn't found out. It's bad enough that you keeping breaking your marital vows, but I'm betraying my best friend and I think that's even worse."

"What brought this on? You know I'm capable of loving both of you," He reached to bring Rhonda to him but she pulled away. "No, Dave, this is it. It breaks my heart because I love being with you but I don't love you. I love your wife in the purest possible way. It's over."

"We've has this discussion before, Rhonda. We're not hurting anyone. Please, I want you, I need you in my life. I'm a better husband and father because of the reprieve you offer."

"Dave, it hit me this morning in church. Pastor Morton talked about choosing one path in life and how a little bird couldn't straddle two branches for any length of time before he fell through the widening distance between them. It's going to catch up with us, Dave. You have to be true to Linda and the boys." It took all the strength she had to show him to the door. " I will miss what we've had but you have to choose the branch with Linda and your sons."

"I can't do it," Dave had said but agreed it was over only when she threatened to tell Linda.

Rhonda had cried after Dave left, and Monday morning she was still morose over the decision it was necessary to make. With fake bravado she said out loud, "Oh, well. Nothing like wearing a new ensemble to cheer up a gal." She chose a tan pants suit, which the storeowner had referred to as "pecan", and an ivory silk blouse. Newly purchased leather heels and purse, in a little darker tan, completed the ensemble. When she stepped outside to give her pup one last time to relieve himself, she decided it was too hot for the jacket and left it behind. At the clinic she stopped in Linda's office to show her since her best friend had been with her when she bought the blouse on a recent girls' weekend in San Antonio.

Free of responsibilities, they had such a great time shopping and staying at a hotel that once was a convent on River Walk. They had enjoyed a dinner cruise on the river. Delicious food. After the cruise ended, they topped off the evening with a stop at the Rocky Mountain Chocolate Company. Rhonda had taken a photo of Linda with the company's signature bear, and a stranger took a picture of both of them on one of the bridges. They had prints made for each of them of that. Who could have foretold the photo of two attractive women, one blonde, one brunette, would wind up a police department evidence room?

Linda always was fun. Sometimes, like last Monday, they shared such foolishness. She'd shown Linda the perfect accessories she's bought to wear with a fall pants suit and the pricey silk blouse Linda had talked her into buying in San Antonio. Rhonda had urged her friend to feel the butter-soft leather pumps and purse. After running her hands over the purse, Linda made a big deal of kneeling at her feet and putting her hands all over the shoes. What if Dr. Ron or another staff member had walked in on them? Rhonda smiled.

She recalled how late that same morning she was seeing her last patient, a pleasant older woman with mild arthritis, when she heard a familiar loud voice in the hallway. There was no mistaking that voice. Felicity Ritter, Sandra's old customer. Rhonda delayed her patient longer than could be justified in hopes she could avoid an encounter with Miss Felicity. But, as she proceeded to leave the building, Felicity saw her and because her sister looked like her, called her "Sandra Lewis". She'd have some explaining to do since she told everyone that she had no family. Rhonda and Sandra had made a deal -- if someone discovered the connection between the sisters, it would be expedient for both to leave Corpus. To Rhonda that meant the end of her career, her friends, her home, everything. Rhonda always had feared the possibility of being mistaken for Sandra and the complications this would cause. *That's why I wrote a will and diverted all my assets to her.*

The plan when she left the clinic was to withdraw all her money from the bank and credit union and be on her way to Mexico before anyone at the clinic realized she was missing. But time-consuming impediments delayed her. First she found a text from Dave. She texted back. He'd meet her at the Vega Building around 12:30 for what he hoped would be a quick persuasive talk, or else.

She stopped at her bank to withdraw all her money, but that didn't happen. It was her money but there was a limit to how much she could withdraw. After nabbing the limit, she paid a visit to her safety deposit box and took out all of hers and Sandra's important documents plus a large chunk of cash. She made a big deal of feeling safer with her valuables in a safety deposit box during the end of hurricane system, when most hurricanes hit the west Gulf coast. She remembered the teller speaking condescendingly to her, "The storms they're talking about now are going towards Mexico, and they aren't supposed to turn into hurricanes anyway. But you're smart to keep your valuables with us --this building has eighteen-inch hurricane strength concrete walls that are cabled from the roof and anchored below the ground."

Rhonda went into a restroom on the same floor. In the stall she asked herself out loud. "How can I do this? Shirk my responsibilities? Abandon my poor patients? My colleagues? Linda, the best friend I've ever had? Poppy? Oh, no, in all the happenings today I hadn't even thought of Poppy. She disguised her voice to call the office at the complex to tell the manager a little dog was barking, and he'd better check on it. The line was busy.

She didn't know an elderly woman, washing her hands, watched Rhonda go into a stall and listened to her normal voice and the disguised one, and jumped to all the wrong conclusions.

Did she have the courage to do the right thing? To go back to the clinic, confess to Ron, and suffer the deserved consequences? She couldn't muster the courage to do the right thing.

Instead of escaping, maybe -- she sobbed a little-- the best thing for all was for her to end her life. She always carried a scalpel for protection. She knew how to use it but all the blood she'd leave for someone to clean up? She couldn't. There were other ways. She couldn't swim, as she once had told Linda. All she needed to do was cross the causeway to North Padre, go to the beach, attach some weights -- like the ankle weights in her gym bag -- wade out into the waves and keep walking.

No! She needed her sister Sandra to do the thinking. She wouldn't be so cowardly. A few minutes later the lives of Rhonda and Sandra collided in the restroom on the same floor as the Community Credit Union.

Over coffee and cinnamon rolls from room service, Sandra also relived the Monday a week ago. It was too unsettling to recall what she'd done when she and Rhonda met in the restroom outside the credit union so she skipped that part.

Locating Rhonda's car, Sandra had put the doctor's purse and heels on the seat to make it look like an abduction. First she thought it was prudent to wear Rhonda's outfit so if anyone from the credit union saw her by the BMW they'd think it was Rhonda. Then she was afraid as soon as Rhonda was reported missing, they'd be looking for a tall blonde in nut brown and ivory. Sandra had no idea a man had spotted the car and could have seen her; but tired of waiting, he had gone inside to look for Rhonda right before Sandra left the restroom. They had missed each other by less than a minute. He would have thought Sandra was Rhonda, and Sandra would have recognized him from a photo Rhonda had shown her sister. A picture of her lover, Linda's husband, Dave. Sandra was far from perfect, but it disgusted her that Rhonda slept with a married man. Rhonda kept this affair very quiet to protect her stellar image.

Sandra spied Rhonda's gym bag in the back seat and put on her black hoodie that would be uncomfortably hot with afternoon temps reaching the high 80s; she'd have to put up with it because it covered most of her hair and all but the top of the blouse. She remembered the scalpel left behind in the restroom and returned to get it. Sandra intended to put it in the trunk after wiping off her fingerprints with some hand sanitizer found in the gym bag but there was such an odor coming out of the trunk that she shut the lid and slid the surgical knife into the gym bag. The keys she tossed under the car since neither she nor Rhonda had further use for them.

Vacating the ramp, Sandra bought a newspaper and called an ad for a car. A kid met her at a Stripes that was within walking distance. She ordered two burritos and dipped them repeatedly in the hot sauce she's learned to love in Corpus. She was so uncomfortable that she'd unzipped the hoodie. Then carelessly she'd dribbled sauce all over Rhonda's lovely expensive blouse. She dabbed it with a paper napkin, which just spread it and made it look worse. She wound up zipping up the jacket to cover the stain, only until she could buy some other apparel.

She purchased the kid's car for a ridiculous amount and then stopped in the Stripes restroom before driving to a Wal-Mart. She wanted to get rid of Rhonda's phone. She scrolled through recent calls. There was the one she'd made to the car seller and the last one Rhonda had made, presumably to let her know where to meet her. Actually that one was to the office of the manager of the townhouse. She tossed the phone in a toilet and flushed. It swirled around but wouldn't go down. She wasn't about to fish in a public toilet for it. Probably the water had ruined it. *Should have done something else with it, like throw it down a storm sewer or into the bay.*

At one of the many Wal-Marts in the area she bought scissors, hair color, some toiletries and a few articles of clothing. She then looked for a motel where no one would picture Rhonda, the seedy Liberty Motel.

After playing beauty salon, she'd napped, eaten a pizza, and stopped to see if Poppy was barking himself to death. She had escaped detection, twice, by a cop in front of Rhonda's townhouse, after thinking she'd damaged the car's muffler in a monster pothole and before she tossed trash from her car, got gas and started towards Brownsville. In a downpour she'd stopped to ditch the scalpel, which would rust away for decades beside the Brownsville road. Then she was hailed by a trooper, who unwittingly aided her in escaping to San Antonio until the weather favored her Mexico escape.

By then it was Tuesday morning. She found a nice motel but ditched the car because it had occurred to her it was hotter than she'd been in the hoodie. As long as her plan for a quick get-away had failed, she decided to stay another night and accessed the Internet for news from Corpus Christi. As she anticipated, police searched for Rhonda. Sandra patted herself on the back for doing what's she'd done to keep from looking like the person of interest. Then she read about the stolen Taurus. She returned to it and
locked the keys in it.

The rest was one misadventure after another. The security fiasco at the airport, missing her plane to Houston, all the flight delays, sleeping and suffering from food poisoning in the SA airport, finally reaching Chicago, having Brian turn down her plea for help and still being in Chicago right now.

CHAPTER THIRTY-NINE

Withholding

Maria proceeded to headquarters after her discovery at the clinic. She should have reported her findings about the forged credentials to the Chief and Belkin but she didn't. After all the Chief closed the case and said he wouldn't reopen unless they found her body; Stan had agreed. Rhonda, it seems, had promoted herself from hairdresser to doctor; but if Ron didn't press charges, it wasn't a police matter. Just for her own curiosity, she called Rhonda's attorney.

"This is Maria Gonzales with the SCCPD in regards to the missing doctor. We need to know the name of her one beneficiary.

"Not without a warrant."

"I'll bring one."

She knocked on the Chief's door. "I need to go to the missing woman's attorney with a warrant. I think this will tell why the doctor left town."

"Gonzales, what don't you understand about a case being closed?"

"Sir, I received more information from San Antonio that will prove that the doctor did buy the Bennetts' car and drove it there."

"And? Did she commit a crime?"

"Possibly, but to protect my source, it has to be kept out of the papers."

"I already told the media the case is closed."

"And no one wants to press charges against her."

"Then why is this so damned important?"

"It's important because then there will be proof that she is not a missing person, just as you said from the first.

"Gonzales, you're driving me nuts. I'll sign the warrant if you'll promise me you won't pursue the case any further than this." Maria agreed though, like a grade school girl, had her fingers crossed behind her back.

Maria received the information she needed from the attorney. The beneficiary named to Rhonda's estate: Sandra D. Lewis. *Rhonda's disappearance was premeditated; once she was declared dead, Sandra aka Rhonda would get the money. Unless Sandra could make it look like Rhonda died and obtain the money -- her money -- sooner. I still need the DNA report to prove Rhonda and Sandra are the same person.*

The attorney's arrival intruded into her thoughts. "I have another document related to this." He handed her the copy of a separate letter naming Linda Hernandez, executor.

As she had gotten to know Linda better, Maria couldn't believe the woman had any part in this but now doubts crept into her mind. She had to ask, "Does she receive funds for that?'

"She could collect a fee for selling the car, the town home; but that isn't spelled out. As I recall Dr. Collins said she wanted someone local to take care of things in case of death since the beneficiary lived in Chicago."

Maria thanked the attorney for his time as he asked, "What happened to my client?"

To Maria's noncommittal response, he added, "What a fine, gracious woman."

CHAPTER FORTY

Secret revelation

That evening Linda felt ready to pour out her heart to her husband. As she began to talk, Dave realized how sleepless nights and loss of appetite had taken a toll on his wife. She'd lost weight; her lively brown eyes looked dull and sunken. He put his arms around her and realized how much he loved this woman and how fortunate they were to have Rhonda out of their lives. Dave encouraged Linda to talk, hoping it would help.

Even though proven wrong, she first explained her theory that her friend had assumed the name Rhonda when she went to med school, probably so an abusive husband wouldn't find her. She told him how in Mazatlan Rhonda had told her about a secret which could ruin everything. "It bothered me so much when she referred to the secret and said she might have to do something uncharacteristic. Now I understand what she meant."

Dave swallowed hard and looked tortured when he heard that and worried that Rhonda had told Linda about the affair, but Linda didn't seem to notice as she continued. "Today Officer Gonzales checked Rhonda's records, and we found out what her secret was. She never went to med school. All her records -- faked. Ron wants this kept quiet because only he and I were told, but we agreed we could tell our spouses."

For a second, Dave enjoyed relief as to the secret's content but then he felt as stunned as his wife. How could Rhonda have lived a lie like that? And gotten by with it? What if..." His thought was the same as anyone who learned the truth about Dr. Rhonda. What if, through her lack of education, she had harmed or even killed a patient, maybe a small child?

Linda began to sob, "I thought I knew her, and that she understood she could tell me anything." The friendship she thought had meant so much to both of them. Even though Rhonda had betrayed her, Linda still felt that her friend had a good reason for doing what she did and that their friendship and the happy memories they shared were genuine. She felt as if she was being ripped apart with sorrow.

Afraid she would awaken the boys, Dave attempted to calm her. He knew what he had to tell her certainly wouldn't accomplish that, but now he hated Rhonda as passionately as he had loved her and wanted his wife to realize her so-called duplicitous friend wasn't worth her tears. He was willing to risk all by full -- at least partial -- disclosure about the woman everyone had thought was near Perfection.

"Linda, I can't bear to see you so upset. Rhonda isn't worth it. She betrayed you and everyone else."

"But she must have had her reasons," Linda argued and pulled away.

"No, I think Rhonda just dreamed of being a doctor and found some con artist who could sell her the credentials she needed. That's an insult to you and any other doctor who worked so hard to get through everything necessary for being a doctor. I remember how you sweated out the boards. All she did was have her credentials manufactured. She played all of us for fools."

Linda, somehow, wasn't ready to give up the illusions of her friend. "But, Dave, she was my dearest friend, we had so much ..."

"Linda, you know you could have gone to jail because you wanted to help her. What would that have done to our boys?"

His wife didn't seem to hear him as she whispered through tears," But she was such a good doctor and such a good friend."

Dave couldn't stand it that Linda still defended Rhonda. He raised his voice, "Good doctor, maybe, but not a good friend."

"How can you say that? She was a great friend."

Dave had reached the boiling point. "Linda, she doesn't deserve your dedication. I love you and I never wanted you to find this out. It happened soon after you introduced Rhonda to me. We had a very brief affair."

Linda choked. She had tried to understand what would have driven Rhonda to lie about her credentials but this was beyond comprehension. Her best friend, the woman who seemed so virtuous, had betrayed her in the most personal way. And so had Dave. Her husband and best friend?

Too shocked to speak, beyond tears, Linda just stared in disbelief.

"Linda, you have to believe me, I love you and only you and always have. I have regretted this more than anything. I've never strayed before and our affair didn't last because both of us felt so much remorse that we agreed that you should never know and that it never would happen again."

Seeing his wife's look of anguish, he lied lamely, "I was the one who broke it off."

CHAPTER FORTY-ONE

Case Really Closed

By mid-October the Taurus had been returned to Corpus Christi, and all of the DNA reports were in Maria's grateful hands:

Rhonda's and Bennetts' DNA and prints in the Taurus
Rhonda's and Linda's in the BMW
Bit of Linda's hair but no prints at Rhonda's home
Rhonda's DNA and prints in abundance at home
Hair on hairbrush, hair from the BMW, hair in Taurus: all matched Rhonda's DNA

No third person involved. Case closed. Case really closed.

Smiling broadly, Maria leaned back in her chair. *I'm glad I persevered. Stan was right, but I proved it. Rhonda ran, and we know why because I thought to check her records and followed up things he wouldn't. The clinic isn't going to press charges so this case really is over. Unless we can find Rhonda and charge her with I don't know how many criminal counts of felonies, misdemeanor and infractions.*

The detective expedited arrangements to return the Bennetts' car, even though she didn't look forward to telling them the car had been stripped of its sound system. She drove the car to the family's home while Officer Vargas, who originally had been assigned to finding the Taurus, followed in a patrol car for the return trip to headquarters.

Bill Bennett answered the door and smiled when he saw Maria.

"Here's your car, Mr. Bennett. It's in good condition but I'm sorry to say at some point someone removed the sound system."

Nodding with sadness, Bill spoke. "I know. Austin confessed he sold it first for drug money and later sold the car."

"How is . . . are all of you?"

"Right now Austin and my wife are in Minnesota, where he's going through rehab at Hazelton. Gloria is attending a support group for parents there, and I'm going to one here. We compare notes daily. We're all going to be fine, and we owe it to you."

Maria smiled and gave him the keys to the car and an unprofessional but welcomed hug.

On the way back to the station, Maria told Vargas that it seemed miraculous that the car in his case wound up being the get-away car purchased by the missing person. She didn't expect a compliment but Vargas praised her. "You're the one that discovered the link between my car and your missing doctor."

Back at headquarters something still nagged Maria. She'd been thinking about Dr. Linda's husband. The more she had thought about him, the more suspicious his reactions seemed. They should have brought him in alone for questioning. *Maybe Belkin was right that he and Rhonda had an affair. I wonder if Mr. Hernandez wanted to break-up, and Rhonda threatened to tell his wife so he tried to do away with her. Or, maybe he just paid her to get out of town.*

Marie knew she'd have an impossible time convincing the chief to reopen the case when she had no evidence, but if there was a link between Rhonda and Dave Hernandez, they could have come to the wrong conclusion about Rhonda leaving on her own. (Not long after she would learn that Dave, indeed, had cheated on his wife, and unbelievable as it would have seemed to her today, she was the one who would urge Linda to try to salvage her marriage.) Maria decided to accept the Chief's ruling just as he stopped in her office to ask if Officer Gonzales would mind switching to the night shift the following day. She agreed and enjoyed her day off, catching up all she'd let go with her life while consumed with her first case. Something unexpected awaited her when she reported that night.

A hand-lettered banner greeted her with the words, "Congratulations, Maria, Rookie of the Year." A cake with similar lettering sat on the dispatcher's desk.

Stan stood there grinning, and then among the blur of colleagues chanting, "Speech!" and "Cut the cake!" Maria saw special faces: Xavier! Her parents and brother! Sydney! Obviously, Belkin was behind this party including the assemblage of her loved ones, who listened as the Chief said, "Quite frankly, I thought this woman was a pain in the you-know-what but I have to give credit for her attention to detail in solving the mystery of the Famed Missing Doctor and for putting up with another pain to all who know him, Detective -- or as the media called him -- Defective Belkin."

Amidst loud guffawing, Maria protested, "I'm guilty as charged for being a royal pain, but both you knew the doctor wasn't a crime victim from the first. I just proved what you figured out."

Belkin handed her a wrapped gift.

Maria put her fingers to her mouth in mock horror. "I sure hope it isn't what we found in the doctor's trunk."

"No, the forensics department hasn't found the cause of death in that case yet," Belkin quipped.

From the laughs Maria knew Belkin had made certain everyone knew what they'd found and how she had reacted. She postponed opening the gift as one colleague asked, "Well, what did you learn from busting your first case?"

Maria thought of many things, which included learning to work with a know-it-all partner, and keeping her emotions under control most of the time, but instead she smiled broadly and quipped, "A gal can change her hair color, but that color won't change her DNA."

CHAPTER FORTY-TWO

Moving on

Two weeks later, on a beautiful October day Linda called her brother-in-law, Tom Cantu, regarding a phone call she had received from Rhonda's attorney. "When Rhonda made out her will, a few months ago, she named me executor. She told me if anything happened to her, I should sell her house and car, with the proceeds going to her beneficiary."

"Did she ever tell you the name of her beneficiary?"

"No, Rhonda said she couldn't divulge the person, I never saw the will. I only have a letter from the attorney about being executor. But I know I now because of the police investigation. It's 'Sandra Lewis', 'Rhonda' was the alias."

"Rhonda diverted funds to Sandra. In other words, she faked her death and named Sandra beneficiary. The will is fraudulent and thus null and void, or will be as soon as someone contests it."

"That's what her attorney said, and why I called you. What will happen if I contest it?"

Cantu answered, "We will prove the will is fraudulent, and asserts will be frozen. Whatever name she's using will not be able to touch her accounts. The letter you have is a separate matter. We'll ask that you be authorized to sell the house and car now and be given a percentage of the proceeds as executor. Then this won't hang over you until 'Rhonda' is declared dead."

Linda hadn't been saying much more than necessary to her unfaithful husband, but she told Dave about the visit to Rhonda attorney and he exclaimed, "Go for it! I don't want her to be able to collect a cent of her ill-gotten money. It will be nice to add to the college fund for that imposter's 'nephews'."

Still retaining some feelings for Rhonda, part of Linda wanted to warn the woman who had been her friend. Under pressure she contested the will.

CHAPTER FORTY-THREE

Life goes on

Weeks had passed since the SCCPD closed the Missing Doctor Case and they had issued their statement to the press. The public longed for more news, but the media had gone on to the next much less appealing story of Corpus Christi's need for massive road repair.

Wal-Mart cashier, Marlys, and her friend, Leah, had a hard time believing that the doctor hadn't been abducted and killed. Hadn't they given the detectives incriminating evidence? To satisfy her curiosity for more information, Marlys called the PD. One of the detectives in charge of the case convinced Marlys the evidence they found was a hoax, but assured her that the find had been very important. Marlys took on new status at Wal-Mart as the cashier who helped solved the missing doctor case. Likewise, Muriel Martin, with a smug look on her face, told anyone who would listen that she had cracked the case with the recital of the incident in the restroom. The eyewitness in Stripes sought no publicity and was glad the case had ended.

Life went on at both the PD and the Cielo Vista clinic. Detectives Belkin and Gonzales worked to find vandals who had sprayed graffiti on several homes off Rodd Field Road. Maria often heard from Mr. Bennett, who most recently said his wife and son would be home for Thanksgiving. Dr. Ron hired a physician to replace Rhonda and had an attorney check the man's credentials and call all his references. Melanie's

Auntie Fe suffered a relapse but now had regained both her speech and use of her right arm. She planned to come to Corpus Christi on Christmas Eve.

Dave and Linda had work to do to repair the damage to their marriage. Remorseful, Dave tried everything beginning with roses, which were met with indifference. He offered a weekend alone for two. She refused that. Finally she softened when he did something a good husband and father should have been doing all along. He volunteered to take the boys and dog on an outing so she could have time to herself. Dave found he enjoyed doing a Dad Thing with his sons and realized he'd grown to like the little dog. He and Linda had told their boys that Poppy could stay with them forever because Auntie Rhonda wasn't coming back.

Despite the difference in ages, Linda and Maria became friends and enjoyed pleasurable lunches together those rare times their schedules meshed. Unofficially, Marie and Linda worked together to see if they could locate Rhonda.

Linda confided in Maria about Dave and Rhonda. Maria told her about announcing her engagement at Christmastimes with a wedding in June. Linda promised to do anything to help with the wedding.

Maria felt she knew Linda well enough to suggest therapy. "I know you are a physician and understand about the treatment of personal problems but I'd suggest you find a therapist to help you with the suppressed anger and grief you are suffering. Perhaps couples counseling, too."

Linda accepted both suggestions and she and her marriage benefited.

Sandra had been in Chicago for two months, long enough to hold Brian and Grace's newborn daughter, Sadie, and long enough to feel the bite of Chicago's November winds and first snowfall, destined only to worsen. She longed for the warmth of the Texas coast, and she had run through a large portion of Rhonda's available money. Time to make a new plan.

She finally hit on an idea. Return to Corpus Christi, the scene of her crime. She knew Brian was right. She didn't consider herself a bad person, in spite of what she'd done that September afternoon in Texas, but it would be freeing to go to college and earn a degree on her own. She planned to spend as much time as feasible walking on the beach in the fall and then would register for the winter quarter at Texas A&M.

First I need to tie up a few loose ends to make up for all the distress Rhonda caused. The best approach is to write a letter to Dr. Brooks and explain what happened to his award-winning employee.

She wrote:

Dear Dr. Brooks,

I am sorry I haven't reached you before this, but you will understand when I tell you why Dr. Rhonda L. Collins left so suddenly. She had a psychotic breakdown and wound up in Chicago, where I live. I'm her half-sister, whom she sometimes visited here. It took a while to convince her but she finally admitted herself to a mental facility and will be unable to return to her position. She gave me Power of Attorney so I shall move to Corpus Christi to take care of her assets. I can only imagine what anguish her disappearance caused you and others not to mention the waste of taxpayers' money. I know how much she loved her job and working for you. *Blah, blah, blah I'll finish this later. When I get there the first thing I'll do is contact Rhonda's attorney to see if he could draw up a legal document confirming I have Power of Attorney. Then I could have access to Rhonda's checking and saving accounts as well as her stocks, which, of course, I will need to pay poor Rhonda's medical bills. I wish I could take over her career, but I can live in her townhouse, drive her car, enjoy the lifestyle she did. At least, until I run out of money, which* *should last until I have my degree. If not, I'll sell the townhouse and move on. I'm nothing if not flexible!! Life is good! I've always made the most of my opportunities, and this is no different."*

Now that she'd made up her mind, Sandra wanted to travel to the Texas coast as soon as possible; but first she studied herself in the mirror. Her hair looked shaggy, and long blonde roots needed attention. She did like the shorter hair but the color, not so much.

While the stylist in the hotel cut and colored her hair a lighter shade of brown, Sandra worked out her travel plans. Having a credit card, she could make a plane reservation, but flying still caused too much anxiety. *I took a bus when I left Arkansas, and I can do it again.* Thinking of a battered little blue suitcase, she decided, *All I have to do is buy a couple large suitcases, nice ones, for all the clothes I've bought while I've been here, thanks to my Nordstrom's card.*

Two days later Sandra took a taxi to the bus station and bought a one-way ticket to Corpus Christi. She found herself looking forward to the long ride, which would give her plenty of time to check her new life plan for flaws, to think about the rest of her life. Running away had provided her with valuable time for introspection. She rather liked living in her mind, all those amusing inner dialogues and monologues.

Sitting down to wait for the bus, she considered what it would be like if Rhonda, instead of Sandra, returned to Corpus Christi. Blissfully unaware of what had transpired while she holed up in Chicago, Sandra decided Rhonda could explain her mental breakdown to Dr. Brooks and say she now had her condition under control with medication. He'd forgive her but most likely not rehire her.

Doubt reared its formidable head. *What if he'd found out that her credentials had no validity. Then he could press charges. But he wouldn't do that, would he? No, from what I know about him, he'd be worried about his clinic's reputation. But her reputation would be ruined and she'd probably lose her friends, too. She'd want Poppy, but the Hernandez boys would be so attached to him, she wouldn't want to snatch him away. No, in reality it's better that the poor woman perished. If anyone asks I don't know what really happened to Rhonda, but I know only I, Sandra Lewis aka Ronnie Lee Jackson, am left. And, of course, big sister Rhonda, who stole my name. I wonder what she has been doing these past eight years.*

Suddenly seized by the conscience usually kept well suppressed, Sandra knew her life of lies could not continue. From the time she left home, she had lied to survive. As she hitchhiked, she lied to people who gave her rides, she lied to Lurene about her name and her "cousins" who were her little sisters, she'd lied about having teaching credentials the year she taught, and she lied for years about being a licensed hairstylist. She'd lied about Rhonda's breakdown in the letter she had started. "I'm tired of changing names, changing jobs, lying to get those jobs. I can't do it anymore."

But she lied so easily now she wondered if she could stop. There was only one place she'd never told a lie and where she needed to return. The place where she started was the place where she could start over.

Sandra hurried back to the ticket counter and asked, with a hopeful smile, if she could exchange her ticket.

A frown crossed the clerk's dark-complexioned face as she looked at the striking woman in clothing that shouted "pricey". She'd been watching her and saw how she stood out among the other casual to ragged bus travelers. "Having a little trouble making up your mind, Missy?"

"I guess I seem a little undecided, but now I know exactly where I want to go."

"Are you sure?"

"I've never been so sure about anything in my life. I'm starting over."

"All right, I'll see what I can do about exchanging your ticket so it won't cost you any more."

"How sweet of you!"

The transaction completed, Sandra reclaimed her seat. She hoped the wait for this bus would be shorter, but unfortunately it would take longer for the new ride. Her usual traveler's luck. *But there's something I can do while I wait -- I'm going to call Linda Hernandez. Linda was such a good friend that she needs to know what happened to Rhonda.* She took out her cell phone and punched in the memorized clinic office number. *It's good I haven't sent the letter to Dr. Brooks. If anyone deserves the truth, it's Linda.* A voice she didn't recognize, that of a new receptionist hired to make work easier for Carla and Amy, answered, "Cielo Vista Family Clinic."

Good! Someone new. Makes this easier as Carla and Amy surely would have recognized her disguised voice, "May I speak to Dr. Hernandez?"

"One moment, she's in her office,

Good. If she was unavailable, with a patient, I might lose my courage."

"Dr. Hernandez, speaking."

"Hello, Dr. Hernandez."

Even though Linda finally had convinced herself she no longer cared what had happened to the conniving woman, she couldn't help herself from reacting to the voice she never again expected to hear. "Rhonda!" she exclaimed while hitting a button to record the call, which Maria had assured her was legal in Texas.

"No, I'm her sister. People say we sound alike, and we sure do look alike. She came to visit me several times in Chicago when she lived in Texas ..." Her voice broke.

Linda wanted to scream, "Liar!" but she had practiced what she would say if this call ever came in order to keep

Rhonda on the phone. "Rhonda never mentioned a sister, or any family."

"That doesn't surprise me. I knew all her secrets and you might say I was her worst nightmare. I visited her in Corpus Christi many times."

Rhonda never mentioned a sister or a visitor. She sure didn't tell me everything. Like sleeping with my husband. I must keep her talking. "What's your name?"

Sandra took a deep breath. "It's Sandra Lewis."

"Do you know Felicity Ritter?"

Gulp. "Yes, why do you ask?"

"I believe she has mentioned you."

"No big deal. We both lived in the Oklahoma panhandle, and then we both wound up in Tulsa, where I had a beauty salon and Felicity became a regular customer. My sister hardly knew her. Again, why's this important?"

Linda replied with another question. "Why are you calling me?"

"I received all the messages you left for Rhonda, and I thought you deserved to know what happened to her." Linda said nothing so Sandra rattled on. "I don't have much time as I'm waiting to board. *Let her think I'm boarding a plane even though I never will again.* "About two months ago, on one of my visits, I met her in a restroom by her credit union, where she insisted I come. She was an emotional wreck, told me she was in big trouble, and wanted to give me some documents and money to safeguard for her. She also said she wanted to change clothing because she'd be too upset to wear that particular outfit again so we shared a stall and changed. She gave me her shoes and purse, but I remembered her feet are bigger so I couldn't wear the shoes. By then, she'd left the stall. I thought she was combing her hair, but -- and I'll never forgive myself for this -- when I came out of the stall, she'd left."

The speaker paused and her voice grew teary. After sniffling a little, she described what happened next. "I immediately ran out of the building to look for her. I spotted her car, but she wasn't in it. I found the keys in her purse and unlocked the car. I put her shoes on the passenger side, and then I decided to leave the purse because it matched, you know in case she changed her mind and came back. The shoes and purse were really quality. Anyway I saw a blue gym bag in the back, and I claimed it because I needed some place to put the documents and the money and the contents of the purse I traded her."

Linda's voice indicated grave doubt in spite of this all making some convoluted sense. "Were you wearing gloves?"

Sandra, surprised by the question, began rapid blather, words tumbling over each other. "No, it was a hot day. I sure didn't need gloves, not like in Chicago. But, why do you ask? If she had gloves that matched she didn't give them to me, and why would she? It was almost 90. She said the outfit had a jacket but too warm to wear it. Said I could get it at her place."

Taking a much-needed breath, Sandra pursued another tangent. "Were gloves found in her car? If they were, I didn't see any. Maybe someone else put them in the car after I left. That's possible because I don't know if I locked the car. The keys I know I tossed under the car."

The keys struck a chord with Linda. As Linda and Maria formed a friendship, the detective had shared that early in her partnership with Stan Belkin, she loved to try to get the best of him because he was such a pain. Maria had found keys under Rhonda's car at the parking ramp. She told how she unlocked the car while Belkin tried to open it with a tool, and she and Maria had a good laugh.

So much of what this person said rang true, but was that because she was Rhonda? *I really can't believe a single word or tear.* Finally Linda asserted in a controlled voice, "I'm having a little trouble believing all you're saying. Rhonda isn't dead. The South Corpus Christi PD was able to trace Rhonda to Chicago."

"Actually that would be me," Sandra stated with pride. "I was scared to death so I left the parking lot." *Now I can eliminate all doubt.*

"Why were you so scared?"

"Afraid the police would spot me in Rhonda's clothing with her papers so I made a plan. After I left the Vega Building I bought a car from a kid at the Stripes store that is nearby. I went to Wal-Mart to buy a hair color kit and I registered at a motel to alter my appearance. I did that because my sister and I looked so much alike, just like our mom. I knew the police would be tailing me. I was protecting myself." Pause. " It sounds like I was right." Pause. "Anyway, I drove to San Antonio and flew to Chicago."

"Why Chicago?"

"In my heart I thought, prayed, she'd change her mind and go there, where we have friends."

"The Cavendish family?"

That threw Sandra. *How does Linda know all this stuff?* "Yes, the Cavendish family."

"That's interesting. I talked to both Brian and Grace Cavendish. They said they know you but have never heard of Rhonda."

Grace doesn't but Brian sure does, but obviously he's covering his tracks. Can't blame him. " That's a barefaced lie."

The woman sounded so convincing that Linda began to doubt the conclusions of SCCPD. She faltered. "I don't -- I don't know what to say, everything you've said was reported by the police." *Actually some I heard from Maria after they closed the case.* She decided to add, "I can tell you this, she never returned to her car."

Sandra took an audible deep breath. Her voice turned shaky as if she might be crying again. "That means what I was afraid of, that Rhonda ..." She stopped not knowing quite where to go with this. "Uh, I know how hard this is for you. You were Rhonda's friend, but I'm her sister, and it's terrible for me too." She again stopped as if to compose herself. "I don't know for certain, but Rhonda told me once what she'd planned if something was discovered. I can't betray what it was."

Linda dropped the bomb. "The police found out what she was hiding."

Sandra's eyes widened. "Then you understand why she felt she had to disappear." *What do I say now? I could tell her Rhonda ran to Mexico but she might keep looking for her. I have to give the poor soul closure.* "Anyway, as I was saying, she said if she was found out, which you say she was, she'd just walk into the Gulf and keep on walking. You see, we were poor when we were kids so never had swimming lessons so she couldn't swim."

Linda remembered the time in Mazatlan when Rhonda had told her that. *Am I being played or is this Sandra telling me the truth? In my heart I know this is Rhonda, that lying, conniving husband stealing ...*

"I'm afraid." Sandra sobbed, "that she took a taxi to North Padre or Port Aransas and put on her ankle weights -- I never saw them in her gym bag -- and drowned herself."

Linda surprised herself by sounding so cool and objective, "No body has turned up."

Sandra was rattled but made it up as she went along. "I'm not surprised. With the stormy weather in the Gulf at that time it's hard to tell where my sister's body will turn up."

Just then Sandra heard what she thought was the announcement for her bus. "I have to go. It's time for me to board. I'm sorry, Linda, I know you were best friends, and she thought the world of you and would want you to remember…"

Linda interrupted, "Please, tell me where you're going."

She heard only dead air.

Maria had suggested that Linda tape any call she might receive from either Rhonda or Sandra. That evening Maria came to Linda's home, and both listened carefully to the tape. Maria commented, "Two women in one stall. That jives with what one witness said. What she did after she left the Vega Building is what we figured out, but I think there's something not right about this."

"All the time I talked with her, I felt like I was talking to Rhonda," Linda clarified.

"The DNA and fingerprints do not support the presence of another person."

"I asked her if she wore gloves. She said it was too hot."

"That's incriminating. If she were telling the truth, there would have been additional fingerprints and DNA in the car."

With resignation and anger, Linda grabbed the phone. "Sandra and Rhonda have to be the same person. I'm giving her a call."

Having rehearsed just what she wanted to say, Linda put quite a speech on voice mail that would have saved Sandra from counting on her financial future. Too bad Sandra deleted the voicemail without listening to it.

"Rhonda, Sandra, whatever you're calling yourself, I know for certain you lied to me. You also had an affair with my husband. I've forgiven him but I don't know if I can forgive you. You betrayed a friendship that meant so much to me."

She continued, "Law Enforcement figured out your little scheme to get your money back when authorities declare 'Rhonda' dead. Unfortunately for you, Rhonda, I protested your will. The court declared it null and void, your assets frozen. However, since you named me executor on a separate document, your attorney suggests I sell your properties and receive a fee for that. I think our boys will have a nice college nest egg. I also can claim money to care for Poppy for the rest of his life. The remainder of the money and your other assets will go to the great state of Texas. You were smart to decide not to come back here, where you could be prosecuted for breaking a long list of laws, everything from abandoning a pet to falsifying credentials and a will, misleading the police. I could go on and on, but I'll just say. "Have a nice life, my..." Her voice wavered, "Rhonda, wherever you are."

Both Linda and Maria had triumphed in solving the case of the missing Rhonda. For Maria this gave her the much-needed esteem she needed to continue as a detective. Linda had to believe Rhonda suffered from a mental illness. She no longer blamed her husband for his infidelity. The beguiling, unforgettable Rhonda had bewitched both of them.

CHAPTER FORTY-FOUR

Love the color

Sandra almost boarded the wrong bus. Still two hours to wait before the right one. The story of my life on the run, waiting: waiting for rides when I hitchhiked, waiting for the kid to come sell me a car, waiting for the rain to stop, waiting for planes, waiting for buses. It's never been easy but I've persevered! In time I'll enjoy the fruits of all the years working as a doctor in beautiful Corpus Christi.

As she munched on stale popcorn from a machine, her cell rang. She saw it came from Linda Hernandez, and let it go to voicemail. I don't want to hear anything else she has to say so I'll just delete it. I'll never return to Corpus until enough time has passed so I can have my poor sister Rhonda declared dead.

Sandra concentrated on the image of the scared teen-aged Ronnie Lee with the small battered blue tin suitcase, the gangly girl who'd climbed on a Greyhound bus to run away. That's when she started lying, but the woman, who had learned so much and developed so much confidence, never needed to lie again.

Her bus arrived. She flashed the driver her most radiant smile as he loaded her two large expensive gray suitcases into the compartment under the bus. Feeling buoyant, Sandra Dee/Ronnie Lee stepped up the stairs to the bus.

Immediately she heard someone call from one of the aisle seats, "Sandra! Sandra Lewis!"

Her eyes locked with the woman who called out her name. In astonishment she answered, "Sue-Ella! I mean Rhonda!"

Rhonda patted the seat next to her, and her stepsister Sandra sat down. "What a coincidence. Both of us on a bus heading to Arkansas."

"Yes, I'm tired of bouncing back between Oklahoma and California and decided what I needed is a trip back home. The trees can be so magnificent in the Ozarks this time of year. I love fall!"

"So do I. In South Texas I missed the change of seasons, especially fall colors. That's one reason I decided to come home."

"Sandra, it's been so many years since we saw each other that I almost didn't recognize you. Especially with that hair. Love the color!"

THE END

THE AUTHOR

Alice Marks, born, reared and educated in Wyoming, moved to Minnesota with her husband and the first two of their four children. When illness prevented Alice from continuing a career in early childhood, she began writing. After Alice's husband retired, they moved to an island town, Port Aransas, Texas. Alice joined a dedicated writing group and began publishing short stories and poetry in anthologies and non-fiction pieces in magazines. She published two major humor pieces on an Internet humor site, and wrote Biblical comedies that have been performed at several churches. For her extended family she has written fictionalized memoirs of their ancestors. With 104-year-old Beulah Whitehead, Alice co-authored an autobiography called Sweet Memories: Over 100 Years in the Life of a Texas Woman. Missing their children and grandchildren, Alice and her husband returned to Minnesota. They live in Duluth with two dogs and a cat in a 1920s bungalow featuring a view of Lake Superior. Alice teaches Creative Writing, co-leaders a writing group and serves on the board of the Lake Superior Writers. Alice is working on another suspense novel.

Contents

MISSING 1
DEDICATION 3
INTRODUCTION 4
CHAPTER ONE 6
CHAPTER TWO 12
CHAPTER THREE 16
CHAPTER FOUR 27
CHAPTER FIVE 33
CHAPTER SIX 43
CHAPTER SEVEN 52
CHAPTER EIGHT 59
CHAPTER NINE 68
CHAPTER TEN 72
CHAPTER ELEVEN 75
CHAPTER TWELVE 81
CHAPTER THIRTEEN 92
CHAPTER FOURTEEN 100
CHAPTER FIFTEEN 104
CHAPTER SIXTEEN 113
CHAPTER SEVENTEEN 123
CHAPTER EIGHTEEN 127
CHAPTER NINETEEN 133
CHAPTER TWENTY 140
TWENTY-ONE 144
CHAPTER TWENTY-TWO 153
CHAPTER TWENTY-THREE 157
CHAPTER TWENTY-FOUR 161
CHAPTER TWENTY-FIVE 169
CHAPTER TWENTY-SIX 174
CHAPTER TWENTY-SEVEN 179

CHAPTER TWENTY-EIGHT	181
CHAPTER TWENTY-NINE	186
CHAPTER THIRTY	189
CHAPTER THIRTY-ONE	194
CHAPTER THIRTY-TWO	196
CHAPTER THIRTY-THREE	201
CHAPTER THIRTY-FOUR	206
CHAPTER THIRTY-FIVE	209
CHAPTER THIRTY-SIX	214
CHAPTER THIRTY-SEVEN	216
CHAPTER THIRTY-EIGHT	220
CHAPTER THIRTY-NINE	228
CHAPTER FORTY	230
CHAPTER FORTY-ONE	233
CHAPTER FORTY-TWO	237
CHAPTER FORTY-THREE	239
CHAPTER FORTY-FOUR	251
THE AUTHOR	253

Made in the USA
Middletown, DE
26 February 2022